The Devil Incarnate

Eyes closed as she waited for the killing blow, Mary heard a sound almost like thick wood about to splinter. She felt the concrete floor tremble just a bit and heard a thud, as if the trunk of a tree had somehow fallen inside the warehouse.

It was only when she heard Ben gasp and felt his grip on her hair loosen that she decided to open her eyes.

The first thing she saw was Ben, a surprised and worried look on his face as he stepped backward. The knife was still clutched in his hand, but his arm hung loosely at his side. He was staring, with some concern, directly over Mary's head. No sooner did she begin to relax at the thought of being free than she tensed up again from the realization that whatever Ben was backing away from in terror was right behind her.

She looked over her shoulder and nearly fell onto her back from surprise. A huge man, maybe seven feet tall and wide as a door, his ill-fitting black clothes making him look as if he'd climbed out of a coffin, had stepped from behind the broken wall and did not seem pleased. The low sound she'd heard was his voice. He was growling, warning Ben off, like a dog would. An enormous dog on two legs . . .

Other Universal Monsters™ novels from DH Press

Dracula™: Asylum
by Paul Witcover

The Creature from the Black Lagoon™:
Time's Black Lagoon
by Paul Di Filippo

FRANKENSTEIN™

THE SHADOW OF FRANKENSTEIN

Stefan Petrucha

DH Press™
Milwaukie

Dear Reader: Please be aware that if you have purchased this book without a cover it was reported to the publisher as "unsold and destroyed" and neither the author nor the publisher have received any payment from its resale.

THE SHADOW OF FRANKENSTEIN © 2006
Universal Studios Licensing LLLP. The "Universal Studios Monsters" are trademarks and copyrights of Universal Studios. All Rights Reserved.

No portion of this publication may be reproduced or transmitted, in any form or by any means, without the express written permission of the copyright holders. Names, characters, places, and incidents featured in this publication either are the product of the author's imagination or are used fictitiously. Any resemblance to actual persons (living or dead), events, institutions, or locales, without satiric intent, is coincidental. DH Press and the DH Press logo are trademarks of DH Press. All rights reserved.

Book design by Debra Bailey and Krystal Hennes
Cover painting by Stephen Youll

Published by DH Press
A division of Dark Horse Comics
10956 SE Main Street
Milwaukie, OR 97222

dhpressbooks.com

First DH Press Edition: July 2006
ISBN-10: 1-59582-037-X
ISBN-13: 978-1-59582-037-2

Printed in U.S.A.
Distributed by Publishers Group West

10 9 8 7 6 5 4 3 2 1

Chapter One

The North Sea didn't care for the steamer *Cargaggia*. Rather than help it on its way, it dogged the small ship with high waves and dreadful winds. Were nature's ill will not enough, strange sounds issued from the second, supposedly empty, cargo hold, as if something large and living stumbled about inside, moaning like a confused, lost ghost.

"Who's there?" Sven called into the vast space as he crouched on the steel steps. He tried to sound authoritative, but all he felt was small. The hollow space dwarfed him, like the dark womb of a metal goddess. Even his thick voice seemed tiny as it reverberated off the hull, tinier still as it faded into a ringing that mixed with roaring sea.

If a stowaway was making the sounds, he didn't answer. *But,* Sven thought with a sigh, *why would he?*

He brought his hurricane lamp deeper into the dark. Being a crew member on a steamer was a nuisance, but Nature had made his brain ill-suited for book learning. She made up for that by giving him sharp eyesight, a strong, broad back, and strong arms.

"Hello?" Sven cried again. More echoes.

Only a fool would answer.

The *Cargaggia* was a small steamer, propelled by twin diesels, delayed on the last leg of its regular route from Egypt to England. One of its two holds was filled with cotton, but this second supposedly held only rats. An earlier storm had forced them into Bremerhaven, a German port, where they picked up the baggage of a vacationing baron. Ever since the storm started, the crew had heard heavy thumping down here, and growls only vaguely human. But what sort of fool stowaway would be so loud? Maybe he was sick.

"Hey, hello!"

When nothing answered Sven's cries, some old hunting instinct stirred, so he doused the lamp and fell silent in the darkness. Then, instead of shouting like an idiot, he waited, trying to quiet his breathing and adjust his eyes to the near-dark. He crept down the steel stairs, keeping his balance in the rocking, timing his footsteps to the loud crash of the waves to hide the sound.

By the time he reached the steel plate-and-rivet floor, his eyesight came round. He could make out the edges of a few bare crates here, remainders of their last shipment, and even distinguish one section of high wall from another.

He heard a light scampering he instantly recognized as a rat, but then, to his right, came a far heavier scraping, and a rustling like thick cloth tight against skin. Sven smiled, tickled that his simple ruse had worked. Who said Sven could not think? He was strong *and* smart. He waited a few moments more, to pinpoint the stowaway's location, then tiptoed toward him, contemplating yet another devious plan.

He'd light a match, quickly, out of nowhere. That would frighten the stowaway into submission, maybe even make him piss himself. Sven laughed inwardly at the look he imagined on the poor fellow's (or woman's?) face.

He slipped the matchbox from his trouser pocket and slid out a single stick. There was more scraping. He could even hear breathing, deep and regular. He assumed from the deep sound that it was a man, and not a small man, either. This didn't worry Sven—he was six feet himself, very wide, and he would have the advantage of surprise.

Even so, his heartbeat quickened and he feared he would somehow give himself away. To complete his adventure successfully, he'd have to light the match in one stroke, and, at the same moment, shout, long and loud.

Well, as my English friends say, on with it, then . . .

One . . . two . . . three . . . strike!

Hissing, the match-head flared into a white circle that at first washed everything into bright nothing. It dimmed quickly into a steady flame, but the shout Sven planned on making never occurred. It stuck like an apple lodged in his throat, as his sharp eyes went wide.

The stowaway was taller than Sven by at least a head. The skin of its face and arms, white as a corpse, stood in sharp relief from its worn, black clothes. Impossibly, the top of its head was completely flat, covered with a smattering of freshly grown black hair. The skull came to a nearly straight edge and suddenly dropped down at a right angle into a broad, flat forehead. At the edge where forehead met skullcap, on the right, Sven caught the glint of three metal bolts, one large, two smaller, that seemed to hold the top of the skull in place like the lid on a ghoulish box. The brow was heavy, Neanderthal-like, the cheeks sunken. One sallow cheek carried a wide burn-scar, but there were many other scars on it as well, some thin, with stitch marks pinching the skin together. On either side of its neck, also glinting, twin metallic protrusions rose.

A fire victim, was the first thought Sven had. *Hideous,* was the second.

It was also the last.

The sudden light had disturbed it, the tiny flame at the end of the matchstick more so. It growled and lashed out.

There had been many men in Sven's life: father, friends, mentors, teammates, rivals, and, of course, those unseen masters who built the civilized world in which he was forced to live. It was even a man, or at least something like one, that was killing him. Even so, as the stowaway squeezed his powerful fingers easily past the thick cord of muscle in Sven's neck and crushed the bone beneath, his last word was, "Mother."

When they saw him, they called him *the monster*, so that was what he called himself.

He held the body a very long while before it finally stopped quivering. When it did, the monster marveled that such a frail and paltry thing could so easily achieve what he could not.

"Dead," the monster said. He was neither sad nor pleased.

He laid the corpse gently down on a few bales of cotton he'd found lying about the massive cargo floor, and even tried to cover it with the loose bits. Gently, he petted the forehead, used his fingers to close the eyes, then leaned back on his haunches and returned to his waiting.

"We belong dead."

He'd said the same thing many days ago when he stood in the gloom of the watchtower laboratory, the place that'd been both his birthplace and torture chamber. He'd said it to Dr. Pretorius as his stiff, mismatched arms pulled the lever the sharp-nosed man warned would blow them all to atoms.

There'd been an electric crackle. Bright, white heat swarmed the monster's senses like lightning. It filled him, making him shiver, burned and caressed him. The watchtower shook, then tumbled like rain. Misshapen boulders, loosed from ancient mortar, crashed into one another, making a loud dull sound, like thunder. Lightning, rain, and thunder—death was just like birth.

Through the downpour he caught a glimpse of the woman made, like him, from the dead, to be his friend. She twitched her head, bared her teeth, and hissed at the collapsing world, exactly the same way she'd hissed at him. He remembered touching her long fingers, feeling the soft back of her gauze-wrapped hand. It was as gentle as the flowers a child gave him once.

His lips fluttered into a brief smile, then he fell and was buried by the collapsing building.

For the longest while all was silent as the grave. Shadow plays danced in his still-working brain. Faces, feelings, voices rose and fell. He caught fleeting images of a life he'd never lived, in which he was a person he'd never been. A person, not a monster. He hoped this was death and wondered if now everything would finally stop hurting.

But it didn't. The aching returned. Real rain, wet and cold, splattered his face. His heavy eyelids opened and he stared up through the cracks at the clouds of a clearing storm.

This was not the death he'd seen in the graveyard. This was not the stillness of bones, the quiet of dried flesh.

"Frankenstein," the monster growled, enunciating each syllable as if they were separate words. It was one of the few words he knew, and the one he hated most. If his maker had lived, could he do what the explosion couldn't, make his creature really dead?

It would, the monster thought, please them both.

Not knowing or caring how long he'd been there, he pulled himself free from the rubble, then made his way through the woods and to the high gates of Castle Frankenstein. There, he hid in the shadows of the old growth that lined the stone fence, and peered at the bustling activity in the courtyard.

Two coaches waited, impatient black horses huffing at the head of each. Fretful servants stuffed one coach with baggage, pausing occasionally to whisper and cross themselves. Then, from the castle proper, the maker came, Frankenstein, dour and pale, walking his bride, she wrapped in blankets. He hurriedly slipped her and himself into the second carriage.

There was something wrong about her face. Was she sick? The monster had been careful not to hurt her when he'd taken her prisoner, but they were all so weak and soft, with bones like dried twigs, that he couldn't be sure he hadn't.

Seeing his maker, the monster stepped forward from the shadows, but the sight of the milling servants and the bright torches they carried forced him back.

Nothing hurt like fire. Not stones, not pitchforks, not bullets from guns. Nothing.

Alternately snarling and whimpering, he waited by a gnarly old oak until the iron gates creaked open and the coaches lurched out. As the first passed him, the one that carried Frankenstein, he snatched at it, but it was too fast. When the second came, he braced himself against the tree trunk and leapt, landing on its back with a crash that rattled the carriage and threatened to tip it into the dirt.

"Aieee!" an old woman screamed. "You'll kill us both!"

Clinging to the back of the coach, the monster held tight and watched as the woman swatted the plump driver with both her gnarled hands.

"Quiet yourself, Minnie!" the driver grunted back. "And keep your hands off! We've hit a ditch s'all!"

"A ditch, he says, a ditch!" the woman said to no one. "More likely you've been hitting the spirits! We're lucky the axle didn't split and kill us dead! The baroness will have my head if her luggage doesn't arrive safe and proper!"

He grunted at her, "Ach! Mine, too!"

She grunted back, "Ach! So it wouldn't be a *complete* waste, then."

They rode on in silence, trying to catch the first coach. Satisfied they wouldn't stop to look for him, the monster slipped into the back with the rest of the Frankenstein baggage.

A few hours later, the creature heard a wooden crack, like

the sound of a falling tree. At once, the coach slumped and fell on its side. Bags and boxes pelted him as everything turned about.

"Now you've done it!" Minnie screeched. "You've lost a wheel! We'll miss the ship!"

He heard them move and clamber about. Shifting slightly, the monster peered up, through the carriage's window where he saw the chubby driver survey the damage.

"The wheel cracked! What could've done that? The baggage isn't that heavy!"

Fearing they'd look inside, the monster pulled the boxes and rough canvas bags over himself. He waited through the night and most of the next day. After hours of hammering, nailing, and the old woman's invectives, the wagon was righted and they started to move again, but slower now, and with a distinct wobble.

By the time they reached the port town of Bremerhaven, the monster understood from Minnie's shouts that Frankenstein was gone.

"What are they going to do in London without their things?" she screeched. "What are they going to do without the most important thing of all, *me*?"

"Thing is right," the coachman mumbled tiredly. "Stay here and watch the coach. I'll go see if I can find us another ship heading out. The dock master's a friend of the baron's. The old baron, anyway."

"Run away, then! You'd be happy to leave me here to be murdered by some mangy thief what's after their belongings!" she called.

"If he made sure you were dead first, I wouldn't feel obliged to turn him in!" he shouted back, his gruff voice thinned by distance.

"Well," she said to herself. "At least the monster's dead and buried. Now maybe the poor baroness' nightmares can end, too. I've never seen the dear so distressed, like she's dancing at the gates of madness, she is . . . such a look in her eyes last I saw her, like for a second, she didn't even know who I was . . . "

The rest of her speech was lost in a lowering mumble of complaints and prayers as Minnie, worn from her journey, drifted off to sleep.

Sensing her quiet, the monster slipped out. He planned to look for Frankenstein, but this place was so unlike anything he'd experienced, so alarming, he just stood by the carriage, gaping.

Buildings, he'd seen those before, but none so large as the warehouses that flanked the alley the coach was in. Lakes he'd seen, but none so huge as the vast body of gray lapping liquid that began where land ended and stretched as far and wide as the sky.

And things floated in it, vast things of steel and wood, chained to wooden platforms. They bobbed, moving this way and that with the waves. It took him a while, but eventually he realized they were floating, like flower petals.

After a time, sharp voices brought him back to the immediate danger, and he quickly stomped to the darkness of an empty doorway to watch.

"It's your lucky day," a tall man with a bush of hair under his nose said. His arm was around the driver as the two came walking up. "There's a ship bound to London within the hour! The *Cargaggia*, at Pier 27. And they say there's nothing but clear weather ahead! I wouldn't be surprised if you reached port before your baron!"

"Wake up, Minnie!" the driver called, jostling her. "We've got to get moving!"

It was easy enough for the monster to see where they brought the luggage, much harder to climb on the ship without being seen. At first, he thought the floating building he'd sneaked upon was called London, and that Frankenstein should be here. But as he listened to Minnie complaining on the deck, he finally understood that they were somehow to be brought to him.

When the twin engines roared to life, he squealed. As the great ship rocked, he panted and clung to the walls. When the ship's whistle blasted, he screamed, collapsed to his knees, pressed his large hands to his ears, and wailed until it finally stopped.

As the ship lurched along, he looked through a murky porthole and saw the receding pier. Finally, he realized the building he was in was moving in the water, and that London, where Frankenstein was, was the place where it was headed.

He tried to be patient, but when the storm started and the ship began rocking violently, he couldn't keep from stomping and crying.

When the man came down to look for him, he quieted until the monster thought he was gone. But when the man lit that fire, it filled him at once with an old, explosive rage.

Because nothing hurt like fire.

So he killed him.

As the monster now looked at the peaceful body, its neck bent out of place, he worried more men would come. But there were plenty of places to hide, and when he wanted, he was getting very good at keeping quiet, as long as they didn't surprise him.

A sharp pain twisted his belly. He hadn't eaten for the longest time. Looking around in the darkness, he saw something small and furry amble across the metal floor. A rat. He recognized them from the laboratory, where they used to steal the bread the hunchback left for him on the floor. He'd followed animals before, in the woods, and sometimes they led him to fruits or seeds. Food. So he stood and stumbled after it.

After a moment, he heard a single loud snap followed by a high-pitched squeal. There was a clattering as the rodent skittered, lopsided, into a corner, trailing a rectangular piece of wood behind it, leaving a thin line of red liquid on the floor.

Curious, the monster moved up on it, then kneeled and leaned in for a closer look. His eyes were good in the dark, but it was particularly black in the corner. Getting closer, he could see that the piece of wood it dragged had a metal strap that had snapped around the rat's leg. It was a trap. Badly wounded, the rat sat in the corner, a large, hairy rock, trembling from its own breathing.

The monster came still closer. He thought he could bend the metal back, let the rat go. Then maybe it would take him to some food.

"Friend? Friend?" he said to the furry brown thing.

He moved his huge hands closer. The rat chattered, shat, then leapt and bit the largest finger in the hand held out in front of it.

"Nyraaghh!" the monster whined, snatching his hand back, rat and trap still attached. A flash of the arm snapped the rodent's spine. Its mouth loosening, it shivered and dropped, the wood clattering on the metal floor.

Pained, the monster cradled his hand, rubbing it as tears fell from his eyes, down into the hollows of his sunken cheeks. The rubbing slowed the pain, but not the surprise. It was strange how some things didn't hurt at all, a boulder falling on his back, and others, like a little bite, hurt so much.

The rat lay at his feet, a small pile of fur, flesh, and bone. He prodded it with his foot. It flopped over onto the trap.

"Dead," the monster said. He wasn't sad about it, or particularly pleased.

He bent down and, after prying its leg free, picked it up. It was still warm, as if a fleeting fire still burned inside it. Then the growling in his stomach returned.

The monster was hungry and the thing in his hand was all he had.

He'd seen others eat the flesh of warm things that had once been alive, burning them first in the fire. He'd tasted meat. This was no different. So with a grunt, and fumbling, awkward fingers, he set about pulling apart and eating the thing he'd just called friend.

Chapter Two

"It's alive," the grizzled captain said, two days earlier, as he stared at the dark and roiling sea. A thick fog made all the world, save the deck the two men stood on, look like a canvas painted in shades of gray.

The piercing eyes of Henry Frankenstein crinkled slightly at the Captain's words, but otherwise his pale, gaunt face betrayed no emotion. He tapped a white cigarette against his hand and noticed it wasn't shaking quite as much as usual. He put the long white cylinder in his mouth, lit, and drew. As smoke curled from his lips, no different in color than the fog, he finally responded by asking, "How do you mean?"

The older man nodded toward the water. "The ocean. It's alive. Much as we try, after thousands of years of sailing, we don't control it so much as try its patience."

Captain Benjamin A. Tucker was a typically brash American, crude and non-deferential. To him, Frankenstein's status as baron meant nothing. On his ship, the old salt bowed to nothing save the sea. Perhaps that was why his career was relegated to smuggling cargo and carrying passengers in need of discretion into England.

Frankenstein didn't mind Tucker's brashness. He rather admired it, and, in any case, couldn't afford to be picky. Twenty-one people from his small village had been killed by the monster he had created and now some young fool inspector wanted Henry Frankenstein himself put on trial for their deaths. Pressed by public outrage, the burgomaster was forced to go along with an investigation, and there could be charges filed. Septimus Pretorius, Frankenstein's deceased professor and latter-day partner, once warned him of the possibility. "It is you, really, who is responsible for all those murders," he'd said.

Frankenstein wanted to face the charges, but couldn't. Not for himself, but for his wife, for Elizabeth's sake. Her fragile nerves had already been shattered by her kidnapping at the hands of the monster. What would become of her sweetness if her new husband was put on trial, or worse, found guilty?

Vacationing for a time, for a rest, seemed best.

Wresting his mind from his troubles, Frankenstein smiled at the captain. "You're talking mere romanticism, Captain. There's nothing out there that can't be explained. The pull of the moon causes the tides, geology explains the channels and the currents. As for the rest, the unseen force that shapes the waves this way instead of that, well, it's only fear and superstition that prevents us from finding out."

Tucker's eyes flared, the yellow at their edges one of the few notable colors in the gloom. He pointed, his finger hopelessly small against a cosmos of mist. "Baron, I swear there are things in those depths, living things, monsters that we're not meant to understand. Some are so ghastly, that simply seeing them would drive us mad."

Henry's eyes crinkled again. He wanted to say that madness was preferable to ignorance, but his heart started pounding, and he felt his hands shake as the extra blood pumped into them.

Maybe it was just the word, *monster*.

Or was he afraid Pretorius was right? Was he responsible? Was all that blood on his hands?

"I'm sure you know more about it than I," he said to the captain, unable to conceal the bitterness in his voice. He tightened the white ascot around his neck, then pulled his long tan coat closer around his thin waist, preparing to leave. But the captain didn't take the subtle hint.

"Baron, have you ever heard of a ship called the *Essex*?"

Frankenstein blinked. "I'm afraid not."

"A Nantucket whaler. Once, fifteen months into a routine voyage she approached a shoal of whales and the crew lowered three boats. While they were killing the whales, they noticed a large bull watching. It was huge, eighty-five feet, eighty tons at least. It got so close they could see that its flat, giant head was full of scars from the attacks of the men that had tried to kill it. Astoundingly, it started to move on the ship, slowly at first, then picking up speed until finally it rammed the *Essex* so hard the hull splintered and the whole ship went down. The monster pulled itself free, rammed the ship *again*, and finally swam off. Now where's the science in that?"

A slight, derisive smile took Henry's lips. "So what if it's true? Some rogue fish explains it neatly. The world is full of misunderstood men called mad, why shouldn't a whale be mad as well?"

Captain Tucker said nothing. He just turned to face the great gray wall of the world.

Fearing he'd offended the man, not needing any more enemies, Frankenstein invited him to say more. "Well, what became of the crew?"

The captain shook his head. "Took to the lifeboats. They were near enough some inhabited Pacific islands, but there were rumors that cannibals lived there, so they headed the other way. When the food ran out, they succumbed, sir, to cannibalism and fed upon their dead."

Without thinking, Frankenstein responded, practically to himself: "Well, what of it? It's just dead meat, same as the rest. Nothing more than clay, once the life's gone from it. Why, if

I'd been captain, I'd have used the lifeboats to find the whale, just to have a closer look, to try and understand what made it what it was."

Tucker turned and regarded him. Frankenstein sensed him stiffen.

Superstitious old fool. Judging me.

"Your wife, sir. How is she faring?"

Frankenstein looked away. "The ocean does not agree with her."

A conspiratorial look came over the old face. He inched closer and spoke quietly. "If I may say, opiates are considered quite good for the stomach, and their calming effect on the nerves is well known. If you wish, I could . . . "

Now it was Frankenstein's turn to stiffen. "I don't care what you do with your self or your ship, Captain. I appreciate your discretion in carrying us, and you'll be well paid for it, but now I'd appreciate it if we were to be left alone for the remainder of the journey."

Tucker nodded, adding in a monotone, "We'll enter the channel soon. Then it's not much farther to London."

With that, Frankenstein moved quickly away, doing his best to vanish into the fog, to put distance between himself and the drug smuggler. He'd known their cargo was contraband, but the fact of opiates on board, especially in relation to Elizabeth, put a shiver in him.

An addict. He'd have me turn her into an addict.

He walked in short fast steps along the deck, barely noticing the way it rocked with the whims of the sea. The cool mist carried the smell of brine, which, while it wasn't as bad as the charnel houses he was used to, made his lungs heavy. The wound in his side, earned when his creation threw him from a burning windmill, ached as he inhaled.

Oh, Elizabeth, where have I brought us? Will I never be able to protect you, like a proper husband?

Approaching the cabin door, he heard her moan beyond it. He knocked softly and said, "It's me, Elizabeth." Without waiting for an answer, he turned the bronze handle and stepped inside.

The lights were out, as he'd left them, hoping she might fall asleep.

"Who's there?" her frightened voice asked.

"Just me, my darling," he said again. He heard blankets rustle and saw her shadow rise on the bed.

"I can't sleep, Henry. I can't even close my eyes. The darkness plays tricks on me. Turn on the light, please."

"All right," he said, stepping deeper in, toward a wall-mounted lamp. Gently, he adjusted it to its lowest setting. "But just a little."

The soft yellow light flushed the darkness and caressed the slight figure of Elizabeth Frankenstein. She lay atop the bedding, unkempt hair carelessly strewn alongside her head on the pillow like thin straw. The rosy blossom in her cheeks that Henry still remembered was gone. Now she wore a pale, gaunt look almost as dreary as his own.

"Sit with me, Henry," she said from the bed.

They were always both high-strung. Antic birds, as his acerbic father called them between pipe puffs. That was what he and Elizabeth had always understood so easily about one another, why he could face her manic flights with tenderness and patience, why she could leave him to his brooding, solitary work, his lonely dreams of changing mankind forever, for the better.

"You seem so distant, my darling," she said. He did not reply, just looked at her as he closed the short distance between the door and her side.

"I'm sorry if it seems that way," he said as he sat on the bed beside her and took her hands in his own. "Mostly, I worry about you."

He touched her long fingers and petted the back of her hand. They felt cold, and he pressed them to make them warmer. "The nightmares will pass in time, I'm sure."

A new expression played on her face, like that of an insane cat, eyes wide, but attention turned inward. "But they're not just dreams, Henry. I see them when I'm awake," she said. As an afterthought, she added, more curious than upset, "Am I going mad?"

"No, no, no!" he said. He forced himself to smile as he gripped her hand tighter. "It's just the shock. You've been through so much. It hasn't even been a week since that horrific business. You must give yourself time, my dear. You must."

He pulled her close, half lifting her into his arms, concerned at how light she felt. He buried his head in her shoulder, and rubbed her back. "There, there," he said and felt her tremble.

She stiffened and pulled back, her humanity suddenly clouded over by fear.

"Elizabeth, what is it?" he said, but he knew. He'd seen the look, the night Septimus Pretorius arrived to drag him back to his experiments, and three times since.

She drew back, curled her spine, and pointed to a spot in thin air, between the wall and the cabin's ceiling. "It's here again, Henry! It's reaching out its bony hand! The angel of death!"

"No, no, Elizabeth," he said, but he knew there was no talking to her now.

She raised the back of her hand to her chin, her voice rising to a near-shriek. "It's pulling at the veil between our world, Henry, and it's terribly strong! It wants to force its way here, to make you pay for your sins!"

For a moment he thought he saw it, too, hovering in the dark above the bed, somewhere between a shadow and a thought. Its face was too familiar, gaunt with sallow cheeks, bolts holding the flat top of the head down to the rest of the skull. It was a monster. Not from the depths of the ocean, or beyond the pale, but from his own hands. His monster.

What a terrible liberation it had been: Pretorius instructing the monster to kidnap Elizabeth, forcing Henry to do that which he secretly longed, to continue his experiments in creating life. Even now, though he was disgusted at himself, the memory of the stitching thrilled him—of touching bone, muscle, arteries, assembling them as if he were an artist drawing form and meaning from dull clay. It was the only time—the only time in all his life!—his hands were as steady as the darkness between stars.

But now it was over. It had to be. All over except the nightmares.

He shook her till she faced him. "No! Elizabeth! There's nothing there! Nothing at all! You're safe! We're safe! There is no angel of death coming for me, my darling!"

She calmed momentarily, but then something lost and animal took her eyes and her lips curled into the grotesque mockery of a smile. "You? Oh, no, my Henry. It doesn't come for *you*, this time! It's *me* it wants! Me!"

He believed it when he'd told her the delusions would pass, given time. But here and now, the mad glint thriving in her eyes, he was no longer quite so sure.

"It's dead, Elizabeth. They're all dead. Nothing could have survived that explosion. Nothing."

"Nothing?" she said weakly.

"Nothing," Henry said reassuringly.

Not the monster, not Pretorius, not the female creature.

"Nothing."

But he could tell that, much as she wanted to, she couldn't bring herself to believe him.

Chapter Three

"Well that's ducky, 'innit?" Mary Blyss said as she knocked back her whiskey. "Women've been pushing life out between their legs for a million years. One snot-nose bloke comes along, makes himself a monster, and thinks he's the bloody king of England . . . "

On the surface she was a short, feisty thing with a small, round face that made her look a bit like a cute monkey. Adding to the impression were her mischievous green eyes, fluffy light brown hair that formed a gay mane around most of her head, and a smart, disarming laugh.

But inside Mary was still trying to calm down. Not an hour ago, Dilke, a nasty brute she barely knew, had spun her about, hiked her skirt, and pushed her into a wall. He could have had her for a few coins, but he was too drunk to ask. As he pressed his foul-smelling mouth closer, she wanted desperately to scratch or kick him, but for all her years as a prostitute, for all her years here at the Whale and Watch on Thrawl Street, Whitechapel, she never could raise her hand to a man. Something inside her just froze.

So when the tall, blond, blue-eyed German, Inspector Erik Krogh, pulled Dilke off her like a leaf on her shawl and ran the drunken fool out the front door, she'd sidled up to him immediately, hoping to make him a regular customer.

Ever since, she'd been trying to get a rise out of him, a smile or a wink, or even a nod, but so far, no such luck. His manner was stiff, self-conscious, even after a few drinks, and his rugged

face held a kind of perpetual sadness. Mostly he seemed interested in telling his monster story.

"I know it's fantastic, but it's true," he said, flatly. "And I in-
tend to see the young baron behind bars."

She shook her head sympathetically, and made a "Tsk,
tsk" sound with her tongue. He didn't react. Probably
didn't hear, what with the raucous late night—or rather early
morning—crowd.

They sat at a small table, just beyond the privacy screen, so
Mary had a view of the bar and the front door, in case Dilke
returned, or any of her regulars came 'round. The old Victorian
screen had been hit by so many flying tankards and fists, it
looked more like a bunch of cracks than like frosted glass. At
night, when one couldn't see quite so clearly, the dark wood
paneling, leaded lights, and windows all still looked lovely, not
unlike the slightly aged prostitutes who met their clients here.

Centuries back, the Whale, like a lot of local pubs, was a
monastery. Then Henry VII formed the Church of England
and dissolution destroyed the monasteries, forcing the monks
to make more ale than prayers. A room in the back still held
a few ancient casks under its flying buttresses, and nowa-
days provided a quiet spot for a quick tryst, when the alleys
seemed too dangerous and you didn't want to walk all the way
home. She could have taken Dilke there if he hadn't been such
a lout.

But he'd really put the fear of God into her.

Sure, each month saw its share of beatings and robberies,
each year its share of murder, but just last month, two women
had been found cut up so badly that the lazy press, rather than
go out and find itself some real, respectable news, started trum-
peting the return of Jack the Ripper. Mary didn't believe the
nonsense that Saucy Jack was back, neither did anyone else in
the neighborhood, but she was acquainted with one of the victims,

a woman named Daisy Spatz, and that, more than anything else, had her anxiously watching the shadows. After all, the way she froze up, what would she do if attacked, other than curl up and wait to die?

Oh, but this Krogh fellow sure didn't seem the rough sort, and that was worth some time. She comforted herself that she was usually right about a man's character, except, of course, for her husband, Mr. Benjamin Blyss, but she was too drunk to stand the night she let him into her life and he locked the door behind him on his way in.

If ever there was a man she wished she *could* raise her hand to, or hurl a frying pan at, or dip in boiling oil, or draw and quarter, it was Ben.

But how to get to Krogh? She'd had some schooling as a girl, unlike a lot of the others, so maybe she could think her way in. He was a serious fellow, a little lost in London, and all about this monster thing. Maybe she should try to draw him out a bit on it? She buried her practiced cheeriness, scrunching her face to make it look as close to grim as she could, and asked, "So, did this monster hurt one of yours?"

Krogh nodded. "My son, Rikard. A boy of four."

Mary opened her eyes wide, reached out, grasped his arm, and said melodramatically. "Preserve us, was the lad killed?"

Krogh shook his head and took a swig of his whiskey. "No. The monster was ravaging the countryside when it burst into our small home. It was a horrid giant of a thing, more like a storm than a man, its flat, giant head full of scars from the attacks of the men that had tried to kill it. I'd just fixed the door that morning, made it stronger with the best wood I could find, but the creature tore it off the . . . the . . . I'm sorry I don't know the word . . . "

And he was. Genuinely sorry. He even looked down, embarrassed by his ignorance. Mary used the opportunity to rub his forearm a little. "Nothing to be ashamed of. It's not your language, after all. The hinges, love? Do you mean the hinges?"

Krogh nodded and pulled out a small book. He slipped the string around it off and used the nub of a pencil that lay folded in its pages to write the word down. He folded the book closed, then lifted his head and continued. "The creature tore the door off its hinges like they were made of paper. I had my gun. I fired. I'm a good shot. I hit it, but it just came for me, hurling me across the room with such strength that my back cracked an old shelf in half. Then poor Rikard came forward thinking, I suppose, to protect me. It grabbed his arm and . . . "

Krogh swallowed hard. Mary searched her brain, unable to imagine what English word he'd forgotten or didn't know. But Krogh hadn't forgotten the words, he was just having trouble saying them. "And yanked it from its socket, like a dead branch off a tree."

Her little mouth parted, but Mary was speechless. Krogh poured another drink for himself and one for Mary as well. Then he stiffly tapped the bottom of his glass to the top of hers, and poured the contents down his throat.

"That's why I've come. For justice. I'd almost convinced the burgomaster to pursue charges when Frankenstein fled. He thought to escape me, but he was mistaken. True, I have no power here, but Inspector Devin of Scotland Yard has agreed to meet me in the morning."

She wrinkled her brow, bringing her small face together on either side of her nose. "But what are you doing in Whitechapel? The only barons here were just released from the loony bin where they shared their water closet with a dozen Napoleons."

That embarrassed look came over Krogh's face again. "In my small village, sometimes I get a pig as a salary. To come here I had to sell my father's gold and borrow money from family and friends. The lodgings in the East End are such that I wouldn't let that pig live in them, but they're all I could afford."

Mary tried to keep her disappointment from her face: *No money, then.*

Krogh glanced up at the cheap imitation of a nautical clock hanging on the wall. "I'm sorry, Fräulein, for burdening you. I think at last there's enough drink in me to let me sleep before my morning meeting. Sleep has been hard to come by since . . . well, I thank you for your company."

He rose, swaying slightly on his feet, then dug deep in his pocket to produce the few coins he placed on the table.

Cripes, Ben'll kill me if I come home empty-handed.

Trying to force the image of a screaming, one-armed, four-year-old from her mind, she smiled, prettily as she could. And she was pretty. Of course, Krogh couldn't see the long, wide, white scar on her abdomen that Ben gave her last Christmas, instead of a goose. The midwife he dragged her to that night to stop the bleeding was drunk, too, her mouth and fingers so covered with chicken fat she couldn't completely wipe it off on her apron before she took to sewing Mary. Worse, the woman had never done that sort of stitching before, so even the threads and the puncture wounds from her awkward suturing remained, white and raised.

But Mary was still pretty, and it was a rare customer that turned her away.

"Inspector Krogh," she said. He turned his head toward her. "I bet your lodgings aren't near as bad as you say. I'm thinking all they need is a woman's touch. I'm also thinking you could do with a woman's touch yourself, if I could find a few coins in that pocket of yours."

Krogh seemed confused at first.

Gak! Do they even have sex in his small village, or do all the women just lay eggs or take a trip to the baby store? Did he think we were just passing the time with drinks at three in the morning?

Then he looked hurt, and Mary realized he had.

"Fräulein, my dear wife sits at home now, and if she is not changing our son's . . ."

"Bandages?" Mary offered.

"Bandages, yes, if she's not changing his bandages, she prays for my quick, safe return. Only an unthinking brute would break a vow to her now. So, I wish you a good evening."

He whirled, stepped to the other side of the partition, and vanished out the door. His tone was so polite, she didn't even feel insulted, just annoyed. But now she'd wasted an hour with nothing to show for it. Nearly morning and not a regular customer in sight. Ben would likely have drunk through whatever pennies he'd begged for during the day, and if she didn't have more, he'd turn on her. Oh, he'd be too far gone to cut her again, but his fists were strong, and he had a way of flailing that made it difficult to duck even his most awkwardly placed blows.

Why can't I just fight back, the way Cyra or Mitzie do? I bet he'd turn tail and run if I so much as blocked him.

Well, maybe one day she'd just pick herself up and head off. There must be bars and drunken men in other cities, other countries. She might even be considered more exotic there, like Cyra, who had a whole dark-skinned Gypsy act worked out. Maybe she could even make her way to Krogh's little village and marry herself a nice shepherd.

Ha!

She sighed, feeling tipsy and desperately in need of sleep. Maybe she could find a spot to catch a few hours' sleep before the sun rose, then grab a bloke on his way to work in the morning. Ben would be satisfied with a few coins. She'd done it before.

Scanning the tables for familiar faces, she spotted Mitzie. The younger girl, wearing an A-line skirt and cast-off gabardine jacket that hung crazily off her shoulder, was leaning forward across her table to better show her cleavage. The way the pub's dim yellow light twinkled against the black of her eyes made her seem quite smart, though she wasn't. But you didn't have to be bright in this business, just pretty, and Mitzie was that. Mary figured the rough bloke opposite her was probably her fifth for the night.

When Mary first met her, she was surprised such a looker didn't have a husband with an actual job. It made more sense when she got to know her. The girl wasn't totally screwy, but when she was thirteen and her father found her pregnant by the milkman, he threw her down some stairs. She landed on concrete, costing her the baby and flattening the side of her skull. A decade later, she still wore a little cotton cap stuffed with paper to hide the deformity.

She and Mitzie had been friends for years. She had a little flat a block away. Mary could catch a few winks all curled up on the floor.

Mary leaned out and waved to the girl. When there was no response, she whispered, "Mitzie!"

Mary knew she heard, but the strawberry blonde ignored her. Usually, she'd let it go, but Mary's shoes were tight and her feet numb.

"Mitzie!" she said again, not bothering to whisper.

The girl grinned at her unseen companion, then leaned out and gave Mary a hot glare. "What?!" she formed with her lips.

Mary frantically waved her over. Mitzie made a face, said a few words to her customer, and stepped over.

"I'm working!" Mitzie hissed.

"All work and no play, dear," Mary said with a shrug. "Look,

I'm sorry to be a bother but I'm aching to shut my eyes. I haven't got a half-penny and Ben will be in a mood."

"No luck all night?" Mitzie said, surprised. "I thought I saw you with that strapping blond fellow. I was thinking I might be jealous."

She shook her head sadly. "Says he has a wife and sick boy back home, but, truth to tell, I don't think he likes women. Either way, I drank all I made early on and none's left. Ben can get wicked when I come home like that. Let me sleep on your floor?"

"Sure, love, just give me half an hour, okay?" she said, nodding back toward the table. "This one's the last. He's been waiting, and he even paid for some fish and chips."

"Oh, did he now?"

Mary looked through the dark toward the little table, paying more attention now that she knew the man had money. His back was still mostly to her, but he'd shifted sideways in his seat. He seemed short and stout. As he twisted slightly, she caught a glimpse of a carroty moustache and a blotched face. Something about him made Mary shiver. He was not a good-looking man.

"Do you know him?" Mary asked. "I've never seen him, and you should be a little careful after what happened to Daisy."

Mitzie's eyes went wide and she giggled madly. It was the most obvious way her old wound affected her, making her laugh at inappropriate moments. Like right now, unless you knew her, you wouldn't realize that the laugh meant she was afraid.

Mitzie put the back of her hand to her lips and tried to stop herself. "I know! They say it's like the Ripper's back in town."

"More likely she had an addiction and a debt," Mary said. "But this is still Whitechapel, darling. Try to remember what we're famous for."

"Don't worry. I read johns like a book. This one tries to act all educated, mispronouncing big words left and right. I'm sure he wouldn't hurt a fly."

Mary waved her hand in the air. "I'm too tired to fight. Just leave a sock on the door handle so I don't come barging in on you and Sir Isaac Newton," she said. Then she cast another glance at the shabbily dressed man. "Oh, I'm sure he's fine. What difference does it make, right? We're all doomed to hell anyway."

"Not necessarily!" Mitzie said, whirling back toward the table. "This fellow says that when we die we'll be reincarcerated in brand new bodies!"

Mary gave her a wry glance. "I think he probably meant *reincarnated*, darling. Though, in our case, both're probably true."

Mitzie liked this one. She certainly wouldn't let him have a go for free, but she liked him and that made it nicer, easier. He had a quiet way about him. He even kept to himself for a good long time when he came in, like he was watching the scene, not quite a part of things, not even moving. When he did move, that set him apart, too. His shoulders didn't shift as he walked, or his arms sway. It was like his top half was set on wheels, and he slid about like a smooth carriage drawn on ice by invisible horses.

Mitzie'd been sizing him up since he came in. She saw the bill he used to pay for his drink and watched him pocket the change without bothering to count. When she finally went over and got a good look at his face (no prizes to be given there, mind you) she noticed his gaze was as steady as his gait, in the same soft and calm sort of way, like he had all the time in the world.

He also had a funny way of talking. His cockney was thick, but he kept trying to use high-falutin' words. He said "sore" instead of "sir" and didn't want to let her out of his sight for a minute. She even liked the way he broached the business, the way he just said, "What I'll be wantin' most, miss, is to be seein' your room." Or something like that. He tended to swallow the words at the end of his sentences, not from shyness, but kind of like his breath had run out and he wasn't very good at pacing it for speech.

He'd said it twice, maybe three times; "What I'll be wantin' most, miss, is to be seein' your room."

What else could it be?

They made their way to the grime-covered pub door. Though not much taller, he put his arm around her shoulder and she felt the weight of his cloak drift across her back. As he donned his deerstalker, she adjusted the knit cap on her strawberry hair, careful to make sure the paper in it didn't fall out. The doctor had removed a bit of bone on that side, to keep it from pressing on her brain, and now it was soft to the touch. If the spot got so much as a draft, she'd have the strangest dreams for weeks.

Sometimes she dreamt of tumbling down those stairs again, Father looming above her, stooping as if to try to catch her. But then she came crashing down on the concrete landing, where her skull cracked and pressed into her brain. She wondered, sometimes, if she left the very best of her thoughts just below the surface of that landing.

The memory of the dream made her afraid, so she giggled. Good thing this fellow didn't know what she was thinking. He might think her too broken to bother with.

He pushed the door to the Whale open and let it close up behind them, taking with it the soft conversation and the light. Outside, it was one of those typical London nights, ladled with pea-soup fog. There were electric streetlamps on the wider avenues now, but here they were still gaslight. All the flames had funny circles about them, as if someone had taken a paintbrush and outlined their glow.

There were still a few people about. She could hear their scurrying footsteps, even if she couldn't see them. As they walked, some of the shadows turned out to be drunken women, too old to work the pub, leaning up against walls as rickety as they were, wearing ripped stockings.

Mitzie and her customer walked arm in arm, past old buildings, two to four stories tall, all with proper roofs, but some leaning together, looking like they were about to fall over.

As they went, his steps grew more hurried. Mitzie figured he was eager. That made her even more comfortable, because it meant she would be in control. She regarded his face again, the blotchy rashes on ruddy skin, the thick reddish moustache she hoped would tickle, but feared might feel more like a stiff brush against her skin.

They turned right on Plumber's Row and the small set of workers' cottages where she had her room. By now his breathing, which had been so even, sounded raspy. Maybe the cold air was bad for his lungs.

"Just a few doors in," she said, reassuringly. He nodded, as if he'd already known.

When they reached it, she pulled the skeleton key from a pocket in her skirt and lifted the latch.

"Up the apples, then," she said. She took his hand and guided him up the stairs. It was pitch-black, but she knew the way, even drunk.

The door to her small room creaked just a little as she opened it. Inside, there was just space for her bed, her nightstand, and the two of them. She had to press past him to close the door, and caught a whiff of food and alcohol as she did. Remembering Mary, she grabbed a sock from the floor and fitted it on the doorknob.

On the nightstand sat a candle in a candlestick, the room's sole source of light. It added a touch of class, she thought. On it, a fairy, made up of some cheap metal, bent her back and wings beneath the white-wax shaft. She'd found it lying in an alley and never could imagine who would throw out such a pretty girl.

She struck a match and lit the candle. The glow cast his shadow, huge and flat, on the old plaster wall.

"Here's my room then," she said, turning to smile at him. "Not much, but it's home."

"Hike up your skirt," he said. Relieved it would be quick, she complied.

"Higher."

Dutifully, she pulled her cotton slip up, revealing the soft white skin of her smooth belly.

"Like this?" she said, caressing her skin with her fingers.

He didn't react. His eyes were as steady as they'd been in the pub. "Now turn yourself around, put your back to me," he said. "And don't move your arms."

Her brow furrowed slightly. Still holding her skirt up, she waddled in a half-circle so that now she faced the candle. Beyond it, outside the single small window, she could make out the tops of the buildings against the fog. Still too early for any hint of sun. It all looked like a pretty dream.

"Want me to bend over?"

"No," he said.

There was an awkward silence, and a question popped into her head. She probably shouldn't have asked, but she did anyway.

"You really think we all come back after we die?"

There was a quick rustling. He was taking something off. His cloak, she figured.

"Well," he said in that gruff tone of his. "That I can't tell you, but I do know that some of us never leave."

Before she could ask what he meant, she felt a sharp, hard pressure against her throat. By the time she dropped her skirt and raised her hands, she found she couldn't talk or breathe, let alone scream. She tried to twist away, but his hands were powerful, like steel, and she was already feeling dizzy.

"What I'll be wantin' most, miss, is to be seein' your room," he said again, or so she thought. She couldn't tell really, she was blacking out. The window view swam in her vision. Buildings floated in the fog, surrounded by patches of black that grew bigger and bigger, until that's all there was.

The next things she felt were the mattress beneath her, the pillow under her head, and the cold air in the room against her exposed legs and abdomen.

Was it over then? Had she survived? Was he gone?

She managed somehow to open her eyes.

He was standing next to her, a dark shadow save for the glint of metal from the knife he held in his hand.

She only realized then, watching, semi-conscious, as the knife came down and began to open her up from the base of her navel to the bottom of her rib cage, that he hadn't said room at all.

What he'd said was, "What I'll be wantin' most, miss, is to be seein' your womb."

The first cut happened so quickly, she hadn't felt anything but foolish, but as the knife came down again, shining in the candlelight, sliding once more into her abdomen and this time ripping down, the pain began and she couldn't help but do as she always did when she was afraid or nervous, and giggle. Though it didn't sound quite like a giggle anymore, because her throat had been slit.

If her killer thought it odd, he didn't pause in his work. He simply went about his business, skillfully moving the knife in slices both jagged and clean until Mitzie's giggling, and Mitzie herself, stopped completely.

As the drunk wore off, Mary's head throbbed at the temples. The fog and the coal-dust air made her nose drip.

Wouldn't a cold just beat all? Or maybe I'll be lucky and just get consumption.

It was too dark to tell whether or not what she coughed up was freckled with blood. Sighing, she looked up at the Plumber's Row window, the one with the small candle flickering in it.

What could they still be doing in there?

She'd been standing outside Mitzie's flat a good fifteen minutes. The chill had worked its way through her shawl, through her clothes, into her skin. When she opened the front door and saw how dark it was on the stairs, she'd realized she'd make a racket trying to climb them and decided against checking for the sock. She didn't want to ruin Mitzie's trick. After all, coins usually changed hands after the fact.

But now she was getting annoyed. For all she knew, they'd been done ages ago. Mitzie was probably fast asleep, letting the candle burn itself out. Rubbing her temples and coughing, Mary pushed open the door. A sliver of light from a streetlamp tumbled in, hitting a piece of cloth on the floor. It looked a bit like a sock, but it was soaked in some sort of dark reddish oil. Thinking nothing further of it, Mary stepped over it and mounted the steps. Occasionally, her foot landed in something wet and sticky. This was also no surprise in this little corner of hell.

Creeping as slowly as she could, she stumbled and cursed just twice before she found the second-floor door.

It was too dark to tell if there was a sock on it or not, so, trying to suppress a cough, she gingerly felt about for the knob. Her palm made contact with cold metal. No sock, but there was something wet on it. Maybe Mitzie had washed up and her hands were still wet when she took the sock off the door.

It didn't matter. The only thing that mattered to Mary was lying down on a borrowed blanket, getting enough sleep so her sweet, monkey face didn't look all pasty and puffy when she hit the streets again at sunrise. She suppressed a cough again and hoped Mitzie wasn't awake and didn't want to talk. Her throat could use a rest.

But that's not what it got.

When she opened the door and saw, in the candlelight, the pieces of Mitzie laid out on her blood-drenched bed like a cow at a meat market, Mary screamed and screamed and screamed.

It wasn't until the second time she looked, when she stopped screaming long enough to open her eyes and make absolutely certain she wasn't imagining the scene, that she saw the terrible grin on the dead girl's face. That's when it felt like more than shock, when it felt as if a cold finger had reached through her chest and touched her heart, because she knew in a flash from the desperate upward curl of her lips, exactly how frightened poor Mitzie had been when she died.

Chapter Four

Fineries were wasted on Henry Frankenstein, even as a boy. Staring at stars or gently pulling apart the leaves of a plant to study the framework of the veins inside was always more fascinating than being fitted for expensive clothes or having servants waiting on him. It wasn't that he disdained such things, he just didn't care. Decorations held no interest. He longed only for what lay beneath.

As he strutted nervously about the plush beige carpet, rubbing his hands, he was oblivious to the luxurious hotel suite in which he paced, with its wide, long rooms and glorious view of the South London smokestacks that lay just past a Thames alive with freighters and scows. Silk-lined curtains in a jacquard pattern with elaborate tassels hung on either side, making the view seem like it took place on a stage.

Elizabeth was in the other room, resting after their long journey. They'd been at the Savoy two days now. Each night, thinking she was at last asleep, he restlessly wandered the streets or badgered the manager about when the luggage might arrive. When she'd caught him out, he was secretive. Sharing his thoughts might upset her. So instead he promised not to leave her alone again.

But now, all day he'd been like a caged animal, his vexed mind beating, wanting to pursue the dark reason he'd chosen London as a haven. His actual experiments were at an end, but there was a theoretical question he longed to have answered. The implications weighed heavily on him, but there was only so much he could do until the luggage, with his papers, arrived.

It was Fritz, his hunchbacked assistant, after all, who'd brought him the abnormal, criminal brain he'd unwittingly used in the monster. *That's what made it a monster*, Frankenstein told himself. *I'd done everything perfectly. The blood is on Fritz's hands, poor devil.*

Just a few days after his great success, he'd found Fritz's body, hung by the neck, the monster growling as if it was a lion protecting a just-slaughtered meal. True, the hunchback had tormented the creature, gleefully burned it, but still, to come to such an end. It was when Frankenstein first saw the monster's animal reaction to Fritz's torch that he stopped referring to the creature as *he* and started using *it*. Finding his assistant dead froze that decision forever.

He might have jittered about the room that way for hours, but a knock at the door nearly catapulted him out of his skin. He rushed toward the white oak door, making sure the chain lock was secure, and leaned his head in. "Who's there? What do you want? I told you we were to be left alone!"

A creaky, familiar voice answered. "It's Minnie, Master Frankenstein! We've arrived at last!"

Henry never cared for the shrill old woman his late father hired, thinking of her as less a servant and more a final joke from the old baron. Still, hearing her voice meant his papers were here, so he undid the chain and threw open the door.

Minnie, more haggard than usual from her journey, leaned against the frame. Behind her were a league of bellhops accompanying all manner of chest, suitcase, and bag. If his papers were there, he couldn't see them for all the clutter.

With a frantic wave of his hands, he motioned them all in. "Bring it in, bring it all in."

As the belongings were neatly laid on the floor, Minnie

stumbled in as well, plopped herself into one of the comfortable chairs, and fanned herself with a newspaper.

"Oh, what a terrible journey," she moaned melodramatically. "The waves were as high as mountains, and they left my poor stomach twisted like strudel. If you don't mind my saying, I spent more time heaving than I did breathing!"

"Come now, it couldn't have been that bad," Frankenstein said absently. His eyes were riveted on each bag as it came in, searching for the one he wanted.

"Not that bad? I picked up a paper on the corner here half expecting to read about my own death by drowning! That rusty hulk nearly turned over three times! They even think one of their poor sailors fell overboard, that a wave came right up and yanked him from the deck, save us all!"

As she babbled, the old brown leather case came into view, seeming none the worse for wear. He raced toward it, nearly pushing the bellhops out of his way. He grabbed and opened it, disregarded the thick journal that took most of the space inside, and pulled out a thick pile of loose papers.

Fearing the bellhops were watching, he pressed a few coins into their eager palms and dismissed them.

"If there's anything else you need, sir," one said with a smile, obviously pleased by the baron's largesse.

"We are not to be disturbed," he said as he closed and locked the doors.

He fanned the papers and found a pink sheet folded in quarters. Excited, he unfolded it, revealing a handwritten receipt signed by the late Dr. Waldman for body parts shipped to Goldstadt Medical College from the Burke & Hare Medical Supply Warehouse on Chatsworth Street, London. Among the items listed were two brains, one normal, one abnormal. With a shudder, Frankenstein realized how ironic it was that the very brain Waldman analyzed in a jar guided the powerful hands that ended his life.

And it was Waldman himself who explained Fritz had stolen the wrong brain. At first Frankenstein had dismissed the issue. It was only a piece of tissue, after all. For a while, he even rationalized the killing the creature did. Of course it wanted to kill the sadistic Fritz. Waldman died trying to destroy it by dissection.

But if those first killings seemed self-defense, there'd been so many since, innocent children among them, that Frankenstein was forced to consider alternative theories. A broken arm, after all, didn't function the same as a healthy one. Why not a brain?

Waldman's notes mentioned a scarcity of convolutions on the frontal lobe, with a distinct degeneration of the middle frontal lobe, adding that these degenerate characteristics tallied with the case history of the dead man, whose life was one of "brutality, violence, and murder."

Those three words also described the life of his creation, making the conclusion inescapable. The brain was at fault. His experiment had been the victim of an accident, no more. A different brain and he'd be honored now, not reviled. It was better, at any rate, than believing God was punishing him for daring to traipse upon His domain, and create life through manmade science.

But the theory only begged more questions: Was the brain born that way, or had it succumbed to some disease or trauma? What was the life of the donor like?

He had to know.

He folded the receipt and stuffed it in his pocket.

"Minnie," he said. She started as if she'd forgotten he was there. "Forget about unpacking for now. There's an urgent errand I must attend to." He walked over and gently pulled the startled woman out of her seat. "I want you to sit with Elizabeth, keep her company. She's been very upset."

"Of course, sir," she said, grabbing her paper from the chair. "I'll read her from the papers."

Frankenstein put his arm around her shoulder and guided her toward the bedroom. "Be careful what you speak about. She needs to relax, to calm down. You won't speak of anything upsetting, will you?"

She laughed. "Me? Of course not! I'll be as gentle as I would with a newborn babe. We've all had our fill of horror for the rest of the century, if you ask me!"

He opened the door and pushed her gently inside. "Thank you, Minnie. I shan't be long."

She turned and was probably about to say something, but he quickly closed the door.

He felt a twinge of guilt at leaving Elizabeth, but reasoned she'd be better off in the cheerful company of the servant rather than with his hovering and fretting.

Patting the receipt in his pocket, he grabbed his coat and headed for the door.

"Minnie, you've made it," Elizabeth said, brightening as the woman entered. "I was worried."

She lay on a four-poster double bed with a bronze canopy.

"I'm fit as a fiddle, baroness. And I'll tell you my terrible or-deal another day. The baron says you need to relax, and he's right for a change!" she said, waddling in and surveying the scene.

A small fire burned quietly in the fireplace. There was a beautiful bureau topped by an oval mirror against the wall. There was also a washstand with pitcher and basin for decoration, a comfortable chair by the window, and a highboy chest of drawers. But the room was dark, lit by small electric lights, the drapes drawn in front of the huge windows.

Minnie tsked and headed for the drapes.

"Please, I prefer the dark," Elizabeth protested.

"Nonsense, lady, it's a rare beautiful day in London," Minnie answered, and, with a slight flourish, she pulled the heavy cloths back, flooding the room with sunlight.

Elizabeth raised her hand to protect her eyes. "It's useless arguing with you. You're almost as bad as Henry."

"Hmph," Minnie said, displeased with the comparison but unwilling to register the offense. She pulled an upholstered seat up next to her mistress. "Now, what say I entertain you with the latest news of this heaping pile of smokestacks they call a city?"

Elizabeth smiled. "All right."

The old woman's eyes scanned the first page. "Oh, my. It says here a local lady of the evening was found . . . hmm mmm . . . "

Elizabeth leaned abruptly forward. "What does it say, Minnie?"

The servant looked at her overwrought mistress, then back at the paper. "Oh, I can't say. It's too horrible," she said. She kept reading to herself, her face growing paler as she did.

"Tell me! You must!" Elizabeth said.

"Oh, all right!" Minnie said. "Some poor woman was found all cut up. Sliced her into pieces, the murderer did! And in a church, some sort of white chapel!" Minnie said, shaking her head in disgust.

Elizabeth swallowed hard. "Cut her up, did you say?"

"Into pieces, I said," she said, nodding. She scanned a few more lines and paraphrased. "Certain pieces of which were no longer about."

Elizabeth's face went blank. "Parts of the body were missing?"

"Yes, mum, that's what it says right here. Doesn't say which parts, exactly, but I can read further, if you like," Minnie said.

"No, that's all right," Elizabeth answered, slumping back into her pillow.

Minnie grunted with deep disapproval. "Now what sort of man goes about collecting dead body parts?" Minnie said, more to herself than to Elizabeth.

"I think I know," Elizabeth said softly. "Henry didn't think I'd heard, but that inspector back home accused him of murdering a woman for her heart."

Noticing she was shivering, Minnie moved to close the window.

But Minnie knew it wasn't the draft that left her cold and shaking. She could tell, just by looking, that Elizabeth Frankenstein was worried, deathly worried, that her husband was at it again.

Chapter Five

Cutting corners.

Cutting remarks.

Wasted, frightened, but still trying to be strong in the presence of the stiff-lipped, stiff-backed bobbies that flanked her, Mary pushed the gory images of last night's horror out of her mind, but found herself haunted by a word.

Cutting a rug.

Cutting Mitzie.

She tried to keep it out of her desiccated, hungover mind, but couldn't. It was there with her wherever she turned as they led her down a basement hallway. The dress and knitted shawl she'd been wearing since last night were now stained with anxious sweat and tears. Her legs wobbled, threatening to give out, but she managed to keep pace. The police didn't smile or offer comfort, they just led.

Cutting onions.

Cutting beef.

One of them pulled on a door and her nostrils were assaulted by the smell of ammonia mixed in with an odor she recognized from the single time she'd been in a slaughterhouse. The door squealed open, as if its edges were cutting its own frame.

The room before her was big and silent as a graveyard. A sharp silver cone of metal hung like a blade in the center, white light from its bulb sliced the dark beneath it, extending the cone to the table below, throwing gangly, sharp shadows on the tiled floor.

Cutting.

There was a drain in the middle of the floor. She wondered what the devil it was for, then realized it was to make it easier to wash the blood away.

Cutting.

After that she decided to try not to think. Tall and strong, like a good solid piece of wood, one of the bobbies took a few more steps with her toward the table, then backed up as he gently prodded her forward. Puzzled, she looked at his face a moment and noticed a few beads of sweat on his pale cheek.

She guessed he was going to be sick.

She scrunched her small, monkey face and turned toward the body on the table. A stiff white sheet covered most of Mitzie, but you could tell by the strange shape the sheet took that there were things wrong beneath it, out of place, something squished up here, something missing there. There were probably big, pretty words for each and every piece of Mitzie. Latin, like the Mass. All those doctors spoke in Latin. Mary was glad she didn't know Latin. She just stared at the face. Mitzie's eyes were closed. Her death-grin was gone, too, though Mary swore the lips, now a drained dark gray with just a hint of purple, were still just a little upturned at the corners.

Cutting.

There was a voice behind her. "Do you identify this woman as Mitzie Donnor, most recent address being 42 Plumber's Row?"

She turned to see a fat man with white hair reading from a clipboard. He bobbed his head as if he were listening to a song playing in his brain.

"Yes," Mary said, realizing how hoarse and dry her throat was. She coughed a little, careful not to breathe in too much of the smelly air, and tried to speak again. "Yes. That's her. Mitzie. Donnor. Like you said, on Plumber's Row."

She felt awkward, like she was saying "I do" at a church ceremony.

As it turned out, there wasn't anything else to sign or do, so she staggered out of the Commercial Street police station into a too-bright day. The red-brick building with marble details was nothing grand, but it was well made in the Victorian style. Her poor eyes wished it'd been the usual overcast sky, but London cared so little for Mitzie it'd decided to be cheerful on its first day without her for so many years.

It was a good ten-block walk home. No one at the station offered a ride, just an admonition to stay available in case there were more questions. It was a workday, after nine, and the wide avenue was busy with pedestrians and cloth peddlers pushing rolls of fabric on sidewalk carts. In the street, dray horses mixed with an occasional automobile, or omnibus, or lorry going to and from the Smithfield meat market.

What time was it? Noon? Too late to earn a quick one, so there was little hope of giving Ben some money, which meant there'd be hell to pay if she went home. Where to go then? Off to the rails for a jaunt in the country? No, back to the Whale for some hair of the dog, then home to face the dog himself. Maybe he'd forgive her because of Mitzie.

Ha!

Mitzie. Mary told herself in retrospect that she'd known something was off about that man, and in a selfish sort of way, the thought comforted her. Mitzie, after all, wasn't quite right in the head. Someone was always taking advantage of her, not paying enough because she couldn't count the coins up right, or not paying at all. Maybe it was bound to happen to the poor child.

But not Mary. She'd smell a killer like that. He had to reek of something, something deep and predatory. The image of Mitzie, looking like a cow at the butcher's with a human face stuck up top, flashed in her brain. What sort of monster did such a thing? Was the press right? Was it some goblin-child that fancied himself the new Jack the Ripper?

But Mary would smell him. She just would.

Just like I could tell about Ben?

Well, Ben was a piece of work, yes. He'd hit her, yes. But he could never . . .

She put her palm to her plump belly. Through the dress, she couldn't exactly feel the scar Ben'd given her, but the skin on her hand and fingers tingled just the same, as if they could sense the unfeeling tissue.

Cutting.

If only I could raise my hand to him, just once.

Such a look he'd had in his eyes when he'd done it, glazed over, like his soul had slipped out for holiday leaving some diseased cousin behind in its place. Her next thought, the sick thought, welled up like bad food ready to be regurgitated.

What if the killer *hadn't* been Mitzie's john? What if he'd slipped out after the deed and someone else, like Ben, had shown up at Mitzie's flat looking for Mary? What if he'd had his drunk on and his knife out, and thought the girl in the bed *was* Mary?

No, no, no.

She bit the insides of her lip, felt tears well, then beat them back. Ben was a lout, a ruffian. He might even one day kill Mary, but not like that.

As she came to a crossroads the traffic thinned. On the far corner sat, like a fat drunk on a barstool, a two-story wreck of a building that filled the entire block. The crumbly brick behemoth, an old warehouse, once held some kind of textiles. Built before electric lights, the windows were tall to make the best of the natural light. Most on the first floor were boarded, but some above had glass.

Something had happened to it, a fire or somesuch. Now it was a mostly hollow hulk, a fine home for birds and, every now and again, a drifter so far down on his luck he could do no better than its rough floor and open ceiling.

Still, walking diagonal through the building cut the trip round the block in half and lots of working folk from Whitechapel and Spitalfields used it for a shortcut. You just had to keep your eyes up for loose glass that sometimes fell, and down for the sharp bits that might cut or bruise your foot.

She hesitated at the thin, loose board covered with blotches of fraying red paint that was held by one nail to a doorframe. It wasn't fear that held her back, she didn't think anything would happen to her inside, it was bright daylight after all, but she wasn't quite willing to leave the bustle of the crowds for something so empty and lonely.

Aching brain and aching feet argued back and forth about which more deserved a break. The brain was so tired, it let the feet win out, so she pushed the wood aside and stepped into the vast indoors, little realizing she was being both watched and followed.

After he slipped off the ship, the monster found London hellish. There was a village-full of people on each block, they lived inside mountains on either side of enormous streets. Noisy motor cars sputtered by, emitting smoky smells as bad as the electrical odors from Frankenstein's watchtower laboratory. He didn't think for a moment that any of them might help him, and he knew there were too many to kill. There were so many, eventually they might even kill him, tear him to pieces like he had the rat, but that was not how he wanted to die.

Once he'd found the warehouse, though, things had calmed down, ideas drifted more slowly, though rudderless, through the inky blackness of the once-dead brain. Sometimes they even connected with more than simple pleasure or pain. For instance, right now he'd been thinking that everyone had always been bad to him, but then a serene, kindly face appeared in his mind. It was crowned with white wisps of hair laying gentle as a spider's web on the head's thin skin. His eyes were white, sightless, and when he spoke, his voice was as soft and soothing as the violin he played.

"There is good and there is bad."

It was so comforting to remember, the monster smiled and cooed, "Good."

But when the image abruptly faded, it angered him, and his large hands swatted the air as if he could hit whatever had made the memory fade. Wanting it back, he growled a low, guttural warning to the dusty warehouse air.

"Gnrnnnrrrgggh."

He stamped his feet.

"Nrghh."

He would have growled again if he hadn't heard a creaking. Instead his head snapped toward the sound, faster than a cobra toward its prey. His body froze. Some muscles, perhaps not as well connected as others, trembled as he heard the steady sound of light footsteps making their way through the warehouse.

"No," he muttered.

He didn't want to give up this space. He liked the warehouse much more than he had the ship. It didn't rock. It didn't make him sick. It was big and airy like the forests, and on the outer wall there were many cracks from which he could scan passing faces and hope to catch a glimpse of Frankenstein. Sometimes they threw away food. When night came, he ventured out with the rats to retrieve it. He did not want to leave.

The footsteps continued. The monster crept toward the irregular edge of a broken inner wall. There, he waited as the sound came closer. The steps were quick and of little weight, like a deer or a rabbit moving among brush, or like the pretty girl with the flowers he'd once met by a lake.

The pretty girl. Like the blind hermit, she was one of the few who was kind to him. She even gave him some of the pretty flowers to throw into the water. The glistening ripples made them even prettier. The girl was prettier in the water, too. At first he felt bad when she stopped moving, but now that he knew she was dead, that he'd killed her, he thought it was good. Now, she was more like him.

If he had to, he would make them all like him.

Again the image faded.

"Nrgg."

As the footsteps grew closer, the monster decided that if someone screamed or tried to hurt him he would break them with his hands, even if they were a little one. They screamed the loudest anyway, like the boy whose arm he tore. The monster never imagined something so small could make so loud a sound. The boy was louder even than the hanging hunchback, louder than the drowning girl. Though maybe she would have been louder if her cries weren't muffled by the water.

As he braced himself at the sound of footsteps just on the other side of the wall, he decided that this time, he would try to kill whoever it was before they could scream.

Just as Mary Blyss was finally convinced she was alone in the warehouse, she heard the harsh, animal voice behind her. She was so shocked she thought her body would explode, leaving it looking like Mitzie's without so much as being touched.

Heart hammering, she turned and saw who was with her in the large lonely space and felt it was a fact that she'd be sharing her late friend's fate.

Rather than give in to the lump in her throat, she shrieked: "You! You monster, you killed her, didn't you? You're the one that sliced up poor Mitzie! How could you do that? How?"

"What are you on about?" Benjamin Blyss snarled as he

came forward from the shadows. He was a bear, hairy even on the neck and shoulders. His face was squarish, but irregular, like a loaf of moldy bread, with squat, rubbery features and eyes set so deeply under his brow they were perpetually shaded. He wore a black cloth coat and a newsboy hat pulled low over one eye.

"Keep it down, will you?" he said. He pushed his fat hands quickly down in the air to accent his warning. "Someone who doesn't know how daft you are's liable to hear! All Ben needs now is to have the police after him!"

The initial shock fading, Mary's already small eyes narrowed. "How'd you follow me?" she said, but no sooner did she speak then she realized the simple trick. He'd just matched his steps to her own. Of course, he didn't want to confront her near the station house, or even on the street. He wanted to be sure they were alone.

She took a step back. "You *did* kill her, didn't you?"

"Stop saying that!" he growled, coming forward to keep the distance between them scant. She tried to run, but he grabbed her by the arm and pulled her back, close to his face. She caught a whiff of alcohol mixed in with a kind of sickly sweet sweat that rode above the dry dust.

For a moment, anger flashed in her. She imagined herself struggling, scratching his face, drawing blood. But before she could lift a finger, the old paralysis kicked in. He caught the look of terror in her eyes and sneered.

"You'll do nothing, you stupid, lying drunk!"

He swatted her with the back of his hand. Her head twisted to the side from the force, cheek turning red where she was hit.

Then he started talking to himself. "Ben's no idiot. He knows she's pissed all her earnings away again. That's why she was staying at the flathead's flat."

"Stay away!" she cried, but she was putty. She told her hand to rise, her legs to move, but they would not.

He grabbed her by the hair and pulled her closer. Then he put both hands on her mouth and kneed her in the gut.

"Quiet!" He hissed the word so loudly through clenched teeth that flecks of spittle sprayed her face. She could see the muscles of his jawbone throb. "Ben has had enough!"

Watching from his hiding spot, the monster was fascinated by the strange display. He understood from their conversation that they were man and wife. He wondered if Frankenstein hit his wife like that. He wondered if he had hit the woman they'd made for him, she might have liked him more. But no, he'd had no desire to hit her, and he didn't at all like this little man who hit the woman with the monkey face.

Mary doubled over, seeing stars. The drunken night, the shocking sight of Mitzie, the long morning, all left her terribly drained, and now she swooned. Her hands hit the rocky floor of the warehouse, concrete dust rising where she fell. She felt at the grit with her fingers, lowered her knees to get balance.

She heard Ben's fat steps coming up quickly. He was going to kill her, and she wasn't going to do a damn thing about it.

"This'll fix you, you stupid old cow," he said. He came up and kicked her in the side. She rolled, but managed to get onto her knees and face him. He pulled back, ready to strike again.

"No, Ben, don't, love," Mary begged. She tried to get up, but he gripped her hair again, forcing her to hunch over, to scramble from her knees to her feet as he pulled. The spot where he kicked her side hurt so much it made her wince with every move.

He held her hair with one hand as she crouched and waddled backwards into a pool of sunlight cast from a broken window. With his free hand he drew a long blade from beneath the folds of his black cloth jacket coat.

He twisted his head toward her, eyes dead. "Remember the last time you lied to old Ben? Remember what he did with this?"

"No, Ben, please! Don't! I know you didn't kill her! I know it!"

"Ben knows it, too, you addled cow! He was with six mates last night, all night! But now he's thinking that should the police find you here, all cut up just like Mitzie, they'll figure it was the same bloke what did you both, and Ben will get off scot-free."

He took the blade and sliced it down through the fabric of her dress, from breast to navel, exposing the flesh of her abdomen and revealing the long scar he'd given her.

He traced the irregular white line of scar tissue with the tip of the blade, pausing at the smaller, straighter scars the stitching had left behind. He seemed confused by it, as if he were trying to connect himself to it somehow, but couldn't quite recall.

"So what do you think of it?" he said, swaying slightly. "You think Ben could get away with it?"

Weakly, Mary shook her head. "They'll see the old scar, Ben. The one you gave me, and then they'll know it was someone who knew me. They'll know it was you."

He stopped moving the blade and twisted his head back and forth, thinking. Then he said, with a shrug, "I could just cut it all out, then, I suppose."

Her scream rose, then fell off into a sob. Ben pulled his arm back, ready to plunge the blade inside her.

The monster was confused. The mark on the woman's belly looked like the marks on his own body, the places where Frankenstein had sewn the pieces of him together. The woman they made for them had similar marks, smaller and sweeter, but the same. Now this woman. Could she be like him? Could she have been made from the dead? She was with this man, and he, like the monster, wasn't very pretty at all. Would the monkey-faced woman like him, treat him nicely, like the hermit and the girl?

All at once, he did not want to see her hurt.

Eyes closed as she waited for the killing blow, Mary heard a sound almost like thick wood about to splinter. She felt the concrete floor tremble just a bit and heard a thud, as if the trunk of a tree had somehow fallen inside the warehouse.

It was only when she heard Ben gasp and felt his grip on her hair loosen that she decided to open her eyes.

The first thing she saw was Ben, a surprised and worried look on his face as he stepped backwards. The knife was still clutched in his hand, but his arm hung loosely at his side. He was staring, with some concern, directly over Mary's head. No sooner did she begin to relax at the thought of being free than she tensed up again from the realization that whatever Ben was backing away from in terror was right behind her.

She looked over her shoulder and nearly fell onto her back from surprise. A huge man, maybe seven feet tall and wide as a door, his ill-fitting black clothes making him look as if he'd climbed out of a coffin, had stepped from behind the broken wall and did not seem pleased. The low sound she'd heard was his voice. He was growling, warning Ben off, like a dog would. An enormous dog on two legs.

She'd seen worse among the lost souls of Whitechapel, boys home from the war, faces covered with scars and stitches, as if knitted back together, the skin death-like, as if the blood was too frightened to ever come back up to the surface.

But she'd never seen such a face on someone quite so large.

"Here now, this is none of your business," Ben barked as if he'd suddenly remembered he was the one with the knife. "Get away or there's more here for you." He raised the blade and spoke louder. "Hear me, you big lump and bump?"

The growl didn't stop or change pitch. Then the huge, scarred man walked toward Ben, stiff, thick legs pushing, but barely lifting, the large, dull feet.

For some insane reason, maybe habit, Mary thought to warn her husband off.

"Ben, don't," she said, but he either didn't hear her or didn't care.

"All right for you," Ben said. He lunged forward, plunging the blade into the intruder's upper arm, nearly up to the hilt.

The intruder glared at him, goblin eyes livid beneath thick, drooping eyelids. If he was feeling any pain, he didn't register it on his face. As their eyes met, Ben let go of the knife and left it sticking there. The torn cloth at the sight of the wound darkened with oozing liquid, but there was still no reaction from the strange man, making Mary wonder if he was a man at all.

Ben looked briefly worried, but a drunken bravado came over him and he reached for the blade again. Maybe he planned to pull it out and use it again, or maybe he was going to twist it and open up the wound. Whatever his plan, he pursed his lips, reached, and said, "Whoever you are, Ben don't—"

Mary never did find out exactly what it was Ben didn't. Before the next word could come out, the intruder put one heavy hand on Ben's back, then pulled him forward as he rammed his other fist into the center of Ben's chest.

There was a bony cracking sound. A funny rush of air came out of Ben, as if his mouth were the hole in a punctured balloon. Mary had heard something like it once before, again from that trip to the slaughterhouse. It was the sound she'd heard when she saw some men break the ribcage of a cow, on their way to splitting it in two.

Ben caved forward, as if he'd been folded. His body listed to the side, balanced for a moment on the giant fist. Then it tumbled off to the side and collapsed in a heap.

It was only then that the giant's dog-like growling ceased.

"Ben?" Mary asked, but she knew from the way he fell that he was dead. At least his eyes were closed, not at all like poor Mitzie's. She stared at him for a moment before realizing that she was now alone with the stranger.

All the anger seemed to have fled him, but there was something hopelessly brutish about him. He stepped toward her, waving his hands pitifully in front of him, moving his mouth like a baby who wanted food but couldn't speak yet.

"Ahhn . . . Ahhn . . ."

"Easy there," she said, taking a few steps back. She sensed he wouldn't hurt her, but she wasn't quite willing to put that intuition to the test. He seemed not quite right in the head.

He stepped forward again, his feet making loud scraping noises. He moved his hands up, indicating her torn dress.

She made a face. "You want to have a go at it *now?*"

She pulled her frayed dress around her, trying to cover herself, to make it clear she was saying no, but he growled and swatted at her hands.

She raised them to protect her face, letting go of her dress again. "Easy! Easy!" she whined, feeling herself freeze. "I'm sure we can work something out."

But he didn't try to feel her breast or pull her into an embrace. Instead he parted the cloth above her belly and, with a huge index finger that didn't seem to quite match the rest of his hand, he touched the long scar Ben had given her.

"Ahnn . . . ahnnn," he said again, searching her eyes for something.

Maybe someone he loved had a wound like that, or he had one himself. She nodded, pretending she understood. She scanned his face and didn't see any lingering malice in it. Then she looked down and saw thick blood drip from his arm.

"Here, you're hurt," she said, staring at the protruding knife.

"Friend?" he said weakly.

She looked at him, relieved he could talk.

"Well," she said, petting his arm gently, trying to figure out how best to remove the knife and bandage the wound. "I can't imagine anyone wanting to be your enemy."

Chapter Six

"Baron Henry Frankenstein robbed at least six graves and stole warm bodies from the gallows. When these were not enough for his mad purposes, he had a young woman murdered and her heart ripped from her chest. He needed these bodies in order to get the proper pieces to complete his experiments."

Finished with reading the passage he'd painstakingly written out in English the night before, Eric Krogh looked nervously beyond the page and down at the scuffed marble floor. Though his Teutonic will had carried him so far from home, now, before the cool demeanor of an Englishman, he felt weak and foolish.

When there was no immediate response, he glanced up to see Chief Inspector Devin eyeing him from across his paper-strewn desk. He was barrel-chested and balding, but his hair was still as black as a youth's.

"And he did these experiments for the purpose of creating life?" Devin asked.

Krogh nervously rubbed the sides of his pants legs. "Yes. In his own image." After a moment, he added, "Rather than God's."

Devin nodded, leaned back in his worn chair, cupped his hands in front of him, and tapped his thumbs. "But, if he's using body parts, he's not really *creating* life, is he? More like rearranging it, wouldn't you think?"

Krogh's face flushed with embarrassment. He knew full well the story sounded absurd, but he had to convince this dubious man from Scotland Yard that it was real. He had to do this for his son, for himself, for those who'd died, and those whose lives might yet be saved.

"It's all in my file, if you don't believe me," Krogh said stiffly.

Devin raised an eyebrow. "I didn't say that, Mr. Krogh."

Inspector, Krogh thought. *Call me Inspector, please.*

"Then you'll find him and arrest him?"

Devin gave him a slight smile. "I didn't say that, either." He opened his hands toward the unread file. "This is an extraordinary story."

Krogh met the man's eyes, but couldn't read them. "I know."

Just then, behind him, the door clicked and opened. A young man in a dirt-brown suit, red hair slicked back, skin pasty, stuck his head in and raised his eyebrows expectantly at Devin.

"Yes. Good," Devin said, motioning him in. He turned toward Krogh as if in afterthought. "If you'd wait in the hall?"

Krogh rose mechanically. "Yes. Of course."

Outside the office, he found himself a spot on a stiff wooden bench, sat, and looked around. The grand halls of New Scotland Yard were not as he expected. To be sure, the outside of the dignified turreted building, designed in the Scottish Baronial style, was imposing. In his *Ward Lock & Co Guide* to London, he'd read it was made of convict-hewn Dartmoor granite. Here inside though, the walls were plain and white, and along each thin hall, a series of white globe fixtures hung from the ceiling at regular intervals, making the place seem more like a hospital than an investigative nerve center.

Now and then a nondescript aide appeared from what seemed one of a hundred doors, only to disappear into another. As he stared down at his worn black shoes, held together mostly by polish, it occurred to Krogh that even these low-level employees made ten times his salary.

Listening to their echoing steps, knowing they were investigating murders, thefts, and more, scores of *usual* crimes, Krogh wondered if they could handle a case that even he admitted sounded like a folk tale.

Finding Frankenstein himself and killing him would be faster, more certain, but he'd told his son, Rikard, that living by good laws, in service to the community, was the highest goal in life. Even the loss of an arm ("Or both legs!" he'd added with a forced reassuring smile when talking to his son) couldn't stop such a man.

After what seemed an hour, Devin stepped out and stood before him.

"Inspector?" the Englishman said.

It took a moment for Krogh to realize Devin was referring to him. "Yes?"

"Come with me, please."

"Certainly."

He fell into step alongside the stout inspector, quite surprised when, rather than the office, he was led to a paved yard where an officer held open the back door to a police car.

"Bear with me," Devin said, motioning him inside.

Some time into the bumpy ride, Krogh was surprised to recognize the area.

"Is this . . . Whitechapel?" he asked.

Devin furrowed his brow. "Yes. You've been here?"

Krogh shrugged. "My rented flat . . . " he began.

"Ah, yes," Devin said, with a hint of sympathy that made Krogh squirm. Luckily, just about then, the ride ended as the car half rolled up on the curb before the Commercial Street Police Station.

The stark metal sign on the basement door he was led to

said simply, "Morgue."

In response to a knock from Devin, a cheerful, short, be-spectacled fellow with a white bushy beard emerged. The man looked like Santa Claus, except perhaps for his medical uniform and stained rubber gloves.

In the center of the yellow-tiled room with a drain in the floor were twin tables, whatever on them covered by sheets. From the shape of the sheets, Krogh assumed there were female bodies underneath, but there was something definitely wrong around the abdomens.

"They're both ready, just as you asked," the man half sang. Krogh noted the lack of ventilation and wondered if the man had been driven a bit mad by fumes.

"Thank you, Stimpson," Devin said, turning toward Krogh. "Brace yourself. It's a bit gruesome."

Krogh stiffened. "I saw my son's arm pulled out at the socket. I don't believe there's anything left that could upset me more."

Devin eyed him. He seemed about to smile again, but re-strained himself. "Well, we'll see then." He nodded, and the morbid Kris Kringle pulled back both sheets.

Seconds later, someone handed Krogh a pail, the smell of which only made him empty his stomach faster.

Devin stepped forward and patted him on the back while he retched. "I pride myself on a mundane imagination, Inspector, not soaring or unbelievable, like Jules Verne, but capable of imagining what real people do on real days, for good or evil. One thing it's taught me is that you don't need a man to make a monster. God does it quite nicely on His own."

Krogh wiped his mouth with the back of his hand. "Who were they?"

"Two prostitutes killed over the last three nights, strangled, throats slit, then mutilated as you see. Our lads here are split over whether or not the fiend is a doctor, but they agree he has some knowledge of anatomy," Devin said.

He stepped back toward the table and pulled something from his pocket that looked like a pen. In one fluid motion, he extended the device into a long silver pointer. "I don't know how much difficulty you have with the press back home, Krogh, but here they can be a great boon, or a nuisance. So far, we've managed to keep a few details from them, such as this one, so I'd appreciate your discretion. In each case the murderer, with great efficiency, removed, and, so far as we can tell, *kept* the uterus, here and here."

He used the pointed to indicate gaps in the lower portions of each woman's abdomen. The sight of the silver against the bare entrails made Krogh shiver.

"The seat of life. Of *real* life," he muttered.

Stimpson handed him a glass with some golden liquid in it, and merrily said, "Bottoms up, up, up."

Recognizing the smell of scotch, Krogh took a sip as Devin collapsed the pointer.

"Your Baron Frankenstein is a doctor. He was about to graduate from the Goldstadt Medical College with their highest honors, but he abruptly left, dissatisfied with the type of corpses they could give him for his experiments, yes?"

Krogh nodded, impressed that Devin recalled the details.

"Often when he robbed the graves, he and his hunchback would abscond with just one piece of the body; an arm, a leg, or, in the case of one unfortunate woman, a heart. That much, at least, tallies with what we've got here. Do you agree?" Devin asked.

A warm feeling from the scotch invaded Krogh's belly and rose, along his back, to his head as he said, "Yes."

"These two murders also bear more than a passing resemblance to the operating methods of the so-called Whitechapel murderer, Jack the Ripper. I trust that a man as familiar with monsters as yourself has heard the name. Now tell me, is your baron wily enough to try to make his crimes look like old Jack's?" Devin asked.

Savoring the fact that his advice had been requested, Krogh thought about his answer. He reached into his pocket and checked a few pages in his book about Frankenstein's deceptions. Among them were false documents presented to medical supply companies and electrical equipment manufacturers for his purchases.

"Yes. Yes, he could lie like that. He's involved in this, I'm sure. You must help me find him."

For the last time that day, Devin gave Erik Krogh that mysterious little smile.

"Oh, we've found him. That's the information my assistant interrupted me with back at my office. He's staying at the Savoy. We've already sent a car round to pick him up."

Chapter Seven

Henry Frankenstein had the limo pull up directly in front of the squat Victorian storefront. His driver got out, trotted to the passenger door, and held it open.

"Come back in fifteen minutes," Frankenstein said as he pulled his white gloves on and exited. His tone was neither pleasant nor rude, but he didn't look at the driver at all, and certainly wouldn't recognize him if he happened to see him again on the street.

It was evening and the bright sun that made its rare invasion of the city was finally giving up its fight. After years of reading by candlelight and working in the dark, Frankenstein felt a bit of relief at the growing dimness. The shadows of the tall buildings on the tight cobblestone street cooled the stone and plaster, and evened out any contrast in the images.

Frankenstein's eyes fixed on the ill-kept window display of the Burke & Hare Medical Supply Warehouse. Behind the storefront, a much larger building loomed, the titular warehouse, he assumed.

He stepped toward the display. The glass was smudged with some sort of dirt, and inside a thick coat of dust covered the anatomical models for sale. There was a giant model of an eye, with a crude rendering of the lacrimal gland; a male torso with all the viscera exposed; and an intricate skeletal model of the hand, showing, in rather neat detail, all twenty-seven bones. He had to chuckle at the human head that had fallen off its pedestal, its skull cap missing, revealing a particularly poor molding of the brain. One could barely tell where the prefrontal cortex ended and the motor cortex began.

Could this really be where Dr. Waldman procured the samples for his classes? he wondered. Well, it was a difficult business, probably even in metropolitan London. For all mankind's recent advances, society still shrouded the body in reverential fear and folklore, as if by hurting it one could hurt the spirit of the person it once was.

Frankenstein put his hand over his brow as he peered inside. Past some rows of hanging skeletons and shelves of books there was a counter, beyond that a small light glowed in a back room. The proprietor was in, as promised. Heart beating faster, he turned the knob to the mostly glass front door and stepped inside.

The place was silent, so much so, he imagined he could actually hear the dust settling. Other men might be disturbed by all the images of death hanging on hooks or sitting in shelves, waiting to be sold. Other men might think it ghoulish, but to Frankenstein they were like samples of wood to a carpenter planning to build a chair.

"Mr. Burke?" he called.

The gentle voice of someone well trained in the arts of customer satisfaction drifted out from the back room. "A moment, please."

There was a rustling, after which a tall, thin man with a typically Saxon face and a pleasant manner drifted out. "Dr. Frankenstein, I presume? Or do you prefer Baron?" he said, extending the long, bony fingers of his right hand.

Frankenstein gripped the cool hand and shook it lightly. "I prefer doctor. Being a baron is an accident of birth, or, rather, of my father's death. Doctor is a title I've earned."

"Dr. Frankenstein, then," the man repeated, now moving out his warmer left hand to cup Frankenstein's between his. "Jerome Burke, at your service. Simply Mr. Burke."

"Thank you for keeping your shop open for me."

"No trouble, really," he said, still smiling. "I live in a small flat in the back of the warehouse, and you seemed to be in a rush."

Frankenstein lowered his eyes nervously. "Yes, I am. Well, that is to say my enthusiasm propels me, and I've no idea how long I'll remain in England."

Burke nodded sympathetically. "Enthusiasm can be a blessing or a curse. But, since you're in a rush, let's get down to it, then. What can I do for you? You said you were a student of a good customer of ours, Dr. Waldman."

"Yes," Frankenstein answered. He fumbled for the folded receipt in his pocket, noticing his hands were shaking again. He quickly handed it to Burke, hoping the man wouldn't notice the tremors, but, judging from his face as he gently took the paper, he did.

Burke read. "Yes. This is a receipt for two brains. One normal, one abnormal." His eyebrow raised a bit. "The normal specimen fetched quite a high price, but Dr. Waldman is always interested in the best, and, as we used to say, the fresher the body, the higher the price. Are you interested in obtaining another specimen like that one? Of course, given time, we can procure *anything*, but that might be difficult on short notice. Still, if the price is right . . . "

"No, no," Frankenstein said, a little impatiently. "I don't want to procure any specimens. I want to know about the abnormal brain. You see, I'd like very much to find out who the donor was, what sort of man he was, what kind of life he led."

Burke eyed it. "Really? It is, after all, only a piece of dead tissue."

Frankenstein froze a moment and Burke must have noticed the change in his face.

"Is this a spiritual or religious issue, Doctor? We do sometimes have remorseful medical students wander in wondering who it was they cut up, but let me assure you, as I did them, that this is the only way to further our knowledge and help—"

Frankenstein waved him to silence. "It's not that at all. Dr. Waldman noted that this man was a criminal because of the abnormalities in his brain. I want to find out if that's true, and if so, what kind of crimes he committed. It's . . . part of an experiment."

Burke smiled. "Ah, I see, then. That I can understand. Forgive my presumption. Our experiences are not always with such worldwise men. There are a lot of moralists about, even in the medical community. As to the question of who the donor was, well, that would involve revealing how we procured the sample, and that's a tricky business, I'm afraid."

Burke gestured at the dusty displays around him. "This was my father's business and his father's before him. A hundred years ago it was very difficult to study real human anatomy, strictly regulated, even outright illegal. With good reason. The money was so good, relatively, that there were those who weren't above murder to obtain just the right specimen. Now, my grandfather was no murderer, at least as far as my mother and I knew, but he wasn't above a little grave robbing."

Tiring quickly of the family history, Frankenstein furrowed his brow. "Could you get to the point?"

Burke shrugged amiably. "The point? The point? Well, I suppose my point is that maybe things haven't changed all that much over the years. About the murdering, certainly, but maybe not so much about the other issue."

"The grave robbing, you mean?"

Burke shrugged.

Frankenstein suppressed a chuckle. "My good fellow, I assure you, I am in no way associated with the authorities. I'm a doctor, a scientist. To me the ritual of burying the dead is mere superstition. A body is a thing, a piece of bone and meat, a fascinating machine, yes, but just a machine. I conceive of no God who would punish our curiosity, nor do I believe in any law that would do the same. My interest is only in learning about where this brain came from, what the person who had it was like, and if there is a correlation between it and his behavior. That's all. I assure you my discretion will be complete."

Burke lightened considerably. "I'm glad to hear you say it. Sophisticated men such as you understand such things, but there are so many unenlightened persons who do not. The gentleman who leases us this property for instance, refuses to walk under a ladder."

This time Frankenstein did chuckle. "Well, there are a lot of fools about." His voice became raspy, almost pleading. "But can you help me? Please?"

"The fact is we work with a number of individual contractors, those who were called *resurrection men* in my grandfather's day. With the proper impetus, I might be able to crosscheck our records and discover which specific contractor supplied this particular specimen. There'd also be the matter of contacting the fellow, reassuring him as to the sophisticated nature of your character, and the guileless quality of your intentions . . ."

Burke stopped speaking, as if the rest were obvious.

Having bribed his share of officials, gravediggers, and watchmen, Frankenstein knew exactly what Burke meant. He reached into his pocket and tossed two gold coins on the counter.

"For your troubles, Mr. Burke. Kindly tell your *resurrection man* that there will be two for him as well, and a third if my inquiries bear fruit."

Burke indicated the coins with a nod of his chin.

"For that amount, sir, I could procure you three completely new brains of the finest quality," he said back. "Along with their complete histories."

Frankenstein shook his head. "Perhaps some other time. Right now I'm only interested in where this brain came from."

"Give me an hour or so, then."

Frankenstein scribbled his name and hotel on a piece of paper and handed it to the man.

"I'll expect word from you."

Burke grinned. "I'll send it. And let me say again that should your needs change, Burke & Hare would be delighted to provide you with *anything* you require."

Frankenstein nodded and turned to leave, but before he reached the door, Burke called out, "Do give my regards to Dr. Waldman!"

Frankenstein hesitated. For an instant he saw Dr. Waldman's stern face, sitting across from him at a small table at the lab, warning how the creature was dangerous. He pitied him then, pitied his mind for not being able to journey beyond its own animal fear. What had he said then to his beloved mentor?

Dangerous! Poor old Waldman. Have you never wanted to do anything that was dangerous? Where should we be if nobody tried to find out what lies beyond? Have you never wanted to look beyond the clouds and the stars or to know what causes the trees to bud and what changes the darkness into light? But if you talk like that, people call you crazy. If I could discover just one of these things, what eternity is, for example, I wouldn't care if they did think I was crazy!

He eyed Burke and said stiffly, "Dr. Waldman is dead."

Burke's face grew solemn. "I'm so sorry."

Frankenstein whirled back to the door. As he opened it, he saw, reflected in the glass, the tall, gangly Burke, reverentially crossing himself in memory of the dead doctor.

"Superstitious fool," Frankenstein muttered as the door clicked shut behind him.

Chapter Eight

Henry Frankenstein didn't return directly to the Savoy. He had the car drop him several blocks away, at Charing Cross Road by Cambridge Circus, hoping a cigarette and a walk would calm him. But, unable to slow himself even when he wanted, his quick clip brought him to the hotel doors before the cigarette was half finished. Rather than enter, he circled the block twice, until his cigarette was down to the filter. Then he lit another and walked around again.

He told himself he was taking his time in case Elizabeth was sleeping, but the fact was that the taste of his secret journey to Burke & Hare still clung to him, to his fingers, to his mind, and he feared he'd blurt out the details upon seeing her. He hated lying to her. It was an extreme effort, one that filled him with shame, but it seemed telling the truth would only pain her.

On his fourth transit, the concierge, a short, well-manicured man with a good temperament and perfect posture, happened to be standing outside. When he gave the baron an uncharacteristically nervous glance, Frankenstein knew something was wrong. He headed toward the man just as the concierge waved him over.

"What is it?" Frankenstein said.

The concierge, having regained his professional composure, withdrew a white envelope from his pocket and held it out. Frankenstein ripped it open so quickly he nearly tore the sheet of fine hotel stationery inside.

He spoke aloud as he read. "Chief Inspector Devin from Scotland Yard wishes to see me? What is this nonsense about?"

"He did not say, Baron."

Scattered thoughts and images flew through his mind. He remembered the local inspector back at the village, the one making inquiries, who'd prompted their journey here.

"They haven't been to the room, have they? I requested that we not be disturbed. My wife is very frail."

"My apologies, Baron, but they insisted, and we make every effort to cooperate with the police. Dr. Radsworth, our hotel doctor is up with your wife now."

"What?!" Frankenstein shouted.

"He came with the highest recommendations and has served admirably for——"

Frankenstein didn't wait to hear the rest. He raced for the elevators. When one was not immediately available, he ran up the stairs, not bothering to remove his overcoat. By the time he arrived at the door to his suite, he was sweating heavily.

From inside, he heard Elizabeth softly moaning. He pushed in. Minnie was sitting at a table, dabbing her eyes with a napkin, as a stout, balding man with a hawkish nose and thick glasses emerged from the bedroom.

The housekeeper shot to her feet when she saw her master.

"Baron! It's been terrible! The police were here for you!"

Frankenstein pulled off his overcoat and ascot, tossing them carelessly over the back of a chair.

"Yes, I know, Minnie. Is Elizabeth all right?"

"I warned them not to talk to her, that she was feeling frail, but they practically pushed me out of the way, they did. And before they could even ask her anything, she got all hysterical! When they finally left, they said for us not to go anywhere tonight, and if you didn't show in the morning, they'd be back."

Dr. Radsworth rubbed his hands and stepped forward.

"Baron?"

Frankenstein snapped his head toward the doctor. "How is she?"

"I understand that you're a medical man?"

"Yes."

"She seems to be suffering from some sort of trauma, centered on you," Radsworth said. Frankenstein felt the man's eyes heavy upon him.

The fool probably thinks I beat her.

"She was assaulted in our home then kidnapped. I was forced to perform some labors for the kidnappers to secure her release. Will she be all right?"

Radsworth shook his head. "It's difficult to say. For many such a fright will fade with time. For others, it brings out an underlying, chronic condition. Has she always been anxious?"

Frankenstein gave the man a bitter smile. "No more than myself."

Radsworth looked down at Frankenstein's shaking hands.

"I've given her something that should make her sleep."

He placed his bag on a table, and clicked it open. "I'll leave the medication with you. I'd hesitate to use it frequently, but if she becomes hysterical again, it might be necessary."

He pulled out a small, rubber-stoppered bottle and a syringe, laid them on a white cloth, and handed them to Frankenstein. Frankenstein's eyes went wide when he saw the label. Forgetting Elizabeth might hear, he shouted at the doctor.

"This is an opiate! The streets and poorhouses are full of addle-brained beasts enslaved to this so-called medicine. Your country fought a war over it!" Frankenstein said.

"Which is why, Baron, I trust you'll only use it in extreme circumstances, and at the recommended dosage. Otherwise, her hysteria has the potential to make her a candidate for an asylum."

The baron felt as if his chest were collapsing as Minnie screamed, "An asylum! My poor mistress! What's to become of us now?"

Frankenstein shoved bottle and syringe back into the doctor's hands.

"I won't be using this on my wife at all! Get out, do you hear? Get out! I'll tend to her myself!" Frankenstein bellowed.

The hotel doctor bowed curtly, spun, and headed for the door. Just before he left, though, he caught Frankenstein's eye and said, "Whatever you think of me, sir, that woman needs assistance. I pray that you provide it, or find someone else who will." He gently laid the vial and the syringe on a small end-table. "I leave this should you reconsider. Sometimes the sleep it affords is very curative."

His brief fury ebbing to high anxiety, Frankenstein nodded, though perhaps it looked more like a twitch. The doctor left.

He walked up to the table and took the syringe and the small bottle. He planned to throw them out, but a moan from Elizabeth made him hesitate, and instead, he wrapped both items in the cloth the doctor laid them upon, put them in the drawer, and slid it shut.

"Never touch this, Minnie. Never."

"Don't worry, sir, I won't. Ever." She looked as if she was about to say something else, but didn't.

"I'll go see Elizabeth now."

"Yes, sir."

Numbly, he walked to the bedroom door, and pressed his ear against it, listening. He thought he could hear her quick breathing, then realized it was his own, riding tensely above the lower thrum of his drumming heart.

Opening the door, he stepped inside the open, high-walled room. The lights of London by night showed through sheer curtains. Elizabeth was as he'd seen her the last few times, lying there in bed. No longer propped up to sitting, she lay on her back, her head on a single, thin pillow. She gazed at the ceiling with absent eyes, her chest barely rising and falling, soundless. He noticed her gown had been changed, and he guessed Minnie had helped her with that.

He crept across the carpeted floor and pulled a chair up next to the side of the bed. Despite his best efforts, it glanced off the nightstand, making a low thud. She turned to him without blinking, and, seeming to recognize him, smiled. But then her brow furrowed and she let out a soft moan.

"Easy, my darling. The drug that fool doctor gave you has made you woozy," Frankenstein said softly. "There's nothing to worry about."

He unbuttoned his jacket and sat in the chair, taking her hand in both of his. She felt cool to the touch, so he slowly rubbed and warmed her.

"Henry, oh, Henry. The police were here," she said, slurring her words.

"Yes, I know. It's all right."

"They kept asking where you were, where you'd been," she said. Her shoulders tensed as if she were trying to sit up, despite the drug. "What did they want? Why were they here?"

He looked away from her, down at the white hand he was rubbing, hugging with his own hands. "It's nothing my darling. Just some nonsense with our passports, that's all. We left in such a rush, I neglected to fill out some paperwork. You know how the English love their paperwork."

"That's all, Henry?"

"That's all. I'll take care of it first thing in the morning. I'll go in, sign some forms, and be back before you know it," he said. He forced himself to look up at her and smile. She was turned toward him, but her eyes were so glazed over, he wasn't sure she really saw him. But then she blinked, and a bit of the haze seemed to lift.

"It had nothing to do with those poor murdered girls? The ones who were cut up?" she said, her voice full of hope.

Frankenstein started and frowned. "What murdered girls? What do you mean?"

"Minnie read to me about them in the paper. Two girls were found murdered, cut up. Parts of their bodies were stolen."

Frankenstein sighed, inwardly cursing the foolish old woman. "I told her not to upset you. It was probably just some lurid tabloid story. That's what passes for news in this country, I'm afraid."

"But you don't know anything about it?"

"Me?" he said with a little laugh. "This is the first I'm hearing of it."

Her features softened considerably. She smiled. Her breathing slowed. She seemed to be giving herself over to the drug.

"You'll sleep now, darling. I'll be right outside that door all night, Minnie, too, if you need us. Then in the morning I'll go fix this nonsense with the police," he said. He laid her hand across her chest and pulled the blanket up over it.

"You're very good at fixing things, my love," she said faintly, falling asleep.

"It's all I've ever tried to do," he whispered. He kissed her gently on the forehead, drew the blinds, and stepped back out of the room.

Minnie stood near the bedroom door, hands clasped in front of her, slightly hunched over, like a large bird.

He answered her unasked question. "She's better now," he said. "Sleeping. She'll be better still once I sort out this foolish police nonsense."

Minnie handed him a white slip of paper. "A bellboy brought this up."

Frankenstein opened it and read the neat handwriting. At once, he grabbed his coat off the back of the chair where he'd left it.

"I've got to go out again, Minnie. Stay by the door in case Elizabeth needs you."

He didn't wait for her reaction, didn't want to see her face, so he started slipping into his coat, but the old woman came up behind him and helped him get his arms in the sleeves.

"What shall I say if she asks why you've gone and left her?" she asks, disapproval dripping from her voice.

Frankenstein hesitated only briefly. "Tell her . . . tell her I couldn't sleep, that I've gone for a walk and will be back as soon as I can."

Free again of the oppressive suite, he walked quickly down the hall, opting this time to actually wait for the elevator. Could he keep his promise about sorting everything out with the police? What did they want? If it was that fool local inspector, what would the charges be anyway? Making a man? Uncovering the greatest secret of the universe?

They should be giving him awards.

As he reached the front desk and called for his car, he put his concerns about the police behind him. Right now all he had to worry about was finding, in this glorious mess that was London, the right man and the right graveyard.

Chapter Nine

Cobb was a short, alarmingly ape-like man, who doubtless suffered from an overactive thyroid. His eyes had a rounded, protruding quality that Frankenstein instantly recognized as symptomatic of the condition. In comparison with his sooty forehead and three-day growth of black facial hair, the whites of his two, orb-like eyes seem to glow.

He reminds me of Fritz, poor devil, Frankenstein thought.

Unlike the dwarfish Fritz, Cobb's back was straight, but the fellow hunched over anyway, making the shoulders of his ratty wool coat bunch up. He wore a thief's gloves, the sort that covered the palm but kept the scabby fingers bare, and held, over his shoulder, a big sack full of shovels and other tools.

They stood at the corner of Charlotte and Greenfield Street, where Burke's note said to meet. Frankenstein could feel Cobb scanning his groomed, slicked-back hair, his overcoat and ascot, pressed pants, and polished shoes.

The modern-day resurrection man shook his head in disapproval.

"What a piece of work you are," Cobb said in a low cockney.

Frankenstein answered in a jumble of short sentences. "What do you mean? Let's get on with it. Show me the grave. I've got your money."

Cobb shook his head and hissed, "I'm talking about yer these and those!"

Frankenstein stared at him as if he were insane. "I don't understand—"

Cobb rolled his eyes, "Yer clothes! They won't do. Not at all."

Frankenstein realized he was speaking in cockney rhyming slang, using unconnected rhymes, like Uncle Ned for bed, or skyrocket for pocket. Others might find it quaint, but under the circumstances, Frankenstein found it absurd and confounding.

Cobb ambled sideways and indicated the low houses and ill-kept shops and pubs of the neighborhood they were in.

"There've been murders on these fields of wheat the last few weeks," Cobb continued. "Some Jane Shores cut up. The ginger mops are out in force and everyone is on the lookout for suspicious characters."

"Well, what's that got to do with us?" Frankenstein said.

Cobb tapped his chest with his index finger, right where a button was missing from his shirt. "Me, nothing. On my own. You, nothing. On your own. Many such as yourself wander the clubs and pubs here. But together, you and I strolling down the street like China plates? Who do you think'd *forget* seeing us?"

Frankenstein sighed. "I suppose you're right. But what's to be done about it now?"

Cobb looked around to see if anyone was watching, then motioned Frankenstein into an alley. "Come this way." The shovels clanked as he vanished into the dark.

Frankenstein hesitated at the edge of darkness. "See here, you're not going to try to rob me?"

"I'll wait for that until we get to the graveyard," Cobb smirked.

When Frankenstein didn't follow, the little man cleared his throat and said, more somberly, "I won't daisy beat you, sir. Burke knows me and he keeps my Darby Kel nice and full. I'd be a fool to give up what he pays me even for what a baron might have in his skyrocket."

As soon as he translated what Cobb meant, Frankenstein found himself admiring the fact that the man hadn't bothered to deny he'd *like* to rob him. For some reason, he trusted that, so he followed him into the quiet of the dark space. The narrow, lightless space was littered with trash and reeked with the smell of fresh urine.

Grunting, Cobb quickly fished around in his large sack and pulled out a cloth bundle.

"What's that?" Frankenstein said.

"My spares. Usually I change into them after my digging. They'll cost you an extra bob," he said, handing them to Frankenstein. Frankenstein looked at the gray and brown pile. Already, some grime from them had come off on his white gloves. He tossed the pile on a garbage can and pulled off his ascot.

Now and again, Cobb chuckled as he disrobed.

When he was finished, he barely fit into the rags, his arms jutting from the sleeves, his back forced straight by the tight shirt. Cobb eyed him up and down. "Now ruffle your hair," he said, doing likewise to himself. Frankenstein mussed his slicked-back hair, making as much a mess of it as he could.

Cobb nodded. "Let's be off, then."

"Do you know which grave it is?" Frankenstein asked as the two walked along the sidewalk. Sad creatures wandered the street. Were it not for the soot and grime that seemed to cover everything here, they would remind Frankenstein of the villagers back home.

"I don't exactly keep written records," Cobb said. "But that fellow I remember. When he saw the brain, Burke wanted to know all about him, so he paid me a bit extra for the history."

"And what was that history?"

Cobb smirked and quoted, "His life was one of brutality, violence, and murder."

"That much I've read. But can't you remember anything else, man?"

Cobb shook his head. Frankenstein began to wonder if Cobb had made up the romantic history for the sake of impressing his employer.

"A name?"

Cobb raised an eyebrow. "Bob Donning? Something like that, but don't worry, sir, we'll find the spot where I nicked him. I never forget a plot. I'll narrow it down to one or two in any case."

The last few blocks had been nearly vacant of traffic, and now they were quite alone. Cobb stopped at the edge of a high stone fence, swung his sack once, twice, then let it go. It sailed over the top and landed with a thud and clatter on the far side.

"Quiet, you fool!' Frankenstein hissed, forgetting for a moment he was not out with Fritz.

Cobb glared at him, obviously not used to taking orders and not caring for the baron's tone in the least. After a moment he calmed and lifted his foot.

"Give us a leg up, then, will you, sir?" Cobb said.

Frankenstein complied, cupping his hands and boosting the man up the wall. Cobb grabbed the wall's edge, then lifted and twisted himself into a seated position. He patted his legs and laughed a bit. "There, now, that's the easy part!"

Impatient, Frankenstein raised his hands for Cobb to pull him. Cobb, who now had Frankenstein's expensive clothes in his sack on the other side of the wall, hesitated, but then reached down and helped the baron up to his side. Frankenstein turned and saw rows of stone and gravemarkers that went on for a little less than a hundred yards, before ending in another high wall.

It was tiny and unassuming, compared to the vast rolling cemeteries in his native land. The rows were gap-toothed and filled with little markers, some so close together they were almost touching. Piles of older stones lay against the wall. When families died out, their stones would be piled there, the plot opened for a new marker.

Cobb went down first, landing squarely on his feet in the soft earth. Frankenstein followed. The short, beastly man was counting out the rows then the markers themselves. Soon the odd pair stood in front of a small plot with no stone at all, just two pieces of wood nailed together in the shape of a cross. A name and dates were crudely scribbled on them.

Cobb stared at it, his brow squeezing together.

"Well?" Frankenstein said.

"I *think* this is it," Cobb said.

Frankenstein stumbled toward the marker, bits of dirt working their way through the holes in the soles of the borrowed shoes. He leaned down, pressing his hands into the earth and squinting his eyes at the crude handwriting. "Tom Nodding. The date of death seems about right." He turned toward Cobb, "Are you certain? Absolutely certain?"

"I'm not one to be believing in absolutes, but my memories tell me this could be it." He pulled a shovel from the sack. "If the grave's empty, I'll swear to it. That was the only body in years I nicked what had a wooden marker. Usually, I like to leave the poor ones alone. No fringe benefits, if you get my meaning."

The shovel comfortable in his hands, Frankenstein struck the hard earth with gusto.

Admiring the stroke, Cobb said, "You seem to have done this before."

Frankenstein again slammed the blade into the earth and pressed it down with his foot. "Yes, well, sometimes the best specimens are the ones you procure yourself," he answered, smiling grimly.

"Ha! I'm sure Burke would be happy to hire you if you ever got tired of baroning!"

"I'll try and keep that in mind," Frankenstein said.

The baron felt the tense mood between them lighten as they got on with their task. He watched the pile of dirt alongside the sad, untended grave grow higher and higher with the rising moon until finally, the top of a plain wooden coffin, crusted with earth and chipped by their shovels, lay bare.

"There it is," Frankenstein said. "Help me pry the lid off."

Cobb shoved a spade into the narrow space between the lid and the box, then leaned back on the handle. There was a creak, deadened by the dirt walls, as the lid rose a fraction of an inch. Frankenstein kneeled, wedged his fingers in, and pulled. The lid rose, the contents of the box revealed.

"Empty," Frankenstein said.

"Then that's it," Cobb said. "Unless someone switched the markers, your brain belonged to old Tom Nodding."

"Have you any idea who he was? How he lived?"

"By rumor only, sir," Cobb said, wiping some sweat from his brow. He pulled himself out of the hole and stretched his back. "But he died young, not by nature's choice, if you catch my drift. Local Whitechapel man. I think his mother, Emma, is still with us. You can ask around about her easy enough. I'm sure you'll understand if it's not a task I'd want to join you for."

Frankenstein nodded. "Tom Nodding."

Cobb cleared his throat. "Now about that extra gold piece."

"Yes, of course," Frankenstein said, wiping the dirt from his hands as he stood in the grave. "You've earned it. It's in my coat. Get the tools, while I climb out to get it. We can make quick work of filling the grave in."

A woman's giggle snapped both their heads toward the gated end of the small yard. Cobb, still standing and visible, froze as two shadowy figures made their way among the graves.

"Get down here, you fool!" Frankenstein hissed, tugging at Cobb's feet. Cobb made a face at the insult, then slipped back down.

"They'll see the dirt," Cobb whispered.

"Better than having them see you," Frankenstein said. "They could think it a new grave readied for a burial in the morning. But keep quiet!"

Frankenstein peered above the line of the surface and watched in silence as the source of the giggle, a short woman in her late forties, led a taller figure with a cane, a cape, and a deerstalker cap deeper into the small cemetery.

"This way," she said as she pulled him along. "There's a nice clear spot here."

Unsteady on her feet, she took him to within ten yards of where Cobb and Frankenstein hid. Then she lay down on a bare patch of ground, put up her knees, and hiked up her skirt as the tall man hovered over her.

"A whore," Cobb confirmed.

"They use graveyards?" Frankenstein whispered back, perplexed.

Cobb shrugged. "It's cheaper than letting, and quieter than an alley."

All at once, the tall man fell forward, or rather, swooped, down on the prone woman, his cape fanning on either side until it settled and covered them both like a blanket. It ruffled and twisted with movement.

There was a brief audible gasp, then a quiet gurgling that faded into the even, soft rustling of the cloth. Confused, Frankenstein raised his head a little to get a better view.

"What's he doing? What's going on?" Frankenstein said, his brow furrowed.

Cobb snickered as he pulled him back down. "You don't know? And here I understood you were a married man."

"No, no," Frankenstein said. "Look at the folds in his cape. His position is all wrong. He's beside her, not astride, and his right arm is moving up, across, and down."

Moments later, the man quickly rose to his full height. Frankenstein thought he caught a glimpse of something long, sharp, and silver in his hand, but when the man turned in their direction, Cobb nearly yanked him to the ground.

"Do you want us caught?" he hissed.

"Something's wrong, I tell you," Frankenstein said. He stood and looked. The whore was still lying there, motionless. "I think he's attacked her."

With the tall man gone, Frankenstein leapt from the grave and stepped up to the woman. In the moonlight the image was clear. Her throat was slit, her head nearly cut off, but that wasn't nearly as bad as what had been done to her below her rib cage.

"Dear heaven," Frankenstein said. "The woman's been eviscerated!"

He kneeled by her side and grabbed her hand. Still warm. He sensed Cobb beside him then turned to see the little man crossing himself.

"If I had my tools, my needle, some thread, I might be able to help her," Frankenstein said. Gently he pulled back a jagged flap of the woman's abdomen. His face grew even more perplexed. "Her uterus is missing. Who could remove an organ so quickly?"

Cobb looked as if he were going to be sick.

"She's done for," he said. "We've got to get out of here, quickly."

Frankenstein shook his head. "Not just yet. Get me my clothes. If I can reconnect the jugular, bandage some of these wounds, cauterize the larger arteries . . ."

When Cobb didn't move, Frankenstein glared at him. "Hurry,

you superstitious fool! We can't just leave her to die!"

"Why not?" Cobb muttered, but then he walked back to his sack, seemingly to do as Frankenstein had demanded.

But the blood alongside her was pooling, the glow of human presence fading from her eyes. Frankenstein had to remind himself that his own experiments were over, had to stop himself from thinking about which pieces of her he could use. The cuts were jagged, irregular to an untrained eye, but Frankenstein recognized their hasty precision. The killer knew what he was looking for and had found it fast enough.

But what would he want with her uterus?

Frankenstein buried the question as Cobb returned, the sack in his hand.

"Quickly man," he said. "Strip my ascot into small pieces and hand me the matches and a small knife."

Sweat beaded on Frankenstein's head as the thought of once again working on a human body flushed through him.

Cobb gave him a funny look. "You did say your money was in your coat, yes?"

"Cobb, you fool, I told you you'd be paid, but not until—"

Frankenstein never had a chance to finish the sentence. He felt the flat end of a shovel crash into the side of his skull. All that frantic energy that had pooled inside him the moment he saw the body spun round in his head like a whirlpool, and found itself sucked into blackness.

"Murder!" someone shrieked. The cry reverberated between the crude buildings. Whistles blew. Feet stamped. Lights played on the darkness of Frankenstein's closed eyes. The sounds hurt his head.

"Murder!"

Slowly, he opened his eyes and found himself squinting in the face of a bright electric lamp. He raised his hand to his head to shield his eyes only to wince when he touched the large bruise on his forehead. Everything ached.

There were people around him, he wasn't sure how many, but he focused on the feet and black pant legs of one man who stood close by. Frankenstein raised his head, hoping to see a face. He could make out blond hair and squarish features. It may have been a delusion, but he looked like a fellow countryman.

"Be a good fellow and help me up. I've been robbed," Frankenstein said weakly. He rubbed some blood off his forehead, then wiped his hand against his shabby borrowed clothing before extending it to the man who towered over him.

The tall man, surprisingly strong, ignored the hand and yanked his arm nearly hard enough to dislocate it. He pulled Frankenstein nearly to his feet, and very close to the Germanic face and burning blue eyes.

"Here, now, what are you doing?" Frankenstein said. He felt some strength return and tried to pull away. "Is everyone in England a savage?"

The hand wrapped around his forearm was strong, so he flailed and pulled with renewed vigor.

"What is it you want?" Frankenstein said. "If you want money, I'll get you some, just please let me go!"

Then he paused, remembering the face of the young inspector whose efforts had chased him from his homeland.

"Henry Frankenstein," Erik Krogh said, "You are under arrest!"

Chapter Ten

Feet sore and bloody, the throbbing wound on the side of his head untended, the rags he wore that passed for clothes damp with his own cold sweat, Henry Frankenstein paced the small holding cell, a seething mind atop a frightened, animal body. He had a wild look in his eyes, and he rubbed his hands constantly. Occasionally he'd go up to the filthy iron bars that formed the room's fourth wall, wrap his hands around them, and cry out, "You must let me speak to my wife! I must know if she's all right!"

To which some half-asleep drunkard, lying somewhere in the dark distance, doubtless locked in his own tiny cell, would respond, "She's in here with me and we're having a go at it! Now shut up!"

Oh, Elizabeth!

Feeling the blunt, cold, immobile matter of the bars, his heart sank. He wondered if at last the foolish, superstitious daemon of mankind, the one that had mocked, dogged, and frustrated his work every step of the way, had finally won out, and he and all his accomplishments, great or otherwise, would be rent like fresh meat by a pack of dogs, while the calmer, truer minds that existed in such scarce numbers on the planet, would never even see it.

Footsteps echoed in the small hallway. Frankenstein pressed his face against the bar and twisted sideways. Krogh was walking down the hall with a shorter, stouter, older man who wore a neat suit and tie and walked with considerable comfort in his authoritative step.

The young man soon stood before him, his light hair and face marred by the vertical shadows of the bars. Frankenstein lowered his head in a gesture of supplication, and tried to make his voice as pleading as possible.

"Inspector Krogh, is it?" Frankenstein said. "Whatever you think I've done, my wife has done nothing. Her emotional state is very delicate, that's the main reason we came here. Please tell me you haven't dragged her into this?"

Krogh remained still as a statue, but the hatred in his eyes was palpable. Finally, the other man, the older one with the paunch and the moustache, answered for him. "She knows you're our guest, Baron, but not why."

"Thank you," Frankenstein said, vaguely relieved.

Krogh's companion stifled a grin. "It's no favor, it's standard operating procedure. SOP." He paused, then added, "I'm Chief Inspector Devin, of Scotland Yard."

Krogh pulled out a small book, opened it, and started writing.

"I know what you're thinking," Frankenstein said. "But I didn't kill that woman. I do know who did. He was dark skinned, medium height, he wore a cape and a deerstalker cap. The knife was long and thin. He had to be a surgeon to do what he did so quickly. There must have been blood on him."

"Blood like that?" Devin said, pointing through the bars at Frankenstein's stained shirt and hands.

"I was trying to help her! I'm a doctor!"

"And what were you doing unconscious in the graveyard, doctor?" Devin said.

Frankenstein's eyes darted from face to face.

"I'm a stranger to your country, but I do know something about English law. I should like to see an attorney before I answer any further questions," he said.

Devin sighed and looked down. Krogh gritted his teeth.

"That is, of course, your right, Baron," Devin said. "But lawyers so often complicate things. The paperwork alone can take hours, maybe even days, and I hate to see you kept from your wife any longer than necessary."

Frankenstein clenched his fists. "I'm no fool. If you believe I killed that poor woman, you won't be letting me go at all. What do you want from me?"

"Baron Frankenstein, would you consent, of your own free will, to come with us? There's something I want to show you. As a medical man, I suspect you'll find it interesting," Devin said flatly.

"I say we just throw away the key and let him rot," Krogh put in.

Frankenstein raised his head, regarded the men a moment, then said, "Very well."

Devin opened the cell and Krogh held up a pair of handcuffs.

"Is that necessary?" Frankenstein said.

"A precaution," Devin shrugged.

Krogh roughly spun Frankenstein around and clamped the steel cuffs onto his thin wrists. It felt to Frankenstein that his countryman was doing his level best to make the process as painful as possible.

They flanked him as he walked down the long, thin hall. The only other occupied cell contained the drunk who'd shouted at him earlier. They made eye contact briefly, the drunk grunting his disapproval, Frankenstein grimacing in return.

As they exited the holding area and started down a flight of stairs, Frankenstein turned to the older of his captors. "I'm not a murderer, Inspector. It's been the goal of my life to understand death, to restore life, not to take it. Krogh can probably tell you that much, if he's a mind to," Frankenstein said.

"Inspector Krogh has told us quite a bit about you," Devin said. "Notably about how you like to experiment with the dead, cut them up into pieces."

"The dead, not the living. Do you think lifeless flesh so sacred we shouldn't try to learn from it?" Frankenstein said.

Devin shrugged, "I just think it illegal to rob graves in London."

He was led to the morgue, where a short chubby man with white whiskers greeted them at the door. Inside the yellow tiled area were four tables, each with a body under a sheet.

"Once again, all is ready, steady," the chubby fellow said cheerfully. He leaned in toward Devin and tried to whisper, though Frankenstein easily made out every word. "I didn't have time to finish on Mr. Blyss, though, so he's still out."

"That's all right, Stimpson," Devin said. Annoyed, the chief inspector checked the toe tags, and pushed one table away from the rest. Then he waved Frankenstein over to the first of the three. Frankenstein felt Devin's eyes burning into him as he pulled back the sheet.

Frankenstein nodded. "The woman who was murdered last night."

"Her name was Kelly Blaine," Krogh put in. "She was thirty-seven and had two children."

Frankenstein ignored the pointless details. His eyes were riveted on the corpse, dancing up and down the slash marks, the bruises. He twisted his head this way and that, then lurched awkwardly forward, having momentarily forgotten his hands were cuffed.

Regaining his balance, he looked at Devin. "May I take a closer look?"

Devin nodded, but Krogh hesitated.

"You can shoot me if I try to escape, Krogh. I suspect you'd like that a great deal," Frankenstein said with a bit of a sneer.

Krogh released the cuffs. "It is not a duty I would regret performing."

His hands freed, Frankenstein rubbed his wrists, and stretched his fingers. His hands shivered, but not so much that he couldn't control them. He poked the wounds with his index finger, lifted the flap of the abdomen, squinted at what he saw inside.

Then, without asking, he went to the next body, pulled the sheet himself and repeated the examination, this time occasionally muttering things to himself, like, "He was in less of a hurry this time," and, "He certainly knew what he was looking for."

By the time he reached the third corpse, he examined the pelvic area first, and said, with some confusion, "The womb again. What on earth would he want with a womb?"

"Perhaps to assemble a corpse to bring to life?" Krogh said.

Frankenstein laughed grimly. "Yes, perhaps one, if I were building another woman. Two if the first had been damaged. But three? I'm a better surgeon than that."

Then he turned to Devin. "What was it you wanted me to see?"

"I never said this was about you seeing anything," Devin said.

"Ah. You wanted to see how I reacted. Well, I hope I've satisfied your curiosity," Frankenstein said.

"You did," Devin said with that funny little smile of his.

Frankenstein was about to say something when his attention was drawn to the table Devin had pushed away.

"What about that one?"

Devin nodded toward the covered body. "Benjamin Blyss. They found him dead in an abandoned warehouse not far from here."

Frankenstein stepped over to pull the sheet back, but Krogh reared.

"You can't just—"

Devin cut him off. "It is a breach of protocol, but I'd be curious to see the baron's reaction."

So Frankenstein pulled the sheet back as Stimpson, the white-haired coroner merrily filled in the details. "His chest was caved in. I believe a piece of mortar came loose and landed on him. Someone tried to help him, pried it off, but when they realized he was dead, left him there."

Frankenstein leaned over to look at the bruise. As he saw it, he stiffened. His eyes flared briefly, his hands shook, but he forced himself to look as calm as he could.

Devin noted his reaction with interest. "Something?"

"No," Frankenstein said, stepping back. Stimpson stepped up and covered the corpse.

As the two men stood closely for the first time, Stimpson whispered to Frankenstein, "Mr. Burke sends his apologies and his regards."

Frankenstein eyed the coroner, impressed at Burke's reach. His reaction was interrupted by a loud, "Well, well," from Devin.

The stout chief inspector said. "I've other matters to attend. Inspector Krogh, will you kindly walk the baron back to his accommodations here, then join me on the second floor? They've been kind enough to set up a second office for me here."

Krogh nodded.

"See here, Devin, I've done as you asked," Frankenstein said. "You must let me go!"

Devin smiled. "In due time. You've been helpful. I promise things won't be held up by any undue paperwork."

With that, Devin exited and Stimpson went about puttering in a corner of the large room. Frankenstein and Krogh stood there, staring at one another, as the door clanked shut. As soon as he was sure that Devin was gone, Frankenstein waved Krogh over to the fourth table.

"Come here, quickly. Have a look at this," Frankenstein said.

The man tensed instantly. "Do not think to order me about, Frankenstein."

Frankenstein looked up at him. Devin gone, the younger man's face had become a mask of hatred. "Krogh, please. It's vitally important. I was afraid Devin wouldn't believe it, but I know you will."

Stiffly, Krogh marched up to the dead thing. Frankenstein pointed at the large hollow spot in the center of his chest, where bone and fleshed had been pulped and pressed in.

"That's where Stimpson believe's the stone hit him," Krogh said.

"Look closely at the pattern of the bruise," Frankenstein said, indicating the shape as he spoke. "That wasn't caused by any stone or mortar. It was a fist, a large human fist."

To make the point he held his own clenched and shaking hand near the wound. Though the size of the wound dwarfed Frankenstein's hand, it was clear the shape was the same, the pattern of knuckles and thumb unmistakable.

"How?" Krogh said.

Frankenstein fumbled at the pocket of his shirt for his cigarettes, then realized it was Cobb's clothes he still wore. He glanced at Krogh, considered asking him for a cigarette, then thought better of it. He spoke slowly, hoping at least his voice would stay steady. "I only know one thing powerful enough to crush a man's chest with one blow like that."

As realization dawned, Krogh's face went white. "The monster? Here? Did you bring it?"

He leapt toward Frankenstein and grabbed him by the shirt collar. "You fiend! Did you bring your vile creation to London? Didn't you kill enough of us in the village?"

Stimpson, seeing the conflict, said, "Oh dear!" and waddled out of the room.

"No, no, no!" Frankenstein said, pitifully. "It blew up with the lab, I swear it! I saw it buried by tons of stone! Nothing human could have survived!"

"That thing isn't human!" Krogh said, still shaking him. "It never was!"

"That's not the point," Frankenstein said, pulling away. "If it survived somehow, if it's out there, it must be destroyed! You must let me help you!"

"Never!" Krogh shouted, pushing Frankenstein away.

"But in this our cause is the same! I want it destroyed! It must be destroyed! And who better than me to help?" Frankenstein said. "What could I have done to make you revile me so?"

Krogh's head and shoulders shook and the muscles in his jaw and neck tightened as he clenched his fist and shook it in Frankenstein's face. "I saw that monster of yours rip out my boy's arm!"

Shock and sadness swept over Frankenstein. He stepped back from the shaking fist and said, "Good Lord, man! Did you save the arm?"

"For what? One of your demonic experiments?" Krogh howled. Then he pulled back and punched Frankenstein square in the mouth, sending the slight, shaking man back and down to the floor.

From the floor, Frankenstein raised his head, eyes low, and wiped the blood on his lips with the back of his hand. "Krogh, you simple idiot. You reduce everything to black and white, so you take me for a sinner, a maniac who should be punished, but life is much, much more complex than that! If the arm has survived, I could sew it back on, reconnect it, and make your boy whole again."

Krogh froze, speechless, his mouth half open. He seemed uncertain whether to punch the man again or offer him a hand.

Sensing his confusion, Frankenstein shifted his weight onto his shoulders and tried to talk some sense into him. "Damn it, man! I'm not Satan or some foul demon from the pits of an imaginary hell! I'm not offering a Faustian bargain! You can keep your immortal soul, if you're fool enough to believe you have one! I'm talking science, plain and simple. Medical science! The same methods I used to animate the body I assembled could be used on your boy! Keep me in here, burn me at the stake for witchcraft if you like, I suppose it doesn't matter much what happens to me anymore, but if I can undo some of the damage that creature has done, I'll do whatever's in my power! Just tell me, did you save the arm?"

Krogh's stiff face wavered a bit as he said, "It was cremated."

Though his body moved along with machine-like precision, Erik Krogh's stomach was twisted in knots. Could his Rikard's arm have been saved?

No! He is a criminal and a liar!

But what if it was true? What if Frankenstein was right, and they were all just superstitious fools?

No! He created a monster, not a man! He would turn my son into a monster as well!

Worried his inner torment might show, Krogh picked up speed. By the time he reached the door to the small office Devin borrowed here, he convinced himself it was only simple curiosity that motivated the many glances that came his way.

He swallowed hard as he opened the door, uncertain whether he should confess his assault on the prisoner first, or more importantly, raise the issue that the monster might be in London. Unfortunately, he wasn't sure whether or not Devin even believed in the monster.

The square, windowless space was cramped with brown

wooden file cabinets. In the center, Chief Inspector Devin was wedged into a tiny desk more appropriate to a menial clerk. He was so intently scrutinizing the yellowing papers inside an old file folder, though, he didn't seem to mind.

In lieu of a greeting, Devin nodded toward a small chair stacked high with files.

"Have a seat, Krogh."

Krogh lifted the mass of papers and set them on the floor, careful not to let a single sheet fall. Then he sat in the chair, stiff-backed.

"Since we were at Commercial Street, I had them pull some of the paperwork on the original Whitechapel slayings. Do you know much about Jack the Ripper?" Devin asked.

Krogh, surprised at the question, shook his head. "A little, I suppose. A tall, dark man in a top hat, who cut up whores with a sharp knife and was never caught."

"Ah, you see, the press and the popular mind are so fond of muddling things. He was never described as having a top hat, though some witnesses spoke of a foreign-looking man in a deerstalker. There were nine or more killings during the period, but only five generally accepted to have been the work of the same person: Mary Anne Nichols, 'Dark' Annie Chapman, Elizabeth Stride, Catherine Eddowes, and Mary Jane Kelly. All prostitutes, all disemboweled, except Stride, and there it's believed Jack was interrupted in his work. In two instances, the uterus was removed and taken away."

"Frankenstein might know all that and imitate it," Krogh offered.

Devin hesitated, about to say something, but he thought better and mumbled, "Perhaps." Then he turned back to his file. "A Dr. George Bagster Phillips, the divisional police surgeon, performed an examination of Annie Chapman at the crime scene. He said . . . Ah, here . . . *The whole inference seems to me that the operation was performed to enable the perpetrator to obtain possession of these parts of the body."*

Krogh was confused. "I'd understood that the Whitechapel murderer was insane, his killings born of rage. Are you suggesting he had some sort of intent, like Frankenstein, that made him collect body parts? Uteruses?"

"I believe the correct plural is *uteri*," Devin corrected.

Krogh nodded, retrieved his book, noted it quickly, then looked back up. "But all this suggests is that Frankenstein is imitating him directly."

Devin sighed. "Or that someone else believes he is actually Jack the Ripper. You see, the baron has always been interested in *multiple* parts, for reassembly I suppose, and in each of our new slayings, the uterus has been the *only* part missing."

Krogh shivered. "What are you trying to say? That he is innocent?"

Devin put the papers down and withdrew a small flask from his jacket. He pressed his gut into the edge of the tiny desk, to hand the flask over without standing.

"Have a sip," Devin said. "You're not going to like what I have to tell you."

Krogh took the flask, but lowered it to his lap. "I don't drink on duty."

Devin laughed. "That didn't stop you when you first saw those bodies. Besides, you've no official status here, so, technically, you're not *on* duty. And if you do consider yourself on duty, consider this an order from a superior."

Krogh grimaced, spun the cap, and, without even smelling the contents, took a mouthful and swallowed.

"And what is it I won't like?" Krogh said.

"The baron has powerful friends, or at least his father did. Someone, perhaps his wife, contacted them. They, in turn, approached some important members of our government. Now,

I certainly will not be asked to give up the case on him, especially if it's murder, but I am being ordered to either press charges or release him."

Krogh stood sharply, nearly stumbling into the small desk. "No! He's the killer, you know it!"

Devin bobbed his head side to side. "Well that's what I've been trying to tell you. I don't know it, do I? Four witnesses saw the victim and a dark-skinned gentleman in a deerstalker cap walking down Commercial Street toward the church. Two more saw a man of the same description flee afterwards. Splotches of blood led from the churchyard, across the street, and into an alley."

"So? He has an accomplice. The man in the deerstalker."

"Or, things happened as the baron laid them out."

Krogh's mouth dropped open. "You can't believe that's true!"

"It's plausible. There was an empty grave dug up, he could have been there grave-robbing. Then again, there was no body to speak of, making even that difficult to prove. There was blood on him, but he had no weapon, and this body, unlike the others, seems to our doctors as if someone was trying to stop the bleeding, as the baron said."

Devin's face grew somber. He leaned across the desk again, as if to better display his sincerity. "Look, Krogh, after reading your file, he was my chief suspect. That's why I took the unusual step of showing him the bodies. I'd hoped seeing them would make him give himself away, just by the look on his face. But he didn't react the way a killer might. He examined those bodies as if seeing them for the very first time. The only time he had anything resembling a guilty look was when he saw Benjamin Blyss's body. Now, I'd stake my badge on the fact that he knew something about *that* death. Any idea what it was?"

Krogh swallowed hard, now certain that Devin had never believed this part of his story. "He thinks the monster is now in

England. That the creature is the only one who could have caused the wound."

Devin twisted his head slightly and laughed. "Does he? Maybe I confused guilt for madness, or perhaps for him they're the same."

"You're not really going to let him go, are you? I tell you that man is the devil!"

Devin shrugged. "Please do calm down. I'm not your enemy. I trust he's guilty of much, probably everything in your file shy of this monster nonsense, just not these murders."

"But what of the murders the monster committed in my home country?" Krogh said, his tone reduced to pleading.

"My dear man, Frankenstein didn't commit them, nor do you even argue him an accomplice. Even if this fantastic story is true and he did create a monster, what should Frankenstein be charged with? Should we charge parents for their children's crimes?"

"But . . . but . . . "

"Buck up, Krogh, it's not over yet, but I'm afraid unless some new evidence turns up against him, we're going to have to release Henry Frankenstein."

Chapter Eleven

Thoughts jumping about like bees in a bonnet, Mary Blyss tried to calm herself. She and her savage protector were hidden in the backrooms of the warehouse, as far from the murder scene and the police as possible. They were here over a day now, but she couldn't take him with her, and he wouldn't let her leave.

The giant sat there, thick elbows on its knees, head bent down, his twisted expression maybe best described as forlorn. His face, now that she had time to study it, reminded her of a patchwork doll she'd had as a child, all sewn up, the buttons that made eyes and mouth mismatched and cracked.

"Hungry?" she said.

He opened his mouth and put his fingers toward it.

"Food," he said weakly.

It was one of the few words he seemed to know. Friend. Food. Once, she though she heard him say, "Good," but it may just have been one of those growls of his.

She looked at him, speaking slowly. "I'm hungry, too, love. Why not let me go get food?"

She stirred to rise, but his arm shot out to stop her.

"Grrnnnnrrrr."

It was like a steel pole, stiff, hard, and immovable. She sat back down.

She could get him to follow her, she was sure of it, but she couldn't take him anywhere in public, not with her dead husband's knife sticking in his arm. Ben's name was scratched in the hilt, after all. It just . . . stayed there, right where Ben stuck it, like a little stub of a branch sticking out from a tree trunk. You could hang a sweater on the hilt, use the poor slob as a coatrack, and he probably wouldn't be any wiser.

She'd heard of arrows shot into a limb where the pain didn't register, but this was like parts of his body were just plain dead, or at least unconnected to the rest.

The other problem was the fact that the longer they stayed in the warehouse, the more likely the police would find them. They'd carted off Ben's body last night, but she still caught glimpses of their blue uniforms, heard their cheery whistles as they guarded the outside.

They'll think I had something to do with it. Not that he didn't deserve it, but it wasn't me, your honor. I swear! This grunting hulk squashed him like a big, fat, hairy bug. With one punch, if you can believe that!

The giant idly scratched the floor with his index finger, occasionally picking his hand up to smell the fingernail, as if this time there might be something other than dust on it.

Oh, she could just scream and the bobbies would come running, but he'd saved her life. She at least ought to get him someplace safe. If she could just yank out the knife, she might be able to walk him back to Ben's flat on Brushfield, to tend the wound. Folks were used to seeing war victims hobbling, even rolling about.

"Here, love, please let me have a look," she said.

She barely raised her fingers before he let loose with a loud, "Nyrghhh!"

It was scary, that growl, worse than thunder. That and his thick-lidded eyes. They were dead mostly, but whenever her hand came near the knife, they lit up all yellow, like they were on fire, or charged with electricity like a bulb.

She briefly entertained the notion that this was the same

man who'd cut up Mitzie, but that was ridiculous. If he could wield a knife, then any dog could drive a car.

Probably escaped from an asylum, this one.

If she could get off to the Whale and Watch, use the coins she'd taken from Ben's pockets, then come back with some grub, maybe the giant would eat, feel better and she could do something about the knife.

She patted her chest with her hand. "I'll go get food." She motioned for him to stay seated and said each word, nice and slow, like it was a sentence. "I'll. Go. Get. Food. You. Wait. Here."

He grunted.

Was that a yes or a no?

She stood, very, very slowly. He started a bit and looked as if about to grab her.

Quickly she put one hand to his good shoulder and petted him. Then she put her free hand to her mouth, imitating his gesture. "Food. I'll go get food."

"Food," he repeated and started to stand. "We get food."

She pushed down on the shoulder. It was like trying to move a boulder.

"No, you stay here, love."

He looked at her and made a little sound like a lost puppy. So, he understood her at least. Maybe a stricter tone? Sometimes it worked with Ben, if he was already near-out from the drink in him.

"No!" she said sharply. "Stay."

He made a pouting face, but remained still. This time she managed to take a few steps away. He seemed worried, almost ready to cry, but he wasn't following.

"Stay!" she said again, as if ordering a dog. He did, but he looked so lost her heart ached for him. Worried he might be caught, she raised her hands to cover her face and said, "And hide. Until I get back."

He raised his hands likewise and repeated gruffly, "Hide. You get back."

Then he crouched low behind the broken wall they sat near.

Now we're getting somewhere.

As she came to the rotted old wood door and realized it was too late for him to stop her, she exhaled for what seemed the first time in days.

Through a crack in the board that covered the window next to it, she spied a bobby guarding the entrance. He faced the street, his back to her and the building, his eyes on the passing crowd. After all, he was supposed to stop folks from coming in, so this should be easy.

And it was. After Mary waited less than a minute, his eyes were drawn to a pretty young thing struggling with some packages. When she dropped one, the young bobby hopped over to help faster than a starving man to food. Mary slipped out and even walked by him, bold as you please, and gave him an approving nod, as if she'd been on the street all along.

So far so good.

She was on the Whitechapel side of the warehouse, only a block or so from the Whale. It was a quick walk. A lamplighter was tending the gas lamps, and a few folks milled about ending their day or beginning their evening.

She opened the door, feeling almost like herself for the first time in days. Inside, the dinner crowd was just getting started, but the bar was near empty. Weldon was tending so she waved the thin man over with a smile. He was an older chap, lovely fellow, graying hair along the sides of his head to match his shirt, and a cueball up top. He was slow, but good-hearted, though more than a few rowdy drunks were surprised by how strong those thin arms of his were.

First things first. "Draw me a pint, will you love?" she said.

He gave her a look. She grimaced and laid her coins on the

bar. He snatched two up. Before she could object, he said, "The second's for the night before last. You never paid your tab."

"All right. How about some food for the third? Just a loaf and some cheese? Maybe a pitcher of water?" Mary asked.

"A pitcher of water?" Weldon said, perplexed. "Isn't your pump working?"

"Don't ask. It's for an ailing friend."

He pulled out a glass pitcher. "I should get a deposit."

She made a face at him. "That's offensive, it is. It's not like we're strangers. I'll have it back inside an hour."

He made a face. "Is it for Ben, then? I won't be helping the likes of him."

I guess he hasn't heard.

She shook her head. "No. I haven't seen him."

Weldon shrugged. "In that case," he said, scooping some ice into the pitcher, "Any friend of yours."

After a pause, he asked, "Working tonight?"

Mary shook her head and spoke quietly. "Not tonight. Not after Mitzie."

He slid the pitcher in front of her. "Stupid press is all over it, saying Jack the Ripper's risen from the dead like Count Dracula! It's not stopping some of the other girls, though. Cyra and Paulette have been in and out twice already."

He poured off a pint from the tap. Dark liquid swirled in the clear glass.

Mary watched it absently as she muttered, "Poor Mitzie."

She meant to take just a sip, but the warm taste was so invigorating, she found herself draining a good portion of the pint. As Weldon watched, his brow furrowed and he plopped one of the coins back on the bar. "On the house, then. For Mitzie."

Mary raised her glass to him and gave him a sad little smile. "'Ho! Stand to your glasses steady! 'Tis all we have left to prize. A cup to the dead already, and Hurrah for the next that dies.'"

He gave her a little salute. "I'll see what I can round up for that food."

He slipped into the tiny kitchen, leaving Mary to savor the ale that sloshed in her gullet. A pleasant, light dizziness worked its way up her spine and into her head. She looked at the half-empty glass and thought, *What a gift you are, love—both drink and food!*

She looked around. Maybe she could manage a quick customer before heading back to her new friend. Not on the streets, tonight, no thank you sir, but she could bring some nice gent back into the cask room for some quick recreation.

The pickings at the bar were scarce. She stretched to look around the cracked frosted glass of the old privacy screen to the tables. No one sat alone. Cyra was with a nice young sailor, Paulette with some hunched-over fellow in a top hat and . . .

Hold on now . . .

Mary scrunched her little face close together and stretched her neck out even more. The hunched-over fellow sitting with Paulette looked unhappily familiar. Where'd she know him from? She couldn't place the clothes, or the hair, but there was something about his stance, his shoulders, the cut of the side of his face. The memory tingled just out of reach, but she knew it was important and grew desperate to remember.

Unfortunately, the gent's back was to her and the long fingers of his hands, carving up the meat on the plate in front of him didn't provide any clues.

When stretching didn't help, she stood, wobbling slightly. Drunk on an empty stomach, the ale had gone to her head. Where was Weldon with that bread and cheese? She took a few awkward steps to the edge of the screen and stuck her head inside, a little further than she intended.

She must have made a sound without realizing it, or the man simply sensed her presence, for he suddenly wheeled from his meal to face Mary directly. The sight hit her like a slap from the back of Ben's hand, and she took a few steps back. The man's sandy hair-color she didn't recognize, nor was the top hat or pressed shirt familiar, but the shape of his chin, his brow, and those dark eyes was unmistakable.

She gasped and stumbled back to the bar, moaning as she raced toward the kitchen door, nearly slamming into Weldon as he came out.

"He's here!" she cried, grabbing him. She spoke in a frantic, high-pitched whisper. "The one that walked off with Mitzie! He's here, with Paulette! He's changed his clothes and his hair, but it's him! I swear!"

Weldon's face shot toward the tables. "Where?" he said. He grabbed a blackjack near the register, then leapt over the bar and raced into the dining area. Mary followed, right behind him, just in time to hear him ask again, "Where?"

Weldon whirled, this way and that. Mary scanned the faces. Paulette was still there, looking annoyed that now she was sitting alone, but the stranger was gone.

"He couldn't have gone out through the front that quickly, could he?" Mary said, more to herself than anyone else. For a moment, she had to wonder if she'd really seen him? It felt more like a nightmare.

Still tense, Weldon called Paulette over. "The fellow you were with, where'd he go?"

Paulette sneered at Mary.

"He took one look at Mary here and bolted out the door!" she said, hands on her hips. "And I was hoping to call it an early night!"

I did *see it. He* was *real.*

Weldon bolted toward the door, pulling Mary with him. Outside, despite the thickening fog, there was a clear view in either direction. There was also no strange figure to be seen.

"Let's get the police, then," Weldon said.

The police? Her mind shot back to Ben's murder and the poor creature she'd left in the warehouse.

"No," she said. Weldon stared at her as if she were insane. "Look, this bloke's hair was all wrong, his clothes too nice, and I'm so tired."

"That's for coppers to sort out, Mary," he said. "Not you."

"All right, all right, I'll talk to them," she said, shaking her head. "But just as soon as I check in on my friend. Do you have my food ready?"

"Back on the bar," he said, his eyes still scanning the street. His gaze settled on the warehouse, his hand wrapped tightly around the blackjack.

"I heard they found a dead man in there," he muttered. "Wonder who it was."

He blinked, pulling himself out of his trance, then stepped back inside and a second later reemerged with the bag and the pitcher of ice water. She put the bag under her arm and held the pitcher with her hands.

"I'll walk you," he said.

Oh, sure, Weldon, and I could introduce you to my giant friend what killed Ben.

"Blimey! The street is full of people and the police are on the corner! I don't plan to wander into any alleys. I'll be fine," she insisted.

He shook his head. "If he saw that you recognized him, he'll be back around."

She hadn't thought of that, and thinking it now made her shiver. "Okay, then. Just up to the corner of Commercial."

Saying nothing, the tall balding man with the jack sticking from his hand like the black tongue of a wolf kept pace with her as they walked quickly through the street, the ice in the pitcher tinkling against the glass. When the young pimple-faced bobby was no less than five yards away, she paused.

"This is fine, just fine. Weldon, you're a good one. But you have to go find Paulette," she said. "She was sitting with him, after all, and got a better look than me. The police will want to talk to her, too."

Weldon nodded as if that hadn't occurred to him.

Mary laughed a little as she said goodbye and started walking away, alone. It was a strange little laugh, not her usual chuckle. She fancied it sounded a little mad, in a way that reminded her of Mitzie.

She rounded the corner, waited a bit, then peeked back to watch Weldon. Rather than relieve her, the sight of Weldon receding made her feel a little too alone.

Maybe I am going daft.

She looked at the bobby, then at the bag in her arms and the pitcher in her hands. If she went to talk to the police first, how many hours would that be? It'd been half a day they kept her just to identify a body whose identity they already knew. But this? The giant might starve in the meantime. So she made up her mind. She'd get him the food, try to remove that knife, maybe hide him somewhere else, then talk to the police about the man with the hungry eyes.

Getting in was as easy as getting out had been. She walked straight behind the bobby, sticking to the wall like one of the pigeons.

It's a wonder the police catch anyone at all, she thought, a notion which provided no comfort.

It was full night now, but light from the streetlamps cast a few circular pools into the warehouse. As she approached their hiding spot, she whispered, so as not to startle him, "Here, love, it's me."

The hulking figure rose to standing, putting to rest any thought she'd had that she might have imagined him. His face was easier to take now that it was darker, and if she read him right, he was happy to see her.

"Food?" he asked, pointing to the bag.

"Yes, love, yes," she said, handing him the loaf. He snatched it, almost taking her fingers along with it, and pulled huge chunks into his mouth, smiling as he chewed.

"Good! Good!" he said.

"Where are your manners?" she said, jokingly. "Mustn't talk with your mouth full, you know."

She thought she was talking to herself, really, but he seemed to understand. He pushed the largest gob of white into his mouth, closed it, and went back to chewing, making small grunting noises as he went. She was fascinated by how animal he was, as if he'd just walked out of a jungle after having been raised by gorillas. After a while, he stopped and fanned his free hand in the air, waving toward his open mouth.

"Wine? Wine?"

She couldn't help but laugh a bit at that. "It's a bit early for that, but how about some water?"

She held out the pitcher, its clear contents sloshing about with the ice. Like the bread, he snatched it from her hands and drank greedily.

He was a tough fellow to call. Sometimes he seemed pretty quick, others as dumb as a post. Maybe she could explain about the knife?

"You know you killed Ben, don't you?" she said.

He looked up from his drinking. She pointed to the knife, making sure he understood she wasn't planning to touch it.

"Ben. The bloke who stabbed you."

The monster nodded and grinned. "I make him dead. Like me."

She furrowed her brow. "No, no. You're not dead."

He nodded vigorously. "Yes. Dead. Frankenstein made me

from dead."

Now she was really confused. What was he babbling?

He put down the pitcher and pointed to a long scar on his forehead. "He made me from pieces of dead."

Then he reached his long arm forward and pointed to the spot on her abdomen, now covered with her dress, where her own scar was. "You dead, too? Like me?"

She shook her head. "We've both been cut, love, you worse than me, but we're not dead."

"If I might interject, miss, that's only because whoever did the cutting, didn't know how to do the job."

It was a low voice, like wheels rolling over gravel, with a thick cockney accent.

She and the giant both whirled, though he with a little animal grunt. Standing less than a few yards away was the man from the bar. He was all silhouette in the darkness, looking flat with his tall top hat and the cap draped on him. The only part of the image that had any depth was the silver sheen of metal from the long thin knife that glowed wickedly in his right hand.

Mary gasped. The monster growled.

The figure leaned his head slightly forward, as if tipping his tall hat.

"That won't do," he said.

Then it seemed as if he just vanished, that whatever shadows composed his figure had all melted into lighter gray. But now Mary heard small scraping sounds, feet against the concrete. She wanted to scream, but fear gripped her tongue.

The giant heard it, too. He rose, slowly, jutting his head this way and that, unable to locate the source because of the confusing echoes. He was snarling, long, low, and steady, his muscles poised to strike.

Instinctively Mary Blyss moved closer to the giant, so he wouldn't lose her in the dark. He'd protected her once before, but she had a feeling that whatever was stalking them out in the shadows would put up a better fight than Ben.

She didn't have long to wonder. An instant later, something pulled her into the shadows, away from the creature. She gasped as she felt an arm, strong, but not inhumanly so, against her chest, and felt the cold edge of steel against her throat. An image of Mitzie flashed in her brain, nearly decapitated by the swipe of such a blade.

A rough, foul breath caressed her ear as that voice came again. "You'll have to forgive me. I'd thought maybe I'd just put the fear into you, but it turns out that I've been at this so long, I don't have it in me to stop without leaving a whore dead," he said.

He tensed to draw back the blade, but before he could, the giant snarled and barreled into both of them. Mary was thrown free, and in the dim light, she could see the giant, his hands wrapped around the killer's shoulders, pulling him this way and that.

The killer whirled, his top hat tumbling off. The giant stepped into one of the dim patches of light, his scars now fully visible.

Mary imagined the killer would be shocked at the sight, but when the shadowy figure spoke again, it sounded pleased. "Ah!" he said. "Looks like someone's already beaten me to the cutting with you. So all I'll have to do is follow the line!"

The giant staggered, confused by the light and trying to find its balance, giving the killer the moment he needed to slash forward, the tip of his blade finding a stitch in the neck. He sliced it open, following it down along the arm, cutting both cloth and flesh as he went.

"Nyarghhhh!" the creature howled. Unlike Ben's blade, this time the creature felt it.

Surely that'll bring the police! Mary thought.

She considered running for them herself, but the two men blocked her nearest exit, and she could too easily lose her way in the dark and wind up alone with the killer.

The monster lunged forward with his right arm, the one that still held Ben's dagger, and slapped the killer's arms away, sending him into a spin that almost made him drop his knife. Moving fast for a giant, he closed the distance and wrapped his arms around the figure before it could stab again. He squeezed.

Now it was the killer's turn to cry out. "Ahhh!"

His voice had jumped an octave, making him sound more like a frightened man than a shadow-monster. Seeing the knife lodged in the giant's arm, he slammed into the hilt with his forehead.

The giant stumbled back, enraged and in agony.

I told you you should've let me get that out! Mary thought to herself.

The killer straightened himself and regarded the tall, raging thing before him.

"Now, I'm from the devil's hell, but what grim god imagined you?" he said.

Ignoring him, the giant lumbered forward. Mary, having watched many a brawl between men, bemoaned the fact that there was not an ounce of strategy in him. As the giant came forward, growling, the killer ducked low, whipped off his cape, twirling it toward the giant's legs.

Such a move would likely not work with a normal man, but the giant was already unsteady on his feet and seemed forever about to fall. The killer had noticed and now took advantage.

The cape wrapped around the giant's legs, entangling them. He looked confused for a moment, then off-balance, his arms rising to alter his center of gravity. But before he could regain his balance, the killer slammed into his chest, knocking him down and backward. The giant landed with a heavy thud in a pool of vague light, the sound impossibly loud for a man, and more appropriate to the felling of a wall or bronze statue.

In seconds, the killer was astride him, his long, thin blade raised in the air. But, as he looked down at the giant, with the giant's wounds now far more visible than previously, he hesitated, and his gruff face, which until now had been a killing mask, registered an almost childlike curiosity.

"Can such a thing be?" Mary thought she heard him say.

Whatever had made him hesitate was short-lived and again the blade came down. The giant moaned piteously.

She wanted to do something, anything, throw a rock, throw herself at the killer, but that old paralysis came over her again. She could not raise her hand to a man.

It turned out she didn't have to. At the last instant, the giant twisted sideways, hurling the killer's body to the side. She heard him scream but wasn't sure if it was pain or frustration. In seconds, the shadowy figure was rising, but groggily. She raced over to the fallen giant.

"Wake up! Get up, you lazy bastard, or Jack will kill us both!" she screamed at him.

But then, seeing what the killer had doubtless seen, she too paused in wonder.

Before her very eyes, the stitch the killer had ripped open was mending, the flesh tying itself back together.

What in bloody hell is this?

The killer called to her. It was panting this time, out of breath, but still hollow and terrifying. "I thank you for calling me by my proper name, Mary Blyss. I want to assure you we shall meet again very soon."

She snapped her head back and forth between the receding killer and the prone giant. He was stirring beneath her, so she backed off to give him enough room to rise.

But as he did, more men intruded on the scene.

"Here now, what's all this, then?" a bobby shouted, shining an electric light. There were at least six officers behind him.

As their lights, shouts, and footfalls flooded the warehouse, all the shadows living in it, including the giant, the killer, and Mary Blyss, faded to naught and nothing.

Chapter Twelve

Minnie's gnarled old hands reached once again for the blinds. "You've got to leave these open, Baroness. It's not healthy to stay in darkness all the time like a bat or a raccoon. There's little enough light to be had in this gray excuse for a country, it's amazing they've any plant life at all!"

Elizabeth slumped in her chair, lowering her head to shield her eyes from the light. "I hope I never seen the sun again, Minnie," she said sadly.

Minnie scuttled over, pushed her long dress to the side, and plopped down beside her mistress on the small bedroom couch.

"What do you mean, dearie? The baron's coming back. He'll be here any minute. And between you and me I'm hoping he gives us the order to pack up and leave this wretched place. I've had my fill of this city life. It all looks like one big hotel room to me. And you, m'lady, just a little while ago, so brave and strong, pulling yourself together to make all those phone calls on his behalf. You were like your old self again."

"He needed me. I was strong for him. I love him so, Minnie. I'd even die for him, but sometimes, I'm afraid dying is the next thing I'll have to do," she said.

Minnie made a face. "Poppycock!"

Elizabeth gazed sadly out the window, toward the smoke-stacks across the Thames. They billowed out black clouds, sapping what little color there was from the sky. "This whole place is like a machine, Minnie, just like the devices in Henry's laboratory.

I feel as though we're trapped inside some infernal engine and we'll never get out before it crushes us."

"Tush, tush, dear," Minnie said, patting her hand. "It's just what they call the London smog, you know, from all the burning coal. Coats your lungs, they say."

Elizabeth turned to Minnie and gave her an odd little smile. "You're such a dear, and so kind to me."

"It's a selfish love, Baroness," Minnie answered, blushing slightly. "You and Mr. Henry are the house of Frankenstein now, and houses are only as strong as the pillars that hold them. I've known Mr. Henry since he was a boy, God bless him, he's smart as a whip, but at his best he can't hold up a candle, let alone a whole house by himself. It'd all fall to ruin, like his laboratory, if things were left to him. And then where would I be? So, that leaves it to you to protect him from those that might want to do him harm, and maybe even from himself, if you get my meaning."

"Can I, though? We come here and those poor women start being murdered. Three now. Three more dead for Henry to try to bring back to life. And the papers here all say the killer is a doctor, a surgeon, like Henry," Elizabeth said. She shivered and lowered her head, weeping.

"Now, now. The baron may be a lot of things, but he's no murderer. His father? He could kill you soon as look at you, but not Mr. Henry. When he was a lad he used to sob about the dead wolves the men brought from the hunt. Of course, he spent a lot of time poking about their innards when he had the chance, but that was just natural curiosity," Minnie said.

She meant the story to be comforting, but found herself squeezing her brow at the memory just the same.

Catching herself, she took her mistress' chin in her hands, lifted the baroness' head up, and stared into her eyes. "Now you listen to Minnie. It's high time you pulled yourself together, for the baron and for yourself. He may soon need you to do more than make a few phone calls."

Elizabeth leaned forward, a little panicked. "I don't think I can do it, Minnie. I'm just not . . . "

Whatever word Elizabeth Frankenstein was about to use to describe herself remained unsaid, because the two women heard the door to the suite outside fly open and an excited, familiar voice call from the living room.

"Elizabeth! It's me, Henry! I'm back!"

He raced in wearing a plain cotton suit that barely hung on his shoulders. Minnie had to dodge out of his way as he threw himself on the couch next to Elizabeth and grabbed both her hands in his.

He drew them close to his chest. "I'm so sorry to have worried you with all this nonsense, dear. It's all but settled now. How are you? Are you feeling better?"

The fabric of his jacket felt strange. Elizabeth couldn't help but pull her hands back.

Henry's brow furrowed. "What is it darling? The clothes? They're not mine, they're borrowed. They misplaced mine at the station. I'll have my attorney sue them for the cost."

"Why did they take your clothes, Henry?"

He blinked. "Don't worry about that, darling. It's not important. I swear it's not. What's important is that I'm here."

Their hands still entwined, she lifted his closer to her eyes and looked at his fingers one by one. "You have such marvelous hands, Henry. So delicate, so gifted. You wouldn't ever hurt me with them, would you?"

He stared at her, dreadfully confused. "Hurt you? Why I'd sooner die than see one golden hair on your head come to harm. What's this about? The nonsense with the police and our passports? I told you it was all but settled."

She pulled his hands down into her lap and looked at him. "It's not about the passports, Henry. That's not why the police brought you in, and it's not why they released you. I called a lot of people on your behalf, old friends of your father. It wasn't easy. You're not well liked in our home country, I know that now. But I begged and they finally agreed."

Henry pulled his hands away and sneered. "I see. So the superstitious fools took pity on me, did they? I bet they'd just as soon let me rot."

"You lied to me, Henry."

He shrugged. "You've been so upset, my darling, and I've already caused you so much misery. I didn't want anything further to disturb you. Can you forgive me?"

"Can you swear to me it's not true? That you had nothing to do with the death of those poor women?"

He looked at her, genuinely hurt and shocked. "Elizabeth! Of course not!"

Seeing the sadness in his eyes, she pulled him close to her breast. "Oh, thank you my darling, thank you. And can you swear to me that you'll have nothing further to do with those vile experiments ever again?"

She felt him stiffen. She slowly pulled away to look at him.

He looked so deeply drained as he met her eyes.

"Elizabeth," he said.

"Henry."

He shivered and started talking, "There's just one more thing that I must do, just one more, and then it will be all over, I swear, I just have to find out . . . "

She shook her head, smiled, and put her fingers to his lips. "Hush. Hush, my sweet. He's here now, you know."

His brow furrowed. "I don't understand. Who's here?"

"Death."

"Elizabeth, please . . . "

She nodded at him reassuringly. "It's all right. He's been invited. He is our most welcome guest. Do you see him? His arms unfurled, his dark wings spreading, ready to embrace us both?"

"Elizabeth, please!"

"I used to think it would hurt," she said to the air. Then to Henry she added, "But what could ever hurt more than this?"

She started laughing, quietly at first.

Baron Frankenstein said her name over and over, softly, then louder, as if he were calling to her from the top of a well, but she didn't answer, she just kept laughing.

Terrified, he rose and stepped away.

"He's you, Henry," she giggled, her eyes completely mad. "He's *you!*"

Henry Frankenstein stumbled back. He glanced at Minnie, who sat there, dumbstruck, staring at her mistress, tears welling in her eyes.

"He's *you!* He's *you!*" Elizabeth cried.

Her laughing had stopped and she started to scream.

Shaking terribly, Henry Frankenstein stumbled out of the room and into the suite. He grabbed at a cigarette and was barely able to light it.

I have to think. I have to make things right. Elizabeth's hysterical. She'll calm down. She has before. But I can't deal with this, not now, not with Krogh here, not with the police still suspicious and the monster possibly still alive. There are limits to what any man can handle.

As he heard her howl and moan, he slid open the single drawer in the tiny table and looked down at the hypodermic needle and the small bottle of clear liquid.

It would let her sleep. Give her some small comfort.

A mirror lay above the table, and he happened to catch a glimpse of himself in it. His face was still young, but barely, his black hair had started to recede.

What was he then? What was he becoming?

History was full of the corpses of great men, cut down by small-minded insects. He'd never realized how much their families must have suffered.

He needed help. Elizabeth needed help.

Instead of the syringe, he picked the handle of the phone off the cradle and had the hotel operator place a long-distance call. Some long minutes, several cigarettes, and a stiff drink later, the phone rang and the sound of a familiar voice brought a strange ease to Frankenstein's face, so much so that he almost, but not quite, smiled.

"Victor, old man, I don't want to involve you in my troubles, but I need you to come to London, right away. Elizabeth is . . . well, she's not well and there are thing I simply must attend to that keep me from her side. She could certainly use the company of a friend. You'll come? Excellent. I'll set up a ticket for you straightaway. Don't bother packing, I'll see to it that you have everything you need here. Thank you. Thank you. Elizabeth will be thrilled."

Hugging the receiver as if it were the hand of his best man, he set the phone back down, then slid the drawer with the hypodermic needle shut. Seeing Victor Moritz would do her good, more good than that poison. More good, he feared, than he could himself.

It was no secret that the dashing Victor loved Elizabeth. He wore his heart on his sleeve, but he was too decent a man to interfere with their courtship let alone their marriage. Even when Victor learned of Henry's experiments, he stood by them both. In fact, Henry fully expected that if he'd died, Elizabeth would marry Victor. Henry didn't deserve such a loyal friend, but Elizabeth certainly did, especially now.

He briefly wondered if now, seeing how upset Elizabeth was,

Victor would still feel that loyalty to Henry. He'd called him mad on more than one occasion

It didn't matter. What mattered was that Elizabeth would be watched over, cared for by someone who had her best interests at heart, while Henry was away. And unfortunately, with the monster still about, with him so close to discovering who the brain's donor really was, he would simply have to be away. But once all that was settled, once he was in his right mind again, he would fix everything with Elizabeth.

She would be fine, he was sure.

Holding onto that thought, Henry Frankenstein sat down and smoked cigarette after cigarette until the cries in the other room finally faded away.

Chapter Thirteen

In Whitechapel some days later, two women hid in the cool dark of a second-floor hallway, just outside a half-open door, whispering nervously to one another as they watched a monster.

"We've gone on talking about it long enough. I say we've got to get on with it."

"No. You're daft!"

The creature seemed utterly unaware of them, his entire focus on his food. It was as if eating regularly was a new experience for him, and he approached every meal they gave him with a kind of childish glee. He slurped down the remains in the bowl of milk, letting the overflow trickle down the sides of his cheeks, then pressed as much of the cheese and bread into his mouth as he could. Mouth stuffed to the brim, he tried to maneuver his teeth around the huge liquidy gob.

"Blimey! How much can he eat?"

"At least it keeps him quiet."

Like the mash in his mouth, the monster barely fit the room. The second floor of a two-up-two-down common worker's cottage was a tiny enough space for an average-sized person, but the giant made the nightstand and bed look handcrafted for a midget. His black coat, torn now at the shoulder, lay draped over a small wooden chair. The cloth was so dark and the light so dim, the folds were invisible, making it look like a tent made of shadow.

The creature, still wearing his gallows-black shirt and pants, sat in the center of the bed, making the bed's sad frame creak and bend with his every movement. The knife from his fight with Ben Blyss still stuck from the top of his long white arm, but there was no blood or infection visible at the sight of the blade's penetration.

"Come on! I'll distract him and you grab it," Mary Blyss said. "It'll be out before he knows what hit him. Then he'll be grateful to both of us."

Cyra, a dark-skinned beauty with brown eyes, looked at her friend in horror. "Me? Haven't I done enough for the both of you, then? Hiding you, feeding you? It's not like I'm living the life of Reilly here. Besides, the skin looks like it's all healed up around the blade. I could wind up pulling half his arm off with it," she said. "I don't think he'll be so grateful for that."

"Oh, come off it, darling," Mary said. "You love a challenge."

Cyra smiled a bit, showing the perfect white teeth that let her charge more for her services than most. "A challenge, sure, but we're talking suicide."

"Oh, he's been practically like a baby the last few days! I've *got* to go to see the police today. Would you rather be stuck here with him the whole time I'm gone?" Mary said.

Cyra raised an eyebrow and glanced back inside the room. She and Mary both gasped when they realized the monster was standing right beside them, the door now fully open. They nearly screamed with fright, but wound up laughing instead.

"Quiet as a cat when he wants to be, isn't he?" Cyra said, chuckling.

The monster's mouth twisted into a grin, but the rest of his face didn't quite follow suit. He made a huffing sound, as if trying to laugh along with them. After a moment, he held out the bowl.

"Drink. Drink good."

"Look at him, not so much as a by-your-leave. If he didn't save my life twice, I'd turn him in," Mary said.

Cyra scowled. "Well, he may have saved your life twice, but he hasn't saved mine at all. All he's done is eat what little food I've got."

"Drink?"

Cyra leaned closer to him, arching her neck to look up at him. "Where are your manners? Say, please. *Please* can I have a drink? Can you do that?"

The monster looked confused. He held the bowl out again.

Mary shook her head and tried to pull her friend back. "Don't push the poor thing. I doubt he's seen much kindness at all. Besides, you'd hate to see him angry."

Cyra made a face again. "Coddling him won't help. I had a deaf nephew I taught to speak before he died of the consumption. If this bloke can say drink, food, and good, he can certainly learn how to say please. Just takes a little patience, and a willingness to let him get hungry enough. Here now."

She strained her neck to put her dark face closer to the creature's. She moved her thick lips and spoke loudly. "Please. Please. Please can I have a drink?"

Mary settled back and looked. The giant didn't seem to react at all. Sometimes, when he just stood there like that, so still, he seemed more a statue or a corpse, as if whatever pushed his body about came and went depending on his surroundings.

This time, without making a sound, Cyra just moved her thick lips, forming the words. The monster's brow moved slightly.

"I think he's getting the idea," Mary whispered.

"Please. Say please."

Cyra was just about to give up when the monster pursed his lips and pushed some air through them. "Pluh."

Both women grinned. "That's it, love. You're almost there. Please."

"Pluh. Pluhs."

"Good!" she said patting him on the shoulder, right near the knife hilt. He was so pleased with himself, he didn't so much as blink.

"Pluhs drink. Pluhs give drink."

"Ha! I could teach a cat to dance, I could," Cyra said.

Smiling, she took the bowl from his hands and handed it to Mary. "You heard the man, Mary, some more milk, please!"

Mary nodded and moved across the room to reach for the small bottle that sat outside the window, in the cooler morning air.

"Maybe next we should work on thank you," Mary said.

Cyra went back to smiling at the monster. She clicked her tongue and nodded to herself. "Do it quickly, love, I have an idea."

Slightly apprehensive, Mary poured the thick liquid from the glass bottle to the bowl, filling it halfway. The monster watched her hungrily, but Cyra shook her head. "No. Give him a nice *big* bowl. He did say please."

"Puh-leese . . . " the monster repeated, his eyes now riveted on the cool, white liquid.

"Okay, here's the trick. Don't hand it to him just yet. Just hold it out to him," Cyra said.

Mary kept her eyes on the monster but said to her friend, "I don't know about this, Cyra. What are you . . . ?"

Cyra wiped her hands on her skirt then flexed her fingers, like a pickpocket getting ready to make a pinch. "Just do as I say. Hold it out to him."

"All right," Mary said. She forced a pleasant smile to her own face, matching Cyra's, and held the bowl just out of reach.

The monster raised his hands and leaned forward, about to take a step, but Cyra, still smiling, put her hand on his chest to stop him.

"Just one more thing, love," she said.

He glanced at her, confused. Then with a quick, cat-like move, she grabbed the knife and pulled. It slid out, as if it'd been held in butter.

The monster's face twisted in surprise. His thick eyelids opened wide. Before he could react further, Mary rushed forward with the bowl, singing in a forced, high-pitched voice, "Here's your milk! Here's your milk!"

The monster's head twitched nervously, as if he were torn between trying to figure out what had just happened to his arm and the more immediate pleasures of the milk bowl. With a little moan, he snatched the bowl and drank greedily.

Both women sighed, losing an inch from their height as they exhaled. Cyra presented the blade to Mary, hilt first. "And here's Ben's blade."

Cyra slumped against the wall. Mary smiled and said, "I could kiss you."

"That'll cost you extra, love," Cyra said, laughing.

The monster, milk dripping from his upper lip, laughed, too.

Mary looked at his arm, through the torn shirt and shook her head. "And look at that, barely any blood."

Cyra looked, too. "It's like you said, after the killer cut him, he just healed up."

Mary shook her head and crossed herself. "I thought it was just the light playing tricks on my eyes, but there it is again."

"We could lift the shirt and have a closer look," Cyra said.

"Oh, now who's daft? Just leave him be, I say."

"All right, all right. You'd best be getting back to the police station before they come looking. And try to keep your story straight. Just pretend you never met our friend here."

"Oh, like forgetting about *him's* an easy thing," Mary sighed. "And when am I going to get back to some work? Ah, it could be all day again. They've got some artist I'm supposed to give a description to. You'll be okay?" Mary said.

"I may slip out for a customer or two, but I'll keep him eating. Even if he does show up on the street now the police won't have a reason to arrest him."

Mary nodded, then added, "Regulars only, right? The killer's still out there."

"You've only told me a million times. Yes, regulars only. But I am going to have to earn *some* money tonight, Mary. Apparently I'm supporting the three of us, these days."

Mary leaned over and kissed her friend on the cheek. "You're a saint."

Cyra gave her the eye. "Well, don't go spreading that around or we'll all be in the poorhouse."

Chapter Fourteen

A tattered shawl was wrapped around her head and shoulders. Scores of deep wrinkles rendered the old woman's face a series of squiggles. Some were light, some dark, some sprouted a single strand of thin white hair. There were so many wrinkles, and some so thick and long, it was difficult to tell in the poorly lit bar just where her mouth and eyes were.

Frankenstein hovered near the aged figure. Her appearance was almost enough to make him believe in witches. Almost.

He shifted his shoulders slightly under his simple workman's black coat. At least it was clean, and he hadn't been foolish enough to advertise his wealth. As he came closer, his shadow crossed the old woman. He expected some reaction, but she gave no indication she was aware of his presence. For that matter, she gave little indication she was even alive, other than a slight rising and falling of her shoulders. He'd been warned she was a drunk, and now he feared she was in too much of a stupor to give him the knowledge he craved.

He knew she was short when he spotted her alone at the table, but now, as he got even closer, he realized she was under five feet. There was something about her that reminded him of the little people Dr. Pretorius had grown in his experiments.

"Emma Nodding?" he said softly. He thought he saw a few facial wrinkles rustle, so he spoke louder. "Are you . . . the barkeep told me you were Emma Nodding."

The jaw moved, stretching the pale cheek-skin. Her pink tongue clicked along the few bony stubs in her mouth that passed for teeth. Frankenstein thought she was going to speak, but she just ran her tongue in the space between her teeth and her lips, upper and lower, then smacked her lips twice. She looked more a puppet than a person.

Frankenstein was about to speak again when two thick wrinkles on her face parted, revealing the eyes. They were all but white, just enough of the cornea visible to tell that once upon a time they'd been blue. It was obvious she was blind.

The jaw moved again and she made a croaking noise that sounded like, "What?"

Frankenstein spoke slowly, loudly, clearly. "Are you Emma Nodding?"

"Why? I'm old. I'm blind. Give me a drink or leave me be," she answered. Her shoulders rustled dismissively beneath her musty shawl.

Frankenstein tried to sound pleasant. "I'm a . . . I'm a doctor. I'd like to ask you a few questions."

A rough rasping issued from the back of her dry throat. Frankenstein thought she was trying to spit, then realized she was laughing.

"A doctor? Then you're too late," she said. "It's just that the walk to the graveyard is so long, I'd just as soon wait here for Judgment Day."

Her laughter morphed briefly into a phlegmy cough, then fell back to silence.

"I've been told you know Tom Nodding. That he was your son," Frankenstein said.

The face scrunched. It was a cryptic expression that could have meant simply annoyance or consternation, but Frankenstein took it as sadness.

"Oh, Tom, Tom, Tom. Too late for him as well. They found my poor boy hanged this summer past," the crone said. Sighing, or just exhaling, she felt about the table with her hands, then looked puzzled, as if something she'd expected had gone missing.

"No, you don't understand. I just want to know about him, about his life. I have to find out what he was like, what sort of man he was," Frankenstein said. The old woman went quiet for so long, he wondered if she heard him at all, or if she had, if she understood.

But the coughing laugh came again, or was it more of a moan? "You want to know about my Tom-Tom? About what sort of man he was?"

"Yes, yes," Frankenstein said, excited at even this meager communication. He folded his hands in front of him, to keep them steady. "Will you help me, please?"

"Why?" she asked.

"Why?" he repeated, not really expecting the question, but realizing how reasonable it was. What could he say? He didn't dare try to explain his full reasons. At best they would only confuse and upset her.

"It's a study I'm working on. A medical study—"

He didn't have to come up with the rest of the lie. She interrupted with a weak wave of her stubby little fingers. "No, no. Not why do you want to know. I couldn't care less, I'm sure. My meaning is, why should I help you?"

Here it was again, the need of the desperate and the power of money. It sometimes seemed a force as palpable and effective as the great ray beyond the ultraviolet that first brought life forth from dead matter, though Frankenstein understood it far less.

His experience with the resurrection man had made him far more cautious about bribes. He looked around. There were a few shadowy forms seated at the tables. It was early afternoon, though, and he guessed these were more the sort who were in the midst of drinking themselves to death, like Emma

Nodding, rather than some cutpurse who had the strength to do him harm.

"I'd be happy to pay you a little something for your troubles," he answered in measured tones.

She shook her head. "You know those blind folk you hear tell about who 'see' with their fingertips, or can tell what color a butterfly is by the sound of its wings? I'm not one of those. I'm blind and stupid, I am. For all I know you'd give me blank pieces of paper for bills and copper buttons for coins."

"Well, what then?" Frankenstein asked.

"Well, think of me as one of those auto-machines you put some fuel in and then crank up. I'm here, all set and ready to go and tell you about my poor Tom-Tom, even though it kills me as much to remember as it does to forget. But I need fuel from the kind doctor with his secret research and shaking hands, which in this case would be a bottle of whiskey."

He looked at her hands as they rubbed one another on the table in front of her, wrinkled and bone-like. He held his own out and looked at them for comparison, young, elegant, but vibrating in the near-darkness.

How could she tell?

"Very well," he said. "I'll just be a moment."

He went to the bar where a wide, hairy man in a white shirt, pants held aloft by dirty suspenders, had apparently been listening in. He'd already put a dirty glass and a bottle with some brownish liquid in it on the counter.

Frankenstein put his hand in his pocket to feel for the small amount of money he'd brought with him. The barkeep gave him a wink.

"Don't worry," he whispered. "It's the cheap stuff. Her usual."

"Is she sane enough to talk?" Frankenstein whispered.

The barkeep indicated a spot a quarter way up the unlabeled

bottled with a wet index finger. "Once she gets to around here, she won't be."

Frankenstein nodded, put a few coins on the bar, then grabbed the corked bottle and glass. Returning to the table, he put both close to the woman, letting the bottle fall with a heavy thud, so she'd be certain to hear.

With a liquidy giggle, she felt about until her gnarled hands hit the glass. As Frankenstein pulled up a worn wooden chair that was more scratches than paint, she hoisted the bottle to her mouth and ripped out the cork with her few remaining teeth.

As if sensing his nearness, she hesitated and turned her sightless eyes toward his. "Want to know how I got blind?" she asked.

"If you'd like to tell me," Frankenstein said. He smiled politely, then realized the effort was pointless.

"Someone gave me a bottle of tainted whiskey. Well, they didn't give it to me, I nicked it, but I drank near half before my head started swimming and aching, like there were little worms inside it, trying to chew their way out. Should have died. Last thing I saw was that bottle. See, I was in such a hurry, I didn't even bother to sniff it. So that's what I do now. I take a good long sniff," she said. Then she put the bottle to her nose and inhaled again. "Now, why would you think I'd do that?"

"So you don't poison yourself again, I imagine."

"No!" she cackled. "So I can drink it quicker if it is poison!" Then she laughed and took a long draught.

"Please, can you tell me about your son, Tom Nodding? I need to know what sort of man he was."

"You might be better off asking if he was a proper man at all," she said. This time the bitterness in her expression was unmistakable.

"How do you mean? Was he cruel? Was he cruel as a child?"

She scowled. "No, no, that's too easy. Have you ever heard of a changeling?"

Frankenstein's upper lip twitched into a bit of a sneer. "The fairy tale?"

"Yes. Sometimes the fairy folk, when they want a child, they take one, and they leave something in its place that looks just like a baby. But it's really a goblin child, a thing of stone, more dead than alive."

"You think your child was taken off by fairies?" Frankenstein said. His heart sank. Perhaps the woman was too mad to offer any useful information.

"No, no," she said, shaking her head vigorously. "Do you think I'm an idiot, taking me literally? That's just the best way to describe him. Tom was just like that, since he was born, that's all. He was my fifth child, so I thought I'd seen everything a little one could throw at you, but from the moment he came out, there was just something not right about him. I had means then, when my husband was alive. He earned a decent wage and we had ourselves a little home, with bread pudding on Sundays. Tom was what put an end to all that.

"First thing you'd notice about my Tom-Tom was that he wasn't near as fast as other kids his age. Second thing you'd notice is how angry he could get. Before he could walk, if there was a pile of blocks that didn't sit just the way he wanted, he'd fly into a rage, tearing up everything all around him. Most of what he'd hurt was himself, but I swear even then, his anger was more like a drunken man's than a child's." She paused and laughed to herself, showing the few teeth in her mouth.

"The third thing, I guess, would be how frail he was. Bones like a bird, and flesh that bruised easy. Even the tiniest insult to his body would bring out a huge blue and purple sore that'd last weeks. The other kids beat him regularly. At first I thought it was because he was such a weakling, but after a year or so, I realized it was more. I know he was my own flesh and blood, my poor Tom, and may the good Lord forgive me for saying so, but there was something about him that just *asked* for it. Maybe it was the way he got all angry and you knew he couldn't really do anything about it. By the time he was ten, I was afraid he'd snap, that he'd do something really awful, just to get back at his tormentors. That was my boy, that was my Tom."

She paused again to take a drink.

"What became of him? Why—" Frankenstein began.

"Why'd they kill him?" she said as she swallowed. Frankenstein nodded, then, remembering she couldn't see him, said, "Yes, please tell me."

"His chief tormentor was Brian, my eldest. Now, Tom was never cruel, you understand, he just had this goblin-thing going on in his head and his heart. He was fine, long as you didn't frustrate him. Brian, though, was cold and calculating in the finest British tradition. He had a handle on it, tamed it, kept it under control. But, upstanding as he was toward everyone else, he always had a special hatred for his little brother. His chief joy in life was in watching Tom go berserk.

"Once he even put a pack of matches in the boy's cap, then lit 'em up. Tom smelled the sulfur and started stamping it out with his hand, but he only wound up burning himself. I know it was Brian that did it, I saw him grinning like some kind of evil monkey. I thought he'd grow out of it, but he never did.

"By the time they were young men, there was this neighborhood girl, Bess, that Tom took a liking to. He never said anything, but you could tell by the way he shivered whenever she came near. After about a year or so, he got up the nerve to talk to her, and she laughed at him, right in front of the whole neighborhood. He flew into a rage and nearly broke both his arms pounding against the door she locked herself behind. There was a big scene and the police had to drag him away.

"Well, that was all Brian needed to see. Straightaway he starts courting Bess, and by then he was a handsome fellow with some means, so her head was turned. He always made sure Tom was watching when he brought her around the house. Poor Tom would hide like a wounded puppy. After that, there was no talking to him at all. I begged Brian to call it off with Bess, but he swore she was the girl for him, so what could I do? But when he announced his engagement, he didn't tell me or his dad first, he told Tom. It was times like that what made me wonder which child the changeling was.

"Anyway, the years pass, Brian goes into the service, and after the war they got a place and had three lovely children. Tom did his best, but he couldn't hold a job, so he falls in with a bad sort, running deliveries for the local mob. It's not much, but at least he can handle it, and eventually he finally had enough money to get his own little squat. He seemed to finally come out of his dark cloud over Bess, so I turned the other way and crossed my fingers he wouldn't get caught.

"It was around this time that I lost my poor Charlie, my husband, to cancer of the jaw. Now the boys hadn't seen each other for years, so Tom had actually been free of Brian, but the whole family got back together for the funeral. It was here that Brian asked around and heard about Tom's job. I saw the look in his eyes, I begged him not to do anything about it, and he promised on his father's grave he wouldn't, but he did.

"He went to Tom's bosses and told them Tom had been snitching on them. I think maybe Brian figured they would just beat up poor Tom, but this lot was for blood. They trashed and burned his poor little place, and started hunting the streets for him. Tom was crushed, furious, he had nowhere to go, so he came back to the house where Brian, Bess, and the children were staying, and begged for a place to spend the night. With his father dead, Brian starts acting all like the head of the household, so he not only refuses, he tells Tom that he was the one who lied about him to his bosses and how it served him right for being a criminal.

"Tom screamed and howled, louder than I'd ever heard him before, and he started pounding at Brian's chest and his face. Brian just laughed, grabbed Tom by both hands, and pulled them back, nearly breaking them. Tom went to his knees whimpering, and Brian kicked him out into the gutter.

"I slapped Brian myself that night. I begged him, I begged him just to tell me why he hated his brother so much, but he could never say, and he never lost this smug look of satisfaction in his eyes, satisfaction at his brother's pain.

"But Tom wasn't done, no sir, not this time. After all those years trapped in that frail little body, after all those years of having Brian torture him, and now, with death at his heels, that very night, he snuck back into the house, into the children's room and he . . . "

For the first time in her long story, the woman shivered, and her voice cracked in a way that made Frankenstein think she was about to cry.

" . . . and he slaughtered them, sir, that's the only word I can think of, slaughtered them. I think he did it, well, because when he saw those little ones there, hurting so much himself, he finally saw someone else he could hurt. He left after that. They say the gang killed him, but I was never sure he hadn't finally done it to himself."

Her eyes closed back into wrinkles, her body heaved, and her face scrunched up. Tears welled at the slits, then ran down along the cracks of her face as she sobbed.

"And that's not the worst of it," she began, trying to catch her fading breath. "No, not nearly the worst."

She put both her hands flat on the table to steady herself, but couldn't stop her convulsive sobbing. "I was the first to find them, to see the babes, lying all broken up in their room.

The youngest, my little Mabel, she whose bright eyes reminded me of my own mother, well, she was still alive, but barely. There was no way a doctor could help her."

She started feeling around for something to balance herself, to keep herself from falling off her chair, or from falling even further into herself.

Instinctively repulsed, Frankenstein began pulling back his own hands from the table, but the slight sound they made gliding across the wood told her in an instant where they where. She grabbed them with her gnarled old hands, grabbed them hard and tight and wouldn't let go. Frankenstein was startled, by her touch and her strength. For all her sobbing, her hands held him more powerfully and steadily than a vise, a vise made of bone.

"So I . . . I put a pillow on her face myself, I did, and pressed down until the crying stopped," she cried.

When she released Frankenstein, to bury her head in her hands, he slumped back in his chair and let his arms fall to his sides.

Weakly, he looked around. Despite Emma Nodding's loud voice, not another patron stirred. Even the barkeep went about his business as if nothing were out of the ordinary. They'd heard the story before, apparently, and accepted its telling as part of their own personal hell.

"I killed my own grandchild," Emma said. "It was out of mercy, sweet mercy, but just the same, can anyone imagine a worse sin than that?"

A word sprang to Frankenstein's lips, but he stopped himself before he said it.

The word was "yes." He wanted to say yes, yes, he could imagine such a sin, but the impulse was wrestling with his sharp and critical mind, the one that still insisted sin did not exist.

But whatever its insistence, it now had to grapple with the fact that rather than feeling free upon learning the source of his creature's brain, Frankenstein felt damned, damned as Emma, damned as the other numb, soul-sick, speechless denizens both here and all over the earth. He felt damned because he could not imagine that mere accident would give a sad, demented figure like Tom Nodding a body with the strength of ten men, a perfect body with which to carry out his pent-up vengeance on those with weaker flesh. Though his mind tore at the logical fabric of the notion, in his heart he felt Elizabeth had been right all along, that behind his work had been the hand of the Devil.

But he didn't tell Emma Nodding that. He didn't say a word. Instead, he tossed a few coins on the table and hurried out so quickly he didn't bother to notice whether or not the tearful old woman was able to put her hands on them. Hoping at least to leave this small portion of Hell behind him, he fled into the growing night.

Chapter Fifteen

It'd already been a long day for Mary Blyss at the Commercial Street Police Station. They'd taken her statement hours ago, then sat her out here on this hall bench along with ten or so other Whitechapel locals, who all seemed to have their own Ripper story to tell.

To make matters worse, a stout, balding man with a long, thin pipe sat next to her, constantly nudging her and complaining. He wore an odd purple coat with a sheen to it that looked more like a smoking jacket than proper wear for the public.

"How dare they keep me here for two hours!" he said quietly, leaning into her. "I am a victim! I deserve assistance! But they ignore me."

She knew she shouldn't respond, but she hoped if he had his say, he'd quiet down.

"Okay then. A victim of what?" she asked.

He lit up, happy for the attention. "Theft, theft, my dear . . . may I have the pleasure of your name."

"Mrs. Mary Blyss, if it is a pleasure," she said, wondering if he'd connect her to Ben, though the story of his death had been buried by the Ripper headlines.

The fat fellow nodded. "Professor Lampini, Mrs. Blyss, at your service. I run a traveling waxworks, currently situated in the Whitechapel market, full of fantastic figures from history and fiction, from Alexander the Great to Jack the Ripper, the real one, not this recent poser. You'd do well to come visit and learn a thing or two."

"So what's your beef, then? Folks slipping in without paying?" Mary ventured.

"Hardly. Three times now I've returned to find my figures disturbed, expensive costumes missing. Someone is breaking in and stealing them. I've been here each time to complain, but still the police do nothing but keep me waiting!" he said, all puffed up with righteous rage.

"Why don't you complain to the desk sergeant?"

He shrugged, seemed to shrink a bit, then whispered to her, "Because, my dear, I am a coward and a fake. They've just to glare at me and I'll sit here for days."

Mary laughed. "You and me both, Mr. Lampini. I've been a coward all my life."

His eyes twinkled at that. "So you know what it's like not to be able to stand up for your own rights, eh? There are many of us, I suspect, afraid even of our own dreams. Look at me, all I've ever dealt with in my waxworks is fakery. Not even very good fakes. They're cardboard cutouts compared to Madame Tussaud's. Yet still I dream to find some real horrors to show the public."

"Why don't you then?"

He sighed some smoke through his nose. "Because I know I'd have to travel the great wide world, risk life and limb to get them, and I am too averse to risk, too afraid of pain, to unwilling to endure even its lesser cousin, discomfort. And, of course, afraid of death."

"Here now, we're all afraid of that," Mary said. "Lately, some of us more so than others."

"The whore-killings, yes. I suppose that's why my needs are so secondary here. But cheer up. Nietzsche once said, that which does not kill us makes us stronger. I believe that, I do. In fact, it is my secret wish to have something terrible happen to me, something close enough to death to make me less afraid, so I can then go out and seek my true-life wonders," he said, taking a puff on his long, thin pipe.

Lampini's eyes lit at something over Mary's shoulder. She turned to see Officer Debner, the man who'd taken her statement, emerge from an office and step toward them.

Lampini ruffled his jacket as if preparing to rise, but Debner stopped in front of her.

"Mrs. Blyss, could you please come with me?"

Lampini's shoulders collapsed.

As she rose to follow, she could hear the man sigh behind her, "They even take a whore before Lampini."

Debner led her into a small office. He took his place behind the paper-strewn desk and began going through the papers, not bothering to invite her to sit. Finding the sheet he wanted, he scanned it.

"Now, according to your testimony, you were in the warehouse because you wanted to see the spot where your husband was killed," he said flatly.

"That's right," she said, finally sitting down herself.

He looked up. "Why didn't you come to the station to see his body first?"

She shivered. Had they caught her? "I . . . I'd been here just the day before and saw my dear friend Mitzie, cut up by the killer. I . . . I . . . couldn't bear to come back is all."

He nodded and scribbled something down.

"And that's where you saw the killer?"

"Yes."

"How do you know he was the killer?"

"His eyes, and he talked a lot about cutting people up."

"Uh-huh . . . " He wrote down a few more words, then withdrew a plastic bag from a drawer in the desk.

"This torn piece of cloth was found in the warehouse. Would you have a look at it, please?"

He handed her the bag. Inside was a jagged section of black cloth, part of it covered with a light-gray substance. She fingered it.

"Does it match the clothing that the man you saw was wearing?"

"Well, yes. It's the right color," she said.

"All right," he said, then he bent down and started writing.

She could tell he didn't believe her, or lumped her in with the dozen other Ripper witnesses that waited outside. How could she get them to believe her?

Idly, she fingered the cloth in her hand, her fingertips feeling the gray bumpy substance. There was something strange about it, but she couldn't say what.

"What's this then?" she said, pointing to the rough substance.

Debner barely lifted his head from his writing. "Dirt. From the warehouse."

"Doesn't look like dirt," she said.

This time he did raise his head and pointed to the piece of cloth. "Mrs. Blyss, our experts have gone over that cloth very carefully and determined that that is dirt from the warehouse. Would you have me accept your opinion over theirs?"

Mary smiled a little. "Well, I do have some familiarity with dirt . . ."

He glared in a way that stopped her from finishing her sentence.

It was going to be a long day.

Cyra's sharp eyes sorted through the people on the darkening street below. She watched one tall fellow with chocolate-brown hair for several minutes. He kept looking at his watch fob, then crossly staring at the crowd. Finally, a younger man walked up, happy as you please, and the two disappeared, arm and arm, into a pub.

"Y'ever notice," she said back into her room, "How folks who show up are always happier than the ones waiting for 'em?"

Her companion sat with his back against the wall, eyes closed.

"You asleep?" she asked, but she was thinking, *You alive?*

No response. She clicked her tongue against the roof of her mouth and wished Mary was home. What could they be doing with her over at the police station? Making her clean the place, probably.

Bored, she poked her head about the giant's immobile form. She took in the chalk-white face, marveled at the bolts in his neck and forehead and the sheer flatness of the top of his skull.

It's like having our own personal Elephant Man. But what happened to him? He couldn't have always been this way.

As she surveyed him, she caught a glimpse of herself in the dirty mirror hanging over the wall. The dark skin of her face was puffy from sleeplessness, bringing out her crow's feet. The stains and tears in her burgundy dress were bigger than she'd remembered, and the makeup she fancied exotic, and may have looked so in an alley or pub, seemed garish.

Well, I wasn't always like this, either, was I? she thought with a sneer.

Suddenly not wanting to be alone, she turned to the giant and said loudly, "Wish you could tell us who you were, love."

She'd meant to wake him, but there wasn't even a twitch in response. Looking around the room for the hundredth time, her eyes fell upon his jacket. Surely Mary checked the pockets. Then again, maybe she didn't. If there was money, she'd spent enough on him in food alone to warrant a share for herself. And there might be some kind of identification. Maybe a reward for returning him to his owners.

Gently, she hefted the jacket from the chair, surprised at its weight. It was good thick cloth, an expensive cut, but more like something someone would want to be buried in, rather than seen in strutting about town. She was impressed with the size until she remembered how his arms jutted out of the jacket sleeves.

Deftly, her practiced hands went through one pocket after another, turning up nothing. Then a shiver rolled up her back, like a drop of hot water somehow rising. She turned. The giant's eyes were open. He'd been watching her go through his pockets.

Acting as if nothing was wrong, she smiled and put the jacket on the bed beside him. "Just trying to find out who you are," she cooed.

He looked at her, perplexed.

"Who you are," she repeated. "Your name, you know, love? Your name?"

He twisted his head to the side, curious.

Well, I did teach him to say please . . .

She pointed to the chair and said, "chair." She pointed to the bed and said, "bed." She pointed to herself and said "Cyra."

Then she pointed at the giant and shrugged her shoulders. He shrugged his shoulders, mimicking her. She sat beside him, put her hands on the sides of his face and twisted his head toward her.

"Okay, pay attention, now," she said. She pointed to herself again. "Cyra. Cyra. Cyra. My name is Cyra."

"Sraah?"

"That's it, love, Cyra."

He lifted a heavy hand toward her and smiled. "Friend."

"Okay, yes. Cyra is a friend. Now, who are you? Who?"

His face got that childish look on it again, the same it had just before he figured out what *please* meant. Whatever it was he had for a brain under that flat dome was putting things together. She pointed at him.

"You? Who are you?"

Suddenly, all the delight in him just drained away, like water from a cracked glass. She couldn't be sure, but he seemed pained, as if having realized what her question was, the answer was causing him anguish.

She was about to tell him to forget about it when his hand rose. He slapped himself on the chest and said, "Dead."

She just looked at him, speechless, so he repeated the gesture and said again, "Dead."

At once, the room felt like a coffin, and Cyra felt like she'd been buried with a corpse. She needed air, fast—air and the company of people who could actually talk.

"Ed?" she said, forcing a smile. She'd heard him, but she didn't want to. "Your name is Ed? Okay, then, come on, Eddie. We'll learn thank you tomorrow. For now, what say you and me take a walk?"

She tugged him to standing.

He seemed pleased by the name she called him, pleased she was leading him about. He was very good as she pulled his jacket back on him, yanking hard to get it over his shoulders.

As they half-stumbled down the steps, she briefly feared he'd fall on her and crush her. There was no one in the hall, so no explanations were needed there. But when they stepped out into the street, everyone who passed turned to stare. He stiffened and raised his hands as if trying to wave the scene out of his eyes.

Quickly, she stepped in front of him, caught his gaze, and shushed him. "Here now, Ed, here now. Calm down. Everything's peachy."

Nearby, a middle-aged, greasy lamplighter took a torch to one of the old gas lamps. When the giant saw the flame, he howled like a babe. Now even folks across the street were staring.

She pulled him off to the side, away from the offending flame, then pointed to the row of dim lights that went off down the avenue. "Hush! It's just street lights, that's all."

He looked at them apprehensively.

"Now, I can't have you screaming like that! You'll scare folks, and with the killer out, who knows what they'll make of you? So you mind me, all right?" she said.

She was already thinking this walk was a bad idea. She grimaced and looked around. If she could get him to the Whale, maybe she could position him at a dark table, where no one could see him. Then she could do some business in the cask room and he wouldn't be more than a scream away.

She tried to eye the path that would put them among the fewest people. Most of the pedestrians had been pulled to their side of the street by his appearance. He was, after all, a full head taller than the top hats that some of them wore.

Spying a gap in the traffic, she grabbed his arm and pulled. "This way. Let's go." Everyone tracked their movements, but, luckily, no one followed. Now, Cyra figured, they would have a few more minutes before he drew another crowd.

As the pair clomped across the filthy avenue, Cyra spotted Dale Abbernathy, one of her regulars. He was strutting along with his head held high, which meant he had money. He was married, with two children, and always quick about his business. He also had a fancy for Cyra's darker skin, having enjoyed reading adventure-stories about the tropical isles as a lad.

Thrilled at the prospect of some quick, painless money, a smile rose naturally to her face and she waved to him. His face lit with recognition, but then, on seeing her companion, he blinked repeatedly, as if trying to focus.

"Hey, now, love," Cyra said, but by then, Dale was shaking his head.

"Another time," he called back, then he sped off as fast as his feet could carry him.

Cyra turned toward the giant and scowled.

"This won't do. Won't do at all, Eddie," she said.

Exasperated, she pulled him into the nearest alleyway, a narrow, ill-smelling place between two food markets which used it to dump unsold goods. It reeked of rotted vegetable, fruits, and urine. Fat rats, made lazy from abundance, moved freely among the trash. Not even the whores used this space. It was perfect for her friend.

She pointed to him. "Stay here. Stay. I won't be long. I'm just going to grab a pint, talk to some friends, and as soon as it's fully dark, I'll try to bring you into the Whale. If I make a few coins, I'll even get you some proper food, all right, then?"

"Food," the giant said.

"But you stay, understand? Stay until I get back. And don't talk to anyone!"

The giant nodded. He stepped back and leaned against the wall, as if resting.

She walked to the head of the alley, glancing back at him occasionally. The crowd across the street had dispersed. With any luck, none of them had called the police.

She called to him one last time, "I'll be back in less than an hour." But he said nothing and she could no longer see him.

She stepped out and headed right, telling herself she did the proper thing. Mary couldn't expect her to watch him forever, now could she? Besides, he must have some survival skills of his own. Mary Blyss didn't give birth to him, after all.

Feeling more herself, she stretched her neck and cracked her shoulders. Far ahead, she thought she caught a glimpse of Dale Abbernathy. Perfect. She could explain the giant as a disabled friend, maybe even hit him up for a few extra coins.

Her pace quickened as she tried to catch the receding figure. She wanted to get a few paces closer before she called out his name, so she wouldn't seem so terribly desperate, but she only made it a few more yards before strong hands reached out from the shadows and pulled her into a completely different dark.

The monster liked the alley much better than the small room. If he looked up, he could see far, far, past the light gray clouds, into the dark gray beyond. There was more space as well. The smell was funny, but there were rats if his stomach started to growl again.

One of the rats waddled across a puddle, leaving a black wake on the slick, oily surface. When the ripples settled, the monster saw his own reflection looking up, grim, expressionless.

"Dead."

That's what he'd said when Cyra asked who he was. Now, as he went back over her words, slowly, he understood he'd been wrong. She hadn't asked what he was, but *who.*

"Mon . . . ser . . . " he said to his reflection. "Monster."

He leaned down, trying to see the blackness in his eyes. They reminded him a little of Cyra's, though something sparkled in her blackness that was missing from his own.

Whenever he saw the watery twinkle in her eyes, it was like the moon shining on a lake at night. It gave him a tingle at the base of his neck that wrapped itself around the back of his head like the music the old blind man played. It was like hunger, but mixed with another sensation the monster didn't understand at all.

A chilling scream pierced his ears, like the one Fritz made when he hung him from his neck. Only the voice was different.

Cyra.

Was she hurt? Forgetting she'd told him to wait, he stormed out to find her. She was nowhere to be seen, but a second scream came from the next alley. The monster barreled toward the sound.

"See-rah?"

The space was wider than the one he'd just left, a gas lamp close enough to cast a yellow half-circle of light inside it. As the scream melted into a wet, gurgling noise, the monster saw Cyra lying on her back in the garbage. Her legs were spread, the old burgundy cloth of her dress covered with dark stains.

A man crouched over her, moving his hands this way and that. He remembered seeing Frankenstein and Pretorius move about a body in just the same frantic way, but it wasn't either of them. The monster had seen this man before, too, but his hair was different now, lighter, like hay. The wolfish snarl in his eyes was the same, though. He was the one who attacked the monkey-faced woman, the one who had cut him, the one Cyra called a killer.

The monster growled and stepped forward.

From the look on the killer-man's face, he recognized the monster, too.

"I hoped hard I'd see you again," he said in a low voice that sounded like grinding stones. "But you took so long getting here I was starting to fear you were a dream. But see? I've already got my little souvenir from your lady friend."

The killer-man slipped something pink, wet, and sticky in a small sack, then stood up from his grisly work, long blade gleaming in the grayness. "Now I think I'll have one from you."

The killer-man came forward.

Still puzzling out the scene, the monster's head twitched between him and Cyra. She was hurt, badly, but she was still moving. Her lips trembled and her knees shivered. Her eyes were wide open and staring up, but she looked to be in such pain.

He preferred the dead to the living, but he did not like pain. Especially not in her.

The killer-man picked up speed as he closed the distance. "Whores are my business, Behemoth. I don't take after men, because they lack what I need. But you're special, so I'll make an exception."

At the last yard between them, the killer-man lunged, cape fanning out behind him like wings, blade slashing forward before the monster could take a step.

But the monster didn't need a step. His reach was so long he just grabbed the arm that held the blade, stopping its motion, dead. The killer-man's body came forward a little, from momentum, but the monster just grabbed his other arm and held him there like a doll.

With a grunt, the monster hurled his slight burden. It sailed ten feet through the air, into the brick alley wall. The killer-man's shoulder collapsed with a sickly thud. The silvery blade flew from his hand and clattered to the black ground. A puppet to gravity now, the body slid down the wall, then flopped to the floor in a moaning heap.

Far from finished with him, the enraged monster came forward. The killer-man twisted his bloody head toward the coming giant and opened one eye.

"Why waste your time with me, Behemoth, when you might still save the whore?"

The monster hesitated.

With his good hand, the killer-man pointed to the trembling Cyra. "The whore!" he shouted, "You daft, idiot! The woman! She's dying right in front of you!"

The monster turned back to Cyra. He turned back to the killer and pointed at him.

"You help Srah!" he bellowed.

Through his pain, the killer-man furrowed his brow. "So it speaks?"

"You help!" the monster said again, stepping forward

threateningly on the last word.

Clutching his shattered shoulder, the killer-man pulled himself to sitting.

"Me? No. But why don't *you* go take a closer look?" he said.

The monster trembled. He did not want Cyra to be hurt. Puffing breath from his nose like a bull, he maneuvered his bulky form back toward Cyra.

"That's it, Behemoth, go take a good look at your whore," the killer-man said.

The monster trudged toward her on heavy feet, not even lifting them all the way, so they scraped against the concrete floor as he moved.

From his back, he heard the killer-man chuckle. "Behemoth and the whore of Babylon."

Cyra was right under him now. Her lips were no longer trembling, and there was a long wound across her neck, but her eyes still had that watery glint. When the monster felt that strange tickle in the back of his head, he knew she was still looking back. But something was wrong. The sparkle was getting dimmer, the light fading from white to near gray.

"Srah? See rah?"

He watched that light in her as if it were the sun Frankenstein let shine down on him those long days ago, back in the watch-tower lab.

"So far he's been kept in complete darkness. Wait until I bring him into the light . . . " his maker had said.

The roof of the lab opened and brightness cascaded down all over his body, warming his face and arms. He reached up for it, tried to touch it, but Frankenstein spun a wheel, and slowly, bit by bit, the light faded back into dark.

It seemed that's what was happening now, in Cyra's eyes. She didn't answer, despite his calls, despite his waving his arms, and the light was going away.

"Please," he said, recalling the word she'd taught him. He kneeled beside her.

The killer laughed. "On your knees, Behemoth? Why not ask for her hand while you're there? Make her an honest woman?"

It was all but gone, now. Blood seeped out on either side of her dress, so he lifted it and finally saw what the killer-man had done. Cyra's abdomen had been split open and her intestines lay outside her body, mixing with the dirt on the alley floor.

The monster reared at the sight. Images flashed in his brain: Pretorius, Frankenstein, the bride. It felt as if the watchtower were raining down on him again.

"Live! Live!" he cried.

He scooped the gore into his huge, awkward hands and stuffed it back into the gaping wound. She shivered, shook, and the sparkle in her eyes died completely.

We belong dead.

The killer-man laughed again, low, long, and loud. But the sound was different now, closer. The monster twisted his head in time to see a flash of silver slicing toward his cheek. He moved, quickly, but the blade was faster, skimming the surface of his cheek and chin. It didn't hurt, not yet, but the monster felt a small piece of his flesh come away and dangle by a gory thread.

Pulling back his good arm, dropping his blade, the killer-man snatched at the loosened flesh with his fingers, pulled, and tore it free. The monster slapped his hand to his face, and felt a sticky spot the size of the tip of his finger.

"And now I have my souvenir from you!" the killer-man hissed.

The monster was still taken aback, dumbfounded, as the killer-man stormed deep into the alley and disappeared into the dark. Regaining his rage, the monster stumbled after him, but soon faced a tall brick wall.

Unable to climb, he beat at it with his hands, making dust of some of the mortar. The wall held. He spotted a low hanging drainpipe and tried to pull himself up with it, lifting his feet at he did, but his enormous weight was too much. The pipe came loose, and he and it clattered to the ground.

He panted, frustrated, then he howled and moaned. He stormed back to Cyra's body, feeling the wound on his face. Seeing the knife on the ground, he picked it up and looked at it, thinking the missing piece of his face might still cling to it.

But all he saw were thin red stains on silver.

A loud sound turned him to the head of the alley.

"It's the killer!" a man cried. "He's got the bloody knife in his hands!"

There was more than one man, and more coming. Some wore blue and blew whistles, some had tall hats, others rags. They crowded the front of the alley, blocking it, spilling deeper in when the group pushing behind them became too large. Still more assembled behind them, swarming into the alley like bugs. They held aloft torches, but had cudgels instead of pitchforks.

The shouts of "Murder!" and "Killer!" grew louder in the street.

The monster dropped the knife and stood, little pieces of Cyra dripping from his fingers.

"We've got Jack the Ripper at last!" one screamed.

The front few took some hesitant steps toward him. He let loose a growl that stopped them dead in their tracks. But they didn't flee. He knew they wouldn't flee, that there were too many now for them to ever flee, but he growled again, just the same.

The monster knew them. He'd faced them before. They'd chased him to the windmill, set it aflame while he was inside. They'd hovered over the remains for hours, watching them smolder, hoping to see his bones.

These were different faces, different voices, but the monster knew it was the same creature as before, a creature with many heads, a creature that, like the monster, could never really die.

Even so, he smashed many of them, even worse than Cyra had been smashed, before they finally brought him down.

Chapter Sixteen

The chains were thick, borrowed from a rail yard where they were used to haul cars with faulty couplings. Now they were wrapped around arms, chest, and legs, attached to the stone wall and floor by huge iron spikes, driven into place by sledgehammers.

When Chief Inspector Devin first arrived, roused from sleep at two A.M., at the hastily modified holding cell at the Commercial Street Station, there'd been no visible give to those chains. Now, an hour later, they rattled every time the prisoner moaned and pulled.

Devin watched, horrified and fascinated. The huge man the mob had captured was like the piston of a steam engine, pulling again and again, fueled by some unknown, and seemingly limitless pool of energy. The long arms relaxed only a fraction of a second in each cycle before beginning again. The night sergeant said he'd been at it now for three straight hours.

The sight reminded the Oxford-educated Devin of the myth of Sisyphus, the man punished by the gods for trying to delay his death. For that, he was condemned to push a boulder to the top of a hill, only to have it fall back down just before reaching the top, forever. Had this man, this *creature* as Krogh insisted it be called, been in that Greek hell, Devin feared he might tear a hole in the very fabric of reality.

Was he a man? Of course. Had to be. Devin just had to push the mundane imagination he prized a little to enlarge his definition of what it was a man could be.

"Still want us to transfer him, Chief Inspector?" the sergeant said.

Devin shook his head. "No. At least not until we figure out how."

"Very good, sir. Shall I have the men slam down the spikes again?"

Devin looked at the pitiful prisoner and nodded. "Yes."

Halfax and Debner, the two tallest, strongest officers in the precinct, looking very short and slight next to the prisoner, picked up their heavy hammers and slammed the spikes deeper into the stone. The prisoner wailed with every sharp blow. When they stopped, the chains could not move again, but the prisoner, without a moment's hesitation, went back to pulling.

Sisyphus.

Devin turned to see Erik Krogh strutting down the hall. He was bleary-eyed, but had a look of triumph and satisfaction.

"You've done it!" he beamed. "You've caught the monster!"

"Not me, Krogh," Devin said. "About fifty civilians and ten officers. Twelve were killed in the process, fifteen are now in hospital."

With a visible effort, Krogh forced the smile from his face. "A terrible price. But now we have him."

Devin turned back to the prisoner, watching the giant as if staring at a work of art he didn't comprehend, or a freak at the circus on display. "I owe you an apology, Krogh. I didn't believe your story about your son, or at least I thought you'd exaggerated. Now I see you spoke the truth in that."

Krogh's eyes lit up again. "Then you also believe me about the baron?"

Devin shrugged. "Made from the dead? No."

"But look at the scars! The stitches! The bolts on his neck!" Krogh said. "I tell you that creature comes from the grave!"

Devin patted him on the back and gave him a smile. "Don't fear for your truth. I'll have the best medical men in London examining him, and if they discover any sort of link to your stories about Baron Frankenstein—"

"Frankenstein?" the prisoner growled. All at once, his perpetual tugging stopped.

Devin fell silent. The gaze of all three men in the room shot toward the prisoner. The only sound for the next few seconds was the sharp echo of the last rattle of the chains.

"That's the first word he's spoken since he's been here," the sergeant whispered.

Devin waved the sergeant to silence and took a cautious few steps closer. He leaned toward the prisoner, then spoke slowly, as if to a child.

"Yes. Frankenstein. Do you know Frankenstein?"

The prisoner's eyelids fluttered and he turned toward the chief inspector. Devin tried not to react, but it was difficult. The eyes were dead, like a lizard's, or one of the wax statues at Madame Tussaud's on Baker Street.

All the more surprising then was the prisoner's concise response. "Yes. I know."

Krogh nearly leapt to Devin's side. "Who is he, then? Tell us who Frankenstein is."

The prisoner moved his head as much as his chains allowed, shifting his glance from Devin to Krogh, then back again. He seemed, to Devin, to regard them both as two heads of the same creature.

"He made me from dead."

Devin heard Krogh sigh. He could practically feel some of the long-held tension slip away from the man.

"All right, Krogh," he said. "Let's have the baron over for another visit, shall we?"

Like lightning, flashbulbs exploded around Henry Frankenstein as he was walked from the limo up the steps of the Commercial Street police station. He was flanked by his solicitors, from the respected firm of Wimbledy & Griffin, while they, in turn, were flanked by police. He wore his coat folded over his hands so the carrion mob wouldn't see his shaking hands.

"Filthy murderer!" one shouted. "Grave robber!" came another cry. The only taunt missing was an enjoinder to burn him at the stake.

That one would come soon enough, he suspected.

A rotten tomato sailed past his head, catching one of the officers on the side of the face. Then the mob pushed forward, pressing the police into his solicitors, and the solicitors into him.

Here it is then, he thought. *I'm to be thrown at last to the dogs.*

Reinforcements from the station poured from the doors, pushing the crowd back and forming a safe path. Frankenstein wanted to thank them, but could see from their eyes that they hated him as well.

At least Elizabeth will have some comfort. Victor will arrive today.

He was taken to a small square room, bare except for a table with two facing chairs. A single bulb within a silver cone hung low above the table, casting a circle of light. It reminded Frankenstein of the morgue, only here the subjects to be examined were still living.

Chief Inspector Devin was seated in one of the two chairs. Frankenstein was a little surprised the fanatic Krogh wasn't present, too, and surmised he must be watching or listening from somewhere unseen.

The empty chair was pulled out by his chief solicitor, Jerome Wimbledy, a walrus of a man whose neck had long ago disappeared into his massive double chin and whose head now threatened to do the same.

Frankenstein slipped into the offered seat and faced the chief inspector.

"Well, Devin, I'm here. What do you want of me?"

Devin slipped off the first sheet from a thick pile of papers in front of him. It was a photograph Frankenstein instantly recognized from the front page of the evening news. It showed the monster, chained from the chest down, eyes livid with rage.

"Do you recognize this man?" Devin asked.

Wimbledy moved in to advise him, but Frankenstein waved him off. "Everyone in London and half the world recognizes that face now. It's your prisoner."

Devin clarified. "It's the man who was found hovering over the body of Cyra Ricolla, the murder weapon in his hands."

"That's what the fools in the street say, Devin, but I expect better from you. Based on what I understand from the papers, he's an unsophisticated brute. That . . . poor fellow . . . can no more wield a knife than I can erase my name from your ridiculous English headlines," Frankenstein said.

"I'm not suggesting he could. Clearly, even if he knew how to hold the blade, he lacks the necessary anatomical knowledge. Shall I state the obvious, then? You possess both the skill and the medical degree, Herr Baron," Devin said evenly. "And our prisoner claims to know you. Says you made him from the dead."

Frankenstein grimaced. "Well, what of it? He's deluded."

"Clearly. But since he knows you, we can now link you to two of the recent murders," Devin said.

Frankenstein's eyes fluttered. "What are you suggesting? That it . . . that he and I killed the woman together? That I somehow fled while he remained behind? You're grasping at straws while the real killer is still loose."

"Now that you mention it, yes, that's exactly the sort of case we're thinking of making, coupled of course with certain information provided by our mutual acquaintance, the visiting Inspector Krogh," Devin said calmly.

Wimbledy bent over and this time succeeded in whispering in Frankenstein's ear: "Ask about the charges." The young baron stiffened and leaned forward. "Would you make your case then, even if it is full of holes, even if it isn't true?"

Devin eyed him. "When I have enough evidence to make a case, I make one. Do I thereby uncover the absolute truth? Who can say? I was raised to believe absolute truth isn't something the human mind can grasp, so I content myself with the closest I can come."

Frankenstein sneered. "We disagree. I believe not only that the absolute truth is attainable, but that all men have a sacred obligation to the future of humanity to seek it out at all costs."

"At *all* costs?" Devin repeated with a smile.

Frankenstein slumped slightly. "Short of murder, Devin. Short of murder."

Devin tapped the photo. "Did you know him before you came to London?"

"He's the madman who rampaged across the countryside in my homeland. When we tried to hunt him down, he nearly killed me by hurling me from a burning windmill. So yes, we know one another."

"And before that. Did you know him before that?"

With every fiber of his being, Frankenstein wanted to scream, *Yes! Yes, I did! I knew him at the moment of his birth, because I did it! He is alive because I made him so! I have discovered the greatest secret of all and the gods themselves have damned me for it!*

But his barrister had already made it quite clear what the result of such a pronouncement would mean for him, and, more importantly, for Elizabeth.

Frankenstein blinked. "No."

Devin smiled. "I would like you to see him face to face. Just to make sure."

Wimbledy leaned in again, whispering, "Under no circumstances should you agree." Frankenstein bobbed his head a few times, then curled his lips in disgust. "No, no, no. I must see it. I must."

The attorney, shaken by the response, raised his hands in defeat and stepped back. Frankenstein turned to Devin. "Very well."

In short order, Frankenstein was led to the row of holding cells where he himself had been kept days before. He was taken to the largest at the end of the short hall. Erik Krogh stood there outside the bars, glaring at the baron. Two officers with sledgehammers stood by as well.

The instant Frankenstein passed before the bars of the cell, the creature stirred, nostrils flaring.

"Frankenstein," it said.

Frankenstein tried to control his own demeanor, but couldn't. He felt his face grow white. "Then it's true," he said. "I don't think I believed it until now. It's alive."

Frankenstein stepped nearer his first experiment, eyes wide with wonder. The monster strained to move his head nearer his creator.

"Not too close," Devin warned, but Frankenstein ignored him.

Frankenstein focused on the spot on the monster's face where a slice of skin had been removed. "Tell him the rest, Mr. Wimbledy. Now's as good a time as any."

Wimbledy cleared his throat with a little cough that sent his jowls quivering. "Very well. This madman, whatever he is, whatever he's done, however he came here, is from my client's village, one of his people. Baron Frankenstein feels strongly he deserves advocacy, so, to that end, we've been appointed to represent him as well."

"No!" Krogh shouted. "It deserves only to die!"

The barrister ignored the outburst. "We will expect all the paperwork regarding the charges, and seek our own medical experts to examine him."

There was more talk, but the conversation receded in Frankenstein's mind as he remembered building the man in front of him, and marveled at how he had changed.

As if through cotton, he heard Devin speak: "Fine. But be warned, in the end it will help my case for you to throw your lot in with him."

Then Wimbledy: "The baron gives support out of pity and a sense of village kinship. This man is obviously mad and we'll see that he be treated as such. Now, is there anything else or do you wish to press charges against the baron?"

"Baron Frankenstein, this man claims you made him from the dead," Devin said.

Distracted, Frankenstein ignored him, so Wimbledy answered. "That was a rumor circulating among the villagers due to their misunderstanding of the baron's medical experiments. We're prepared to show that these experiments were quite ordinary, and totally legal. Even school children will put a current through a frog's leg and watch it twitch. The baron did no more than that, really. This poor brute doubtless heard the rumors, and in his deranged mind came to believe they were true, the way another madman might believe himself related to King George. Now, I assume you'd hoped this farce would provide you with some excuse to press charges against my client. Since you can plainly see it has not, are we are free to go?"

"No!" Krogh said.

"Yes," Devin corrected him. "For now. But the baron should not leave his hotel suite. For his own protection."

The next thing Frankenstein felt was Wimbledy, shaking him by the shoulder.

For the first time since entering the cell, he broke contact with the creature. He glanced at the barrister, then at Krogh, then Devin, as if they were dreams.

"Shall we go, Baron?" the barrister said. "Now?"

"A minute," Frankenstein said.

"Baron, I cannot stress how strongly I advise against—"

Frankenstein sighed. "I know. I know." He turned to Devin, who looked hopeful some slip from the baron might yet turn things in his favor. "Before I leave," Frankenstein said. "I'd like a private word with Inspector Krogh. Right here, if you don't mind."

Krogh raised his eyebrows. "I've nothing to say to you."

"Then perhaps you could just listen," Frankenstein said.

Devin shrugged and eyed the groaning prisoner. "How recently were the spikes changed?"

"As you asked, right before the baron was brought in," one of the officers said. "No more than ten minutes ago."

Devin nodded. "Very well. I'll give you gentlemen five minutes."

"And I would once again strongly advise against this conversation taking place," Wimbledy said.

"I understand. I'll meet you outside in a moment."

So Devin exited, followed by the barrister and the two officers. The door down the hall clicked shut, leaving only the sound of the rustling of the chains and the monster's heavy breathing.

Satisfied they were alone, Frankenstein raced over to the monster, closer than any had yet dared stand, and stared at the cut portion of skin.

"I don't know why you bother asking to speak with me. The only thing I'll tell you, Baron, is to confess!" Krogh said.

Frankenstein turned back to him. "I didn't kill those girls. I haven't it in me to kill anyone. Doesn't it matter to you that I'm innocent of their deaths?"

Krogh shook his head. "Not when I know what you're guilty of."

Frankenstein glared at the taller, younger man. "Get a hold of yourself and think! Even that thing they call a monster attacked that mob out of a sense of self-preservation. What drives you? If revenge is all there is to you, why not take out your revolver and shoot me now?"

Krogh unclipped his holster. Frankenstein started, but then relaxed when the inspector put his hand back by his side.

"Why did you want to talk with me?"

"To tell you what you should have figured out for yourself. The longer the creature is kept here, the more danger. Look how it pulls at those chains! How long do you think they'll hold? We tried to shoot it and to burn it. It was caught in a massive explosion, buried under tons of rubble, but it survived! Do you really think the courts will know what to do with it? Science created him, Krogh, only science can put this right."

"It can still be found guilty and executed," Krogh said.

Frankenstein shook his head pityingly. "Poor Krogh. How hard it must be to have no imagination. Come. Look here."

Frankenstein tugged at the inspector. He hesitated but gave in.

Frankenstein pointed. "See there? Look closely at the wound. The skin is stitching itself together as we speak, as if invisible hands were piecing together the skin and muscle."

Krogh's eyes grew wide. "How can this be?"

Frankenstein pushed his hand up against his forehead. His fingertips vibrated as if they could sense the rush of thoughts going on in his head. "I'm not certain, but I suspect it's the after effect of the great ray itself, the one I discovered beyond the ultra-violet, the one I captured through the lightning, the one that gives life. The manner in which I controlled the exposure was crude, so perhaps the body absorbed too much. Its very bones could be over-saturated with the ray, so that every time it's hurt or near death, the residual radiation restores him."

"Are you saying the creature is immortal?" Krogh gasped.

"No," Frankenstein snapped. "Immortality is for gods, and I don't believe in them. But electrocution won't work, or hanging, or burning. Dr. Waldman was right to attempt a dissection. That might do it, or, if I could find a way to siphon off the energy, that could work, too. Perhaps if I reversed the polarity on the cosmic diffuser. But you must understand, the longer you keep it here, the stronger it will get."

Krogh furrowed his brow. Did he understand? Did he believe?

A low, pained howl from the creature turned them both back toward the prisoner.

"Frankenstein!" the monster screamed.

Frankenstein forced himself to stare into the abyss of its dark eyes. He shivered as he did, but managed to hold his gaze. "What? What is it?"

As it spoke, for a moment, even to its creator, it looked utterly human.

"Make me dead. Please."

The last word struck Frankenstein like a physical thing, forcing him to take a step back. He turned toward Krogh and grabbed the taller man by his jacket lapels.

"In the name of all that's decent, help me destroy it, I beg you. It's dangerous to keep it alive. It's inhuman. No matter what your anger against it, or me, can't you see that this is the right thing to do? Let it die. Let this all die!"

Stiff as ever, Krogh pulled Frankenstein's hands off his person, and pushed the doctor away. "No. I want it on trial. I want you on trial. So you can both be destroyed."

Frankenstein straightened himself and regarded Krogh in a new light. "If you want to call what I've done a sin, so be it, but it was the result of an accident, a mistake. What you do here now, you do fully of your own volition, hiding your hatred behind the name of your son. But know this, there are three monsters in this room. The results of your decision, whatever they may be, will hang on all our heads."

Frankenstein stormed out.

"Frankenstein, please!"

The monster's pleas grew louder, until there were no words any longer, just one, long, piteous wail.

As he glanced back, Frankenstein saw the village inspector standing there between the maker and his monster, his face twisted in sadistic delight.

Chapter Seventeen

The thin, gentle voice began the question even before the door was fully open.

"Where is she? Where is Elizabeth?"

Once, he'd promised to go to the ends of the earth for her. Even time and her marriage to his best friend had not diminished his feelings. Upon hearing she needed him, he'd dropped everything and all but ran to London.

Minnie's face was drawn at first, but her eyes brightened as she recognized the handsome face and thin moustache.

"Mr. Victor Moritz!" she sputtered. "What a ray of sunshine in our stormy lives! Why, we haven't seen you since the wedding!"

The very word, wedding, stung, but Victor was careful not to show it. He bit his tongue and smiled, just as he had through the ceremony. "Forgive me, Minnie, maybe it was foolish, but I felt I had to stay away, to give them some time together. I came as soon as Henry told me there was trouble," he said. "All through my journey I've been reading and hearing the most horrible things. The crowd outside nearly attacked me thinking I was Henry."

Minnie spun away and waved her hands melodramatically in the air.

"Oh, sir, you don't know the half of it!" she wailed.

Victor walked himself in and closed the door behind him. He looked around the lavish suite, secretly pleased to see no sign of his best friend.

"Where is Henry now?" he asked.

"Still at the station," Minnie said. "I don't like this London, I don't like it at all! There's so many people here, filling every nook and cranny, I don't know where they put them all. Now it seems they all want Mr. Henry's neck! The police are talking about pressing murder charges! He could be executed, he could, and for all his grand experimenting, I don't think he can bring himself back from that!"

She slumped into one of the cushioned chairs. "And me, what have I done except serve the house with hard work and dignity? But now, I'm afraid to leave the hotel myself! What if one of those papers wanted to talk to me? I don't think I could lie, or live with myself if I told the truth!"

Victor grabbed her by the shoulders and gazed into her eyes. "Then you think he killed those women, too?"

She raised her eyebrows. "I would never say any such thing to the baroness, but Mr. Henry, he was out practically every night since we got here, sometimes not coming back until morning. Then they found him with his hands all bloodied and buried in what was left of one of those poor girls!"

Victor shook his head somberly. "I admit, it doesn't look good, but there could be some explanation."

The servant eyed him wryly, "Sure, the fairy folk, or maybe Santa Claus!"

Victor gave her a bitter little smile, and sighed. "I'd always feared the nightmare of Henry's experiments would come back at him. If only I'd been able to convince him to give them up, but sometimes he looked at me with such hatred, as if I wanted to steal something from him." He paused a bit, then added, "How is Elizabeth? Where is she? I've been sent to watch over her."

Minnie gave him a knowing look. "The last time the master asked you to do that was on his wedding night, when he was expecting he might be killed. I guess that means he expects the worst. And him, the last of the house of Frankenstein!"

She let out a moan and buried her head in her hands.

"I'm sure it's not as bad as all that, he just wants to be free to effectively fight the charges. Oh, poor loyal Minnie. Can I get you something?"

Between sobs, she pointed to a bottle of scotch in a crystal decanter.

"Of course," Victor said. He rose and poured her a small glass.

Watching, she said, "Just another finger, please."

Victor added a bit more and handed her the glass. She took a sip. "And could you hang your hat and coat by the door? I can't let the place all go to hell, you know."

Obediently, Victor strode to the door, shaking himself free of his coat along the way. His muscles were stiff from the ship and he wished he'd had a chance to freshen up, but his appearance was not the most important thing.

He turned back to Minnie, to ask again where Elizabeth was, but before he could, she nodded toward a closed door. "In there, but brace yourself."

He wanted to run, but suppressed himself to a rapid walk. At the door, he rapped his knuckles gently against the white wood. From within, he heard the murmur of a familiar voice. The soft sound thrilled him. Imagining it had said, "Come in," he opened the door and stepped inside.

He expected the full, vibrant, intelligent face of the vision that had won his heart. Instead, he was greeted by a sallow mask of skin that barely clung to the skull, wide sickly eyes, gaunt cheeks, and drawn lips revealing reddish gums that provided her only color. She was half reclined in bed—neither sitting nor lying down—her unkempt hair lay strewn on either side of her head, like clumps of dried grass.

"Elizabeth," he said, choking back his emotion.

Her eyes turned to him with what seemed fear, but then something familiar pierced through the haze that covered them.

"Victor?" she said, her voice barely louder than the distant rush of city that invaded through the open window.

Heart pounding and confused, he raced to her side and took her fragile hands in his. "Yes, Elizabeth, it's me."

She gave him a slight smile. "Oh, Victor. I thought you were a dream. I haven't slept much lately, you know, so it's hard to tell."

"How could you sleep, with all that's going on? But can't they give you something to help you rest?" he asked.

"The hotel doctor prescribed something, but Henry insists it wouldn't be good for me," she said weakly.

"I'm sure he has his reasons then," Victor said with a smile.

She shifted her head to the side. "I do the best I can, but I hear them all the time now, calling him the Ripper. Asking for his death."

"This country is barbaric. You shouldn't have to hear that at all," Victor said. Though upset by her appearance, he managed to smile as he rose and pushed the window down. "There," he said, slapping his hands together. "I hope everything I do here is as easy as that."

"Dear Victor," Elizabeth said, a pitying smile on her drawn features. "I don't hear them from the window. They're right here, in the room, all around me."

She said it so calmly, so matter-of-factly, that it took Victor a few moments to register that she was delusional. Henry had finally done it, then, finally dragged her into his madness.

He fought to be comforting. "It's this place, this trial, it's all too much for you," he said. "Especially after all you've been through for Henry's sake."

She smiled sadly. "Once, I thought my love for him would save him, but now I see it's only killing us both."

With that, Victor could hold back no more.

"No! Don't talk that way! It's not you that's done anyone any damage. You haven't a callous bone in your body. Can't you see it's him? He's destroyed everything he touches, and now he's nearly destroyed you. If he loves you, shouldn't he move heaven and earth to preserve you, rather than continue his precious experiments? Don't you know I love you, Elizabeth?" he said, surprised he'd found the courage to say it all aloud.

Her smile widened. Were her eyes full of pity, or was it something else?

"Yes, Victor, I've always known. You've always worn your heart on your sleeve. Henry knows it, too, that's why you're the only one he trusts to take care of me," she said. "But he does love me, he does. It's just that his mind is so great, so powerful, no heart stands any chance against it, even his own."

Victor seethed at her words, loathed his trustworthiness. What did he owe Henry anyway? How many times had Henry called him a fool? How many times had his best friend hated him for nothing more than understanding that being human meant being limited? All of a sudden, he found himself caring less about the fate of Baron Frankenstein, and more for that of his bride.

"He wants me to take care of you, then that's what I'll do," Victor said frantically. "I'll take you away from here, far, far away. And then you'll recover, you'll see, Elizabeth, you'll see. There's a ship that leaves for America in the morning. I'll buy tickets at once."

She shook her head and giggled, the loose skin around her neck shivering as she did. "You can try, dear sweet Victor, and I pray you succeed, but the voices tell me you will fail. I will die here, Victor. I will die for loving Henry Frankenstein."

—————◆—————

Exhaust fumes from the limo curled into the fog as it pulled to the curb, white fingers of dirty cotton disappearing into thinning clouds. Though a full two blocks away, the crowd gathered in front of the hotel, the press, the curiosity seekers, the mob that spilled out into the street, could not be missed.

Eyeing them with dread and disdain, Henry Frankenstein stepped from the car, hoping to walk off in the other direction.

"Baron," Wimbledy called, stuffing his thick lips toward the window gap as he rolled it open from within. "Please, come back. We'll drop you off at the rear of the hotel. You can use the service elevator to return to your suite."

Frankenstein shook his head. "They'll see the car. They'll know I'm inside. I'm better off walking. I'd like to stretch a bit, smoke a cigarette before I face Elizabeth again. I'll head straight up."

The barrister shook his head. "That would be foolhardy. If they see you on the street, you'll have no protection whatsoever."

"I'm aware of that. Now, do as I ask."

Wimbledy shook his head, jowls quivering. "You are quite insane, sir, and I don't refer at all to your work, imaginary or otherwise."

"Yes, well, I've been called that often enough," Frankenstein said. Then he turned his back on the car.

Wimbledy's voice became less pleading. "Chief Inspector Devin insists you remain at the hotel, remember that. I've vouched for you, sir."

Frankenstein looked back at him. "Yes, yes. I just need to think, to clear my head, that's all. I won't run away." He paused, then asked in halting words, "That man, Mr. Wimbledy, do you think you'll be able to arrange for his release?"

Wimbledy shook his head. "The insanity defense is well-recognized, but there is a lot of public outrage. If I were you, Baron, rather than worry about that sad creature, I'd pray to God for your own future."

With that, the large man withdrew into the car. Frankenstein watched as the window rolled up and the limo pulled back into the busy Strand. As soon as it covered the short drive to the hotel, the crowd swarmed it. Even from here, he could hear the shouts of "Ripper! Murderer!" and the slamming of fists against the metal body of the car.

He'd thought people might be different in a metropolis such as London, but they were exactly like the villagers, torches aloft, as they cheered the burning windmill.

Slowly, the car pulled away from the crowd. Apparently Wimbledy thought better of handling them.

Scraping feet turned Frankenstein around. A well-dressed man and woman, he burdened with packages, strolled out of an elegant shop. While the man struggled with their purchases, the woman held only a copy of the evening paper, photographs of Frankenstein and the bound creature looming large on the first page. He couldn't make out the entire headline, but *Ripper* was a part of it.

Realizing a sidewalk stroll was not a good idea, Frankenstein pulled away from the couple and headed toward a small alley twixt the store and a neighboring chemist's shop. Certain no one was watching, he slipped into the gray darkness.

It was quiet here, the sound muffled by the buildings. The silence and the two dark lines of the buildings made it seem as if the so-called civilized world simply stopped at the alley's edge. He watched pedestrians and street traffic pass, not seeing him, and he felt no longer part of that world, safe. It was an illusion, he knew, but he'd take it for now. Deeply exhausted, he leaned against a dank, filthy wall, procured a cigarette in his warm, deep pockets, lit it, and drew the hot smoke inside him.

He looked up, and through a rare patch of clear sky, saw a star twinkle in the heavens. Staring at the cold twinkle, sworn to the silence of distance, Wimbledy's words came back to him, "I'd be praying to God . . . "

Praying to God. Ha! Well, here's a prayer then.

Then he said aloud to the twinkling star, "I know what you are, old man. You've got them all scared and fooled, just as you have for millennia, but here and now I know your most precious secret. I know what life is. How that must gall you. Punish me for it if you like, hate me for trespassing, heap whatever blood you like on my hands, torture me, kill me, take Elizabeth from me, as if that were somehow just, but you'll never rob me of the fact that I *know*. And as long as I do, you, up there in your heavens, are no longer quite so alone."

"Nor are you, sir," a gravelly voice said.

Frankenstein snapped his head to the back of the alley. "Who is it? Who's there?" he called.

"Are you the man that made the monster, then? You looked much calmer in the papers," the voice said.

Frankenstein stiffened, ready to run, and raised his voice threateningly. "I said, who are you? What do you want? I've only to shout and the police will come running."

"Then shout, but I ask instead, sir, that you pardon my methodizing and realize if I'd meant harm, you'd be harmed. Men such as we are best in shadow, unless we throw our pearlies a'fore swine." The accent was thick, the words slurred. The voice seemed to be struggling to sound educated, but failed.

"I've no patience for riddles. Go away. Leave me alone," Frankenstein said. By all rights, he should simply leave, but the voice had a predatory, hypnotic quality that held his attention.

It went on, ignoring his objection. "Most think pearlies should not be hurled because it's a waste of pearlies, but it's the swine that get hurt, not knowing what to do. They think the pearls food, try to chew 'em, break their teeth, then blame us for their troubles and turn on us for our good intentions," the voice said.

Some babbling maniac, Frankenstein thought. *But what if he follows me out into the street, calls me by name?*

"I don't know what you're talking about. I'm leaving now. I warn you, don't follow," Frankenstein said.

He spun toward the head of the alley, toward that little line where the civilized world began again, suddenly feeling eager to rejoin it.

The next words from the voice stopped him cold. "What they call me is Jack. The one who really cuts the whores. The Ripper. And we have met afore. I saw you in the cemetery that night, watched you try to save my girl. Your creature tried the same. Like father like son. That's what got him caught, you know. Acting like he was you."

"It can't be. Jack the Ripper should be dead by now."

"Should be. That's the whole point of the killing. But, tell me first, did you admire the lines I made? Just a little? One surgeon to another?"

The image of the bleeding woman and the corpses flashed through Frankenstein's head, the quick, accurate cuts. He peered into the darkness at the back of the alley, trying to sort black from gray, trying to see the source of the voice.

This man, whoever he was, knew about the cemetery, knew about the monster. Someone could've read all that in the papers, but if this was the real killer, some maniac who imagined himself Jack the Ripper, here was a chance to learn what he could about him, to help the police catch the real culprit.

Frankenstein centered himself in the alley so he could see whatever came from the darkness, if it came. Now all it would take would be a step to put him back in the street.

Satisfied he was relatively safe, he crinkled his eyes and asked, "What do you mean, that's the point of the killing? Why do you take the uteri?"

"So I have the grand man's attention. Good. Well now, if I share my trade secrets, will you share yours?"

"How do you mean?"

Something small flew from the darkness and landed a few feet from Frankenstein's black polished shoes. Frankenstein nearly leapt out of the alley, but he quickly saw it was just a small bag, the size of an apple, sealed with a knotted drawstring.

"Pick it up," the voice said. "Have a look."

Frankenstein hesitated, then did as asked. He pulled the bag open and fished around inside. "There's nothing . . . wait . . ."

A small whitish thing, nearly a sphere, rolled out and sat in his palm. It seemed to pulse. He steadied it between his thumb and index finger, gently squeezed, and held it closer to his eyes.

What on earth was this? It had the look and consistency of flesh, but it was perfectly round, no sign of any incision or wound, no real texture to the surface.

"What is it?" Frankenstein said.

"That, sir, is the question. I cut it from your behemoth. Over the next few nights, I watched it knit itself together, like it was healing, until finally it formed that ball."

It's the ray, Frankenstein thought. *Bringing the simulacrum of life even to this tiny piece of flesh.*

But the voice wasn't finished. "The first time I tussled with your man, I'd seen my slicing heal up the same way, and I thought to myself, well, Jack, it seems you've stumbled on a better path of self-preservation, my own methods being so crude, y'see, and drawing so much unwanted attention."

"Your crude methods?" Frankenstein said, thinking again about what he'd seen at the morgue, and again in the graveyard. The incisions were too precise, the part of the body removed too consistent for mere homicidal lust.

Frankenstein raised his head from the little sphere in his hand and focused on the lightless patch of alley he imagined held the Ripper. "The uteri you take. You believe they keep you alive somehow?"

"Believe? Inasmuch as I believe I'm here, I believe. I need the wombs to birth me, vile things though they are. And I congratulate you, sir, for having gotten a way around them," the voice said.

A bitter thought crossed Frankenstein's mind, *That's the first time anyone's congratulated me for my work. And it comes from a murderer.*

The hope that Frankenstein might use this information to catch the killer, or vindicate his name, found itself driven back by a purer, more insistent curiosity.

"If what you say is true, how does it work? How does the womb extend your life?"

The darkness was silent for a while, as if in contemplation. Frankenstein heard a car horn out in the street, the rush of pedestrian steps, and, for a moment, imagined he was alone again. Part of him felt relief, he could go straight to Devin, tell him of the encounter, send them off in the proper direction at least.

But the other part of him, the part hungry to hear more, felt a haunting disappointment. And when he let that rise to the forefront of his consciousness, when he truly gave up on receiving a response, he got one.

"Because of who you are, sir," the voice said, slower this time, hesitant, as if trying to project an air of something. Humility? Commonality? "Because of who you are, of what you've done, the boundaries of common behavior you've crossed, you may be the only other who walks this earth who might understand. So, I'll tell it to you then, the whys and wherefores London's puzzled on since I killed my first whore. Do you know, sir, the tale of Sawney Bean?"

"A Scottish cannibal? Caught hundreds of years ago?" Frankenstein offered.

"The same. The dates vary with the telling, sometimes as much as a hundred years. I suspect that's because old Sawney and his clan lived at least that long. Now me, sir, when I was a young man there wasn't much differing me from the mass of humans, save for an itch to travel and a fondness for local tales. That's what took me to the outskirts of Edinburgh, where I followed directions supplied by a farmer and arrived at what was supposed to be Sawney's cave, the cave from which he and his kin emerged each day to prey on unsuspecting travelers.

"It didn't look like much. A cave same as any other, maybe a bit closer to the sea. And there weren't any bones, which got me to wondering if I'd found the right spot. I was figuring to leave when I came upon a small opening, too small for anything except my hand, which I put inside. I felt something flat and dusty, and pulled out a book. Well, sort of a book. It wasn't held together at the spine and filled with words. It just had pictures, and its pages folded out, each tied to the one before it.

"At first I thought it was a children's book, but the pictures weren't meant for any child. They showed how to cut up a human body and prepare certain parts for devouring. Though done by no great artist, they held the most incredible detail. For the life of me, whenever I tried to see the lines that made them, my eyes just kept seeing what the picture showed, as if it were alive and before me. I'm not ashamed to say they got into me right then and there.

"And the faces it showed of those that did the eating, they

looked so much stronger and younger than when they started, and they held such dreadful fire in their eyes, that I wanted to befriend such as them, to be like them. Those pictures, sir, became more important to me than the teachings of the church or the love of my own mother.

"Soon it wasn't enough to just be looking. Somehow the drawings insisted they be tried. I started with animals, from the butcher's shop, just to practice my cutting. That's another thing, sir, the more I practiced, the more detail in the pictures I noticed. Soon I saw that in order to do it right, your victim had to be alive. So I took to hunting my own: a pig, cats, dogs, I even felled a deer once for my purposes. Over time, my cutting got so good I fancied myself a sort of doctor. And the pictures were there to show me more detail, to guide me further down, the deeper I went.

"Then there came a shining moment, sir, when the pieces fell together, when the pictures melted into one, and I realized there was power in them, sir, the power to rip through the veil of the little half-lived lives we wander through, the power to take from one and give to the other. I knew then old Sawney and his clan were no criminals, but servants, servants to the dark god whose own invisible hand drew those pictures, to reveal to us the true glory of our own hunger, to reveal how right and fitting it was to extend that hunger by whatever means possible, until we glow with the fire of our own creation.

"All that was left was to take the womb from a human, sir, to show myself the true compassion that would let me spit in the eye of Death and live forever. Here was I with these divine instructions, my brain afire to make those pictures real, but even then I misunderstood, and for my first victim took a young girl sick at hospital. She was dying of consumption and I thought a quick death would bless her and me both. But I made it too quick, and I felt sorrow over her passing, so it didn't work.

"You see, sir, for the magic to work, she that dies must feel terror, the lonely blackness that preceded creation, while he that wields the blade has to feel the passion of the killing. She must feel it, and you must adore it, the cutting, the ripping away, to allow it to melt into yourself.

"That was when I happened on the idea of killing whores. I never could countenance them anyway. It became simple after that. No more worrying about this or that, just straight and true to the one real object, to stay alive at all costs. And while I still don't know if it'd be right to cut up a queen or a noble-woman, I figure I'm easily worth the lives of a few whores.

"Now, to bring you round to the point of my grand tale, sir, it worked. I felt the energy flush through me, and all differences between myself and the book melted. I am as alive and young as I was when I devoured that first womb. Though I keep the book still, I covet it no longer, for it is fully inside me.

"Ha! Tell all that to a magistrate, and they think old Jack's insane. But you sir, are different from that mass. You've touched the body in the same way, strived for the same thing. So now, I ask, how could you fail to understand old Jack?"

"Us alike? But you murder them," Frankenstein said, stunned. "You take life."

The response was eerie in its calmness. "Yes, sir, yes I do. Maybe it's my years, but these days I really don't see what the big deal is about murdering. There are, after all, lots of people. It's only meat."

Recognizing the echo of his own words, Frankenstein felt a shiver up his back. "It's . . . it's insanity."

The Ripper chuckled. "Do you mean that as an insult, sir? Funny, if you do, because the way I see it, sanity's nothing more than an averaging of folks' behavior, and who wants to be average?"

Frankenstein felt the world behind him and longed to dive back into it. His head was vibrating, torn between disgust and fascination. If the Ripper's tale was true, what secrets did that book hold? He didn't for a moment believe in any dark god, but if there was knowledge to be had in the strange codex, knowledge he could combine with his own . . .

He snapped the thought from his head.

"I want to preserve life. Not destroy it."

"You're an odd sort, sir. More divided than I expected, unless this is some sort of game you play with strangers. If the killing bothers you so, you yourself could put a stop to it."

"Me? How?"

"Isn't it obvious now? Build me a body like your creature's, and put me inside it. Sure, he's an ugly one, but I don't mind the looks. It's duration that interests me and my god. We plan to be here on the Judgment Day, you see."

Outraged, Frankenstein shouted at the dark as he had at the twinkling star above him, "Never! I won't do it. I'm not like you. I don't sacrifice human beings. I serve science and reason, not superstition."

The Ripper's response was measured. "Science . . . superstition, seems to me different words for the same thing. Me, sir, I'm a strong believer in whatever works. For instance, while I'd hoped my story might sway you to my cause, long life has made me patient and I'm confident I'll find something else that will work."

"No!" Frankenstein screamed. He shouted freely now, hoping to banish the voice by mere force of will. "Nothing could ever make me help you! *I'm* not a monster!"

The darkness chuckled, and then it moved on.

Chapter Eighteen

Once, when she was a young thing, Mary Blyss had been with a handsome soldier just back from the war. She couldn't remember his name, but he said the look in her eyes reminded him of his favorite movie star. He seemed a healthy, strapping fellow, but when they fell to talking, she noticed something not quite right. His eyes were sunken in a bit too far, and every closing door, dropped glass, or clapping of hands, made him tense and snap around.

"Artillery," he explained. "I still hear them."

He said that, during the war, when he first heard the crashing din, the noise only terrified him. But then a man right next to him had the right side of his head blown off (*like a pile of dead leaves in a gale*, he'd said), and the dreadful sound, which traveled slower than the shell, came right after.

The soldier-boy said it was like his body went into shock, but he could still function. By the time his third friend died in a similar way, though, he didn't know who he was anymore, other than a machine, or a dumb animal. He recovered, mostly, but there was still a scar on his soul, which, though invisible, had a specific size and shape. It felt, he said, like the artillery had burrowed a deep, wide hole in his mind, and any time something reminded him of it, everything he was just tumbled in.

Mary didn't know what the devil he was talking about for many years.

But then came the moment when a breathless old woman came running down the street, her arms held straight up, like dry branches twisting in the air. She screamed that Cyra had been found, cut to pieces, just like the others, and her killer was cornered by a mob.

Despite her deadly long day at the station, Mary raced to the scene, ignoring the cries of her stiff, aching body. She slowed only when she saw the size of the still-growing crowd, how people tumbled from the alley for lack of space. In the midst of this carnage strode a tall figure of black and white, starkly visible against the sea of human grays. He moved forward, as if wading through a deep pool, legs, arms, and torsos flying from him, some still attached, others not, leaving the dead in his wake.

They poked him with sticks, clubs, and umbrellas. In exchange, he hurled them about like dolls. He kept saying the word Cyra taught him, "Please! Please!" But either his pronunciation was too garbled, or no one cared to understand.

A voice in Mary's head, maybe her own, screamed she should do something, maybe tell them how the giant was too much a simple Simon to ever be confused with the leering killer she knew from his coal-black eyes. Instead, she felt herself stumble into a black hole in the center of her mind, the one the young soldier described. Understanding finally what he'd meant, she wondered if she'd ever climb out again.

They tried to pile on the giant to bring him down, but he shed them like rain. They tried to throw thick ropes on him, ropes from the docks that held huge trawlers in place, but people pressed so hard on all sides, it was impossible not to ensnare them as well, drawing them closer to the beast. The police had guns, but couldn't fire for fear they'd miss.

A paddy wagon drove slowly through the crowd, siren shrieking. The mob cleared a path for it, but when it reached the giant, he seemed to think it was just another attacker. Furious, he grabbed its grill and rattled the chassis. The terrified driver pressed hard on the gas. The slower members of the mob barely leapt out of the way in time as the paddy wagon slammed the giant, full body, into the solid brick of a tavern wall.

At first Mary thought it was over, that nothing could survive such a powerful blow, but in seconds, the giant was struggling again. In a few more seconds, he was actually moving the paddy wagon back from the wall. The smarter policemen realized what was happening and moved in with their ropes, which this time had a far easier target. One after another, crude lassoes found their mark, and just when they did not seem enough, someone else arrived with chains.

Once they were finished throwing, and wrapping, then snapping on huge padlocks, there was barely any giant to be seen. It took six men, three on either side of the twitching mummy, to lower their impossible burden into the back of the wagon.

As the weight hit, the steel frame squealed and bent as if ready to snap. Finally, the paddy wagon, the giant within, and a pile of officers clinging to the outside, crawled down the street to the wild cheers of the crowd.

After that there was only counting of the dead and the arrival of ambulances.

Throughout, Mary Blyss stood like a zombie, taking it in, letting what she could pass through her. Coming at last back to some sense of her self, instead of trying to see her friend's body, she raced to Cyra's small flat, bumping and jostling her way through the still-thick crowd coming the other way.

Flying up the creaking wooden stairs, she went through the door in a flash. She ignored all the mementos of Cyra's short life: the stained paper doily hung on the wall as if it were a painting, the chipped lemon-yellow ceramic lamp, the frayed photo of a child and her mother, even the cheap bisque bowl from which they'd fed their giant. Mary ignored all these, and felt instead under the mattress for the purse of Cyra's money, the thing that would keep her off the streets at night and alive, for just a little while.

Outside the Whale, she saw Weldon, who told her the police had been by again, that they wanted her back now for even more questions. She laughed, or rather cackled, a little crazily, again reminding herself of the way Mitzie giggled when she was nervous or frightened. Then she hurried off to sit in the darkness, hoping no one would remember the flat she shared with Ben. She settled down on the floor of the small bedroom, afraid to light even a candle.

Arms, legs, and torsos, snatches of cloth with paint, it felt to Mary as if all the horrid world was made of pieces that looked like they might, but in truth didn't, fit together.

The next day, though, she was proven wrong. In the hazy morning, the night burnt off into brittle day, she braved the street to spend some of Cyra's money on a little food. She was careful to avoid her usual hangouts, where the police might still be asking for her and wandered instead to a far corner of Thrawl Street, where she heard the cries of the newsboys for the first time in what felt like ages.

And that's when some of the pieces started to come together, because it was there, a small bit of bread in her hand, she heard the young voices cry, long and loud, about Frankenstein and his monster. Stepping closer cautiously, like a wild animal, she bent over and stuck her head down to look at the first page. There was the picture of her giant next to another photo of a tense, but handsome, dark young man with wild eyes. At once, she recalled the story Erik Krogh had told her about his son's arm and realized that that lost, haunted look in the young German's eyes was probably now reflected in her own.

So the giant was the monster. Made from the dead. That much, she could believe, but the rest, that the monster and his maker were the killers, she knew was ridiculous. She'd seen the monster fight the killer, and one look at the photo of young Baron Frankenstein told her this was not the same man. He didn't have the eyes. Sure, he had a bit of crazy going for him, but not that dread, dead blackness. Nowhere near it.

She rose, thinking she should tell the police at once.

But they wouldn't believe her, so why bother? The only one who'd been civil to her there was that bag of air Professor Lampini, and that was only because they were treating him the same way with his robbery complaints.

Her rent paid up, and her little food in hand, she returned to the flat, locked the door, and sat on the floor. Then she thought how the pompous police were nothing more than a bunch of overpaid fakes, worse than Lampini, posing to be something they weren't while people got murdered on the streets.

Fakes.

She rolled the word over in her mind. It rang, like it should be connecting up with something else. Mitzie? Cyra? The monster?

No, the torn piece of cloth they showed her at the station. The one the experts had examined. It wasn't dirt on it, after all. It was fake dirt. Probably just paint.

So what if the killer wasn't some magical shape shifter? What if he just used disguises? Or, better yet, what if he just *stole* them? What if the jacket was a piece of a costume, painted with some gray spots to make it look dirty? And what was it Professor Lampini was complaining that the police wouldn't help him out with?

Missing costumes. Now who would want the clothes off a wax dummy?

Maybe, she thought, someone who wanted a disguise.

So now something else had come together. She knew the killer, old Jack, could be getting his suits from Lampini's waxworks.

She could tell the police *that*.

They still wouldn't believe her. She wasn't one of their experts, after all.

Maybe she could go to Lampini herself, tell him, and then they could go, two cowards arm in arm, together to the police. Or she could just sit here, waiting for the day when the small amount of money Cyra had saved all her life was gone, and she'd have to wander the streets again, where the killer knew her by name.

All alone now. All alone.

She made up her mind, then and there, to seek out Lampini, but she didn't go immediately. She waited a few days, to build her courage, and to spend a little of Cyra's money on some libations.

Professor Lampini's display, he'd said, was in the Whitechapel market. Late in the afternoon, when the sky was still light, but the shadows had just begun to grow long, Mary Blyss reached it, a bottle in her hand.

The place had the air and the stench of a carnival, which to Mary simply meant the smell of an alley, though not quite as bad. It was a slow season, many of the wooden stalls and kiosks were boarded up, but there were still a few open, their owners peddling pots and pans, fruits and meats, clothes and tools.

The eastern end of the market bordered the backs of a row of shops. That, she was told, was where Lampini had set up his great waxworks, a series of tents, really, but there he was free to use the backs of the buildings as a long wall of his own, lending an air of permanence to his traveling, small-time operation. "Mr. Tussaud," they called him in mocking tones, though they had to admit his little show had been a draw for them all.

Mary picked her way across the market's dirt floor, kicking trash out of her way as she went. She walked past the strings of lights held on wooden sticks that lit the open space at night, and was finally rewarded with a view of a long series of tents half hanging from bare brick walls. There were no windows and doors visible, and a huge sign out front, proclaiming Professor Lampini's Astounding Waxworks, explained that the exhibit was currently closed. The area was also notable for the fact that there weren't many people about, owing, no doubt, to the fact that the only exhibit was accepting no visitors.

She had come too far to turn back easily, but took a good, long swig from the bottle before moving closer.

Assuming the edge of the tent that held the grand sign was likely the entrance, Mary Blyss walked up to the thick tan burlap, leaned in, and called out, "Mr. Lampini?"

There was no response. No sound, for that matter.

She rolled her eyes. "All right then, *Professor* Lampini! Are you in there, please? It's Mary Blyss! We met at the police station! I think I know what's happening to your costumes!"

Nothing.

Was he off, gone, or just asleep inside? Not willing to wait, or ask among the other shopkeeps, Mary started to explore the strange series of tents for some hint of an entrance. Ropes attached to stakes kept the front tied town. On the long side, tent seemed to melt into tent without so much as a flap. Running out of ideas, she walked up to the spot where the burlap met brick wall. While he'd managed to cleverly secure the top and bottom, by tying them to a light fixture and a drain pipe, the middle part was loose enough for Mary to stick her head inside.

There was a small table set up, to collect the entrance fee no doubt, and another sign indicating the entrance. Beyond that, blackness.

"Professor Lampini!" she shouted again. As she leaned further in, she found her shoulders inside as well.

"Professor?"

The dark beyond the curtains still did not give up its secrets, so she picked up one foot, stepped in, then drew the other in behind her. The sounds of the market were more than muffled by the heavy cloth of the tents, they were utterly silenced.

Easy enough to come in here, though, she thought. *If I could, anyone could.*

She peered curiously at the table, then under it, wondering if Lampini was stupid enough to leave his money box around. A glint of metal under the table caught her eye and her curiosity was rewarded with the glint of a coin.

A ha'penny. Probably the price of admission.

She pocketed it, stepping closer to the dark. From here she saw a long row of shadow that ended far off, in a burlap wall lit only by the fading sunlight outside it. The exit, Mary figured. The rest was kept dark on purpose, with black cloth or thicker tenting. She could make out the shape of the waxworks now, though, sections, each one holding a human-sized figure on a pedestal.

"Professor?" she called again.

Well, she figured, she could have a peek at the show, and see if what was missing matched what she'd seen the killer wear. Pretending to be a regular customer, she strolled along. The lights were out, making it difficult to see much, but she caught glimpses of what she thought was Henry VIII, Charlie Chaplin, Bluebeard, and, oddly enough the Whitechapel killer, Jack the Ripper. His top hat and cape were gone, though, and Mary found herself wondering if he'd actually disguised himself as his namesake.

In the middle of the series of displays there was a small closed-off area, again, with no visible entrance. As she drew closer, she thought she heard some scraping from within.

Was it Lampini's bedroom?

"Professor?"

She nearly jumped when she heard the response.

"We're closed."

At once she felt guilty about stealing the coin. "So sorry, it's just I wanted to talk with you. It's me, Mary Blyss. We met at the Commercial Street Police Station when you and I were having our difficulties?"

There was another rustle. A figure emerged from a flap in the closed-off area. He was puffing a long thin pipe, as Lampini had, but was otherwise difficult to make out.

"Of course I remember you," the figure said. "But what are you doing here? Come to sneak a peek at my show without admission?"

"No sir! I mean, I'm sure it's a lovely show. I mean, I can see that it's a lovely show, from what I can see. It's just I had an idea about your missing costumes that might help you get some more attention from the police," she said.

"Do you? That would be most helpful. What is your idea? I can't afford bribes, you know," he said with a laugh.

"I think maybe the Whitechapel killer's been stealing from your mannequins for his disguises."

"But I thought they'd captured him. I thought they knew for certain it was this Frankenstein fellow."

Something in his voice didn't sound quite familiar, but it'd been so long since they'd spoken, and then it'd been so brief, she couldn't be sure.

"No, sir. You see, I've seen him, twice. The first time he had a red moustache and a deerstalker, the second time his hair was dirty blond and he had a top hat and black clothes. Does that sound at all like anything that was stolen from you?"

The figure hesitated. The head bobbed back and forth a bit. Smoke curled from the pipe.

"Yes, yes it does. The missing top hat and black clothing was worn by my Jack the Ripper!"

Then it was true. She exhaled. "And do you use gray paint on any of those clothes to make them look like they were dirty?"

"Why, yes!"

"Then we must go to the police straight away. You can identify the piece of cloth as from one of your costumes and maybe they'll believe us when I say the killer's still loose!"

"Of course," he said. "We shall leave at once."

She wanted to run up and hug the life out of him. But as he stepped forward, a loud shout came from the front of the tent.

"Who is there? Who dares to steal from Lampini?!"

Mary whirled toward the voice and saw the Lampini she remembered, the stout man with rolled shoulders, standing at the entrance to the tents. By the time she turned back to the fake Lampini, he was already upon her.

He pulled his head close to hers and whispered in her ear, "And here I'd thought to retire for bit, since the pieces I took from your friends tasted so good and pure. Still, it's always good to see you, Mary Blyss."

She felt something slide past her side, in and out, then heard Lampini's lumbering run. At first she thought he was running away, like the coward he'd said he was, but then she heard him shout, "You, sir! Get away from that woman!"

The Ripper pushed her to the ground. She grabbed her side, not certain if she was wounded or not. Then she watched as Lampini and the Ripper faced off.

"Back away! My interest is in the whore, and I'd hate to take the life of so fine a tailor!" the Ripper said.

Horror struck Lampini's face. He stopped his advance cold.

"Good," the Ripper said. "Now stay silent just a few more seconds and I'll be on my way. Just this night I've had a conversation with a most intriguing fellow. It's my hope he'll solve me forever. If he does, rest assured, after tonight, I'll have no further need to raid your wardrobe."

But rather than remain silent, Lampini screamed, "The killer! He's here! He's here!"

The Ripper seemed to shrug in the dark. "Very well. Call it self-defense then."

He stepped forward, stabbing his blade into Lampini's huge gut. Lampini made a gurgling sound and fell backwards with a thud.

Meanwhile, Mary had struggled up to her knees and made it to the side of the tent. She tried to lift it, to roll out into the market, but it was lashed down too tightly.

She heard the Ripper spin toward her and felt that old familiar fear rise up in her, the one that stopped her from striking anyone who threatened her.

"Still alive, eh? We'll soon fix that," he said, coming forward.

Shaking, shivering, fearing, feeling tears stream down the side of her face, she tried to raise her hands to defend herself, but she could not.

He laughed. "You sense it don't you, whore? My power, your weakness. You can't do a thing. Not a thing. Just like all the rest. Ha! Now tell me why on earth a pathetic creature such as yourself doesn't deserve to die?"

The Ripper's arm came down. She screamed, forever hopeless, but, at the last moment, whirled out of the way. The Ripper stumbled forward, off balance, and fell.

Speechless, she straightened, unable to comprehend why she was still alive. Then she raced for the front of the tent. Not bothering to look back to see if he was following, she ran into the market. Her hand went to her side where the blade had gone in, but she didn't feel anything wet. Had he missed her?

She wanted to cry out to the people in the market, to scream the murderer was there, but couldn't. She couldn't speak, she could only gasp like a fish out of water and stumble about. She was too afraid.

The police . . . I've got to get to the police . . . she thought.

Feeling an ache in her side and a growing dizziness in her head, she scrambled into the street. For two blocks, if there were any police about, she didn't see them. Finally, she came upon the side entrance of the station. Beyond an open door at the head of a small flight of stone steps, two policemen stood, chatting amiably with one another, the hallway light making the scene glow like a poster for a show.

It was then, so close to success, that the dizzy feeling started to overwhelm her, and she paused to look at her hand. It was thick with red blood. Why hadn't she felt it? Was her hand numb? She looked down at herself. Blood was drenching her skirts, flowing down her legs in small rivulets.

Still mute, she fell onto the first step and started crawling up toward the open door. All she had to do was cry out and they'd hear her, kick over a can or bang on some wood, but she couldn't, so she had to get close enough for them to see.

Just see me!

As she pulled herself nearer, a cry came from somewhere down the hall.

"Baron Frankenstein is here and he claims he's seen the Ripper! All available men to the front!"

Without once turning toward the stairs, the two bobbies raced off down the hall.

With her strength ebbing, she made it up the steps and slid into the hallway. As the lifeblood slipped from her out onto the station floor, Mary Blyss let go of all her pointless terror, rolled her eyes one final time before dying and thought:

Him *they believe . . .*

Chapter Nineteen

"Krogh, I swear every word I've told you is true! Can't you put aside your hatred for me for just one moment? While the police are kept occupied with the creature, the killer is still out there!" Frankenstein said, pacing the small office as he spoke, twirling in tight, angry corners.

Krogh regarded him stiffly. "Very well. Putting aside my hatred for you for a moment, Baron, let's just say I find it terribly convenient that of all the people in London Jack the Ripper himself would choose to appear to you."

Frankenstein stopped pacing to face the seated man. He held the wide-brimmed hat he wore to help conceal his identity in both hands. It shook visibly as he spoke.

"It's *you* who says he's the real Ripper. For all I know he's some delusional fool who *thinks* he's the Ripper and believes he'd found some mythic secret of eternal youth. But don't you see? He's read the stories in the papers. He wants me to help make him immortal!" Frankenstein said.

"Giving you an excuse to continue your work," Krogh said. "You claimed someone forced you the second time, too. It seems you always have reasons for your crimes that are beyond your control."

Frankenstein stiffened and narrowed his eyes. "This isn't getting us anywhere. Where is Chief Inspector Devin? Everyone here pretty much defers to you as his unofficial assistant. I want to see what *he* has to say about this."

"He's at the courts, meeting with the magistrate and your

attorneys," Krogh responded coolly. "Regarding your creature's fate."

Frankenstein bolted for the door and looked frantically up and down the corridor. "Where are the courts? What's the address?"

Krogh rose and put himself between Frankenstein and the hallway. He was only slightly taller than the baron, but because of his straight back and wide shoulders, he cut an imposing figure.

He shook his head at the frantic man. "Your attorneys, the magistrate, and Inspector Devin all agreed you would not attend the meeting, to avoid publicity. However, you may leave a note with me outlining your concerns, and I'll see he gets it as soon as the meeting is over."

Frankenstein's eyes danced back and forth as he processed the information. He glanced down at the ground and up at the walls as he thought.

Suddenly seeming afraid, he looked the inspector in his eyes. "Krogh, the killer threatened me. Not directly, but he said he'd find a way to make me help him. He may plan to attack my family, my wife. No matter what you think of me, surely you recognize she has nothing to do with it?"

Krogh shrugged. "I have no complaint with her."

"Good. I know you have men watching us at the hotel, at least notify them to be on the lookout for anything unusual," Frankenstein said.

"The men are trained to do just that, Herr Baron," Krogh said. "I will pass word along, but you may also place the information in your note to Inspector Devin."

"Yes, of course," Frankenstein said. As he fumbled in his pockets for a pen and paper, Krogh motioned him back into the small office where he presented Frankenstein with a pad and Krogh's own stub of a pencil.

Frankenstein scribbled, covering the sheet in short order with sharp angular strokes.

"I've no reason to trust you, Krogh," Frankenstein said, tearing the sheet off the pad.

"No, Baron, you do not," Krogh answered. "But I am first and foremost an officer of the law. Perhaps you can trust in that?"

Frankenstein folded the note in half. "I suppose I must." He handed it over. "Please see Inspector Devin gets this right away. I must return to the Savoy to make certain Elizabeth is all right."

"Very well," Krogh said. "I'm sure the desk sergeant will be happy to have someone drive you back to your hotel."

Frankenstein nodded curtly, then, as frantic as he had been upon his arrival, he rushed down the hall. Krogh watched him go. As soon as he was out of sight, he opened the hastily written note. There were two English words on it that he was unfamiliar with, *utmost* and *urgency*.

Slowly, carefully, taking pains with the lines his pencil made, which were thicker now, having been worn to dullness by the baron, he wrote the words down in his notebook. Once finished, he meticulously tore Frankenstein's note into quarters and tossed them in a hallway wastebasket.

"Room service," a low voice on the other side of the door said.

"Room service?" Minnie repeated. "Now who in his right mind would be calling for room service at this hour of the night?"

Heading for the door, she immediately stumbled into one of the steamer trunks Victor Moritz had assembled in the suite. He'd spent the last few hours quickly packing all manner of things that simply did not belong to him.

Minnie looked at the luggage and shook her head in knowing disapproval, "It's not proper, that's what it is, planning to rush off in the middle of the night to the middle of nowhere with a married woman!"

Then it dawned on her just who might have called room service.

"Mr. Moritz!" she shouted toward the open bedroom door. "Room service is here."

She heard a rustle of boxes and an exasperated sigh. "Take care of it, please, Minnie!" Victor Moritz said.

"'Take care of it, please, Minnie,'" she repeated under her breath. "All right, all right."

She picked her way across Elizabeth Frankenstein's scattered belongings, marveling at how little the man knew how to pack for a woman.

"There's going to be hell to pay when the master returns," she repeated as she held up her skirt enough to see her feet, so she didn't stumble again.

The knock came at the door again.

"I'm coming, I'm coming!" she said, finally reaching the door. She opened it an inch and squinted through the crack.

"You're a little old to be a bellboy," she said.

In fact, the hairy man seemed barely able to fit into the bellhop uniform he wore, if it was a bellhop uniform at all. There were beads of sweat on his ruddy face and he didn't bear the usual pasted-on smile she'd come to expect from the help at the Savoy. His eyebrows were thick and dark, hanging heavily over deep-set eyes. His hair was black and curly, and had a sheen to it that made it look wet.

Ignoring her comment, the man said, "I have something for Elizabeth Frankenstein."

Minnie narrowed her eyes and glanced at the covered plate in his hand. "The baroness? Well, maybe Mr. Moritz ordered it for her. But where's your cart? They usually bring food in on a cart."

He held the plate a little higher. "It's just one plate. I didn't need a cart."

"Well then, give it to me, and I'll pass it along to the baroness," she said, holding her hands out.

He wobbled slightly.

"Are you all right? You look a bit peaked."

He wavered again slightly and said, "I hurt my leg a bit while fighting with a whore."

"Serves you right for visiting one of those filthy things in the first place. And then I bet you tried to cheat her from her wages!" Minnie said.

"No," he said. "She just didn't want me to cut her up."

With that, the Ripper pushed the empty dish and its metal cover into Minnie's chest, hurling her backward into the room. He came in and kicked the door shut with his foot.

The Ripper grabbed the metal dish cover, then leaned down over her as if planning to hit her with it. Instead, he hovered there and tried to bore into her with his coal-black eyes.

Terrified, Minnie grabbed the plate that had landed near her and meekly raised it between her face and his.

His voice spat into it, hoarse and tired, catching breaths every fourth word. "Fancy hotels and expensive suites are not my usual haunts. I'd just as soon get out of here with as little blood as possible, if only to show your master that I can be a gentleman. So, lie still, stay quiet, and you'll not die by my hand. Understand?"

She lowered the plate, looked at him with saucer-wide eyes, and nodded.

"Good," he said.

He rose and faced the bedroom, but before he could take a step, Minnie flipped over, grabbed his leg, and screamed, "Murder! Bloody murder! Help! Help!"

At first he kept walking, pulling her along the floor with his powerful stride.

"Murder! Murder!"

But then, with a grunt, he wheeled and stomped the boot of his free leg into her face, once, then twice, before her arms let go.

It was about this time that Victor Moritz emerged from the bedroom, awkwardly holding a long, flowing nightgown in his hands.

"Here now, what's going on?" he said as he surveyed the scene. As his face registered awareness of the peril, the Ripper slammed the metal dish cover into the side of his skull, sending him sprawling onto the floor.

Moving quickly, the Ripper stepped over the supine newcomer to examine him more closely. Moritz was still conscious, but barely, muttering to himself, "Elizabeth, must save Elizabeth, my darling—"

The Ripper slammed him in the head again, denting the metal plate cover. This time, Moritz did not move at all. The killer looked around. Minnie was similarly unconscious, and the rest of the room was still, save for the sharp breathing of the baroness in the next room.

Satisfied they were alone now, the Ripper grew curious about Victor Moritz's words, and looked around, noticing the packed bags for the first time.

"Stealing the baron's wife, eh? Now *that* is a priceless thing," the Ripper said. "I'd planned on leaving him a piece of his bride as souvenir, but I think you'll do much better."

Moving quickly, the Ripper pulled some supplies from the pockets of the costume he'd stolen from the waxworks: thick tape, rope, some cloth, and a piano wire.

After securing Moritz's mouth with the tape, and his arms with the rope, he lifted Moritz's leg and pulled his black shoe and sock off. Then he wrapped the belt just above the ankle and pulled it tight, as tight as he could before fastening it.

"To keep you from bleeding to death, sir," the Ripper said, though he knew Moritz couldn't hear him. "But I doubt you'll consider it a favor on my part."

Satisfied the belt was secure, he wrapped the thin, sharp piano wire around the ankle bone. "Now here's a little trick I learned on my travels in the Far East," he said, like a magician about to perform a trick. "Japan, if memory serves."

With one hand wrapped around the end of the wire, he started to pull, back and forth, back and forth, "sawing" the loop tightly around the ankle. When it first broke skin, there was a spurt of blood, like juice from a ripe persimmon. The whole of the leg shivered, but then settled down. He kept at it, pulling back and forth, back and forth, as the wire sliced flesh, muscle, and finally the whole of the bone. The foot, free now of its body, fell to the ground with a plop. Jack grinned to see it.

As he rose, he was tired from his effort, but feeling accomplished. He was quite surprised when Minnie's nails came up from behind him and dug deeply into his face.

"Murderer! Murderer!" she screamed.

The Ripper's ears rang from the piercing sound. He leapt back, smashing her small form into the wall.

"Oomf!" she said on impact, but still she clung to him, so he forced his elbow back and up into her ribcage, then slammed her into the wall again.

"Murd—"

This time, all the breath had been knocked out of her. Her grip loosened. He spun, wrapped his fingers around her neck, and squeezed. A rasping sound came from her throat as she struggled for breath, then her eyes started to roll up into her head. She slumped in his hands. As he let go, she tumbled from his grip and crashed to the floor.

He grabbed his blade and hovered over her, ready to strike, but did not.

"Minnie? Victor?" a thin, womanly voice called from the next room.

The Ripper straightened. He walked toward the open bedroom door and stood framed inside it.

Elizabeth Frankenstein sat at the small table by the window. She was looking out, dreamily, though night and fog rendered any view impossible.

He stood there a while before she turned, just her neck, to face him. Her hair was washed and done up, probably by her servant, red ribbons delicately tied in the flowing locks. Unlike the whores he slaughtered mercilessly, he thought this one a lady.

"Minnie and Victor," she said. "Are they dead?"

The Ripper shook his head. "No, lady. Just a little worse for wear. May I say I find myself a little surprised to see you so calm under the pomp and circumstances, what with my presence here and all."

She smiled slightly, a sad smile. "That's because I've been expecting you, sir, in payment for a life badly led."

"No one expects me, lady," the Ripper said.

"You're quite wrong about that," she answered. "We all do. We're just generally not polite enough to admit it."

Chapter Twenty

The moment Henry Frankenstein's trembling hand grabbed the handle of the doorknob, he sensed something deeply wrong. When he threw the door open, revealing the bodies of Victor and Minnie, he felt as if he'd already seen the scene, in his deepest nightmares.

His pained voice shattered the eerie silence. "Elizabeth! Elizabeth!"

He raced into the bedroom. It was empty. Cold dry toast with a dainty bite missing sat by a full cup of tea on her window table. The bed was made, the sheets barely disturbed. Her dresser drawers lay open and her clothes were strewn about haphazardly.

Her absence was a mortal blow, caving in his chest as surely as the monster's clenched fist. Stricken, he stumbled out of the room, muttering and shaking his head.

"Oh no, oh no, oh no."

He turned his head toward the rest of the room and scanned the two bodies. Minnie's chest rose and fell evenly, but otherwise she didn't move. Victor Moritz moaned slightly.

Feeling as if moving his own body were a struggle to carry a heavy corpse, Frankenstein forced himself to the side of his best friend. He kneeled and hoisted Victor's shoulders up.

"Victor! Victor!" Frankenstein shouted, slapping him in the face. "Wake up! What happened? Where is Elizabeth? Where?"

Victor's head twisted and his eyes rolled, sometimes meeting Frankenstein's impatient gaze, sometimes staring at nothing.

He spoke, but Frankenstein wasn't sure if the words were directed at him, or if they were part of some delirious dream.

"My foot, it hurts so much. What did he do to my . . . "

As Victor felt numbly with his hand down his leg, his attention seemed to focus. The two men looked down simultaneously, both seeing the bloody stump at the end of Victor's leg for the first time.

"Good lord!" Frankenstein shouted.

Victor responded more directly. He fainted dead away.

Frankenstein laid Victor back down and noticed the belt strapped around the stub.

If he'd wanted them dead, they'd be dead by now, but that's not his purpose. He must know I'd never help him if Elizabeth were harmed, so she must be all right, she must be.

Frankenstein stood and panted, not knowing what to do next. He tried to rouse Minnie, but she didn't respond.

Alone amidst the wreckage of his life, thoughts flooded his mind, each one believing they were more important than the last.

Elizabeth! What have I done to you?

Victor's in shock. I should call for help.

What hell is this I've built for those I love?

What help could those idiot doctors give him that I can't give him myself?

Why are all these trunks about? It looks like someone was packing to leave.

Will my persecutions never cease?

I could go to the police, but those fools couldn't even stop the Ripper from entering my hotel suite! What use could they be to me now?

He pressed his hands tightly against his skull, wishing he could push his fingers into his brain and sort the thoughts by hand. Elizabeth. He had to concentrate on her. The Ripper kidnapped her because he wanted his help. Did he leave some clue as to how to respond?

Wide eyed, Henry rushed about the suite searching, kicking over trunks, tripping on bundled clothing, until he finally looked at the obvious place, the small table by the door.

Sitting on the table was Victor's foot, two thick red lines of blood running down the side to a sheet of paper placed beneath. Long used to seeing pieces of the human machine, Frankenstein rushed over to it, lifted the foot, and grabbed the note. The ink on the page was a reddish brown, and Frankenstein quickly realized the note had been written in blood. The handwriting was a difficult scrawl, with many misspellings:

> *Mr. Baron,*
> *The owner was trying to run off with your wife, but I fixed it so he can't. Ha-ha! Now you owe me. Two days at the spot we met. If I read nothing in the papers, I'll assume you and I can come to a beneficial mutual arrangement.*
> *Yours truly,*
> *Jack the Ripper*

Note and foot in hand, Frankenstein slumped to his knees. This was it, then. As much as he'd tried to avoid it, as much as he'd wanted to avoid it, he would have to do as the Ripper asked, to continue his experiments, to cross the line and collect the equipment and the pieces he would need in order to make, from the dead, a body that would satisfy this killer.

He would *have* to.

Numbly, he looked at the severed foot and decided to try and find a bucket of ice to preserve it. It was fresh, so there probably wasn't much tissue damage yet.

In spite of himself, in spite of his love for Elizabeth, his friendship for Victor, in spite of every compassionate urge in him, he couldn't help but admire the way the bone was cut so cleanly, and wonder exactly how it was accomplished.

So rapt was he by the unique technique that must have been employed, he utterly failed to notice that his hands were no longer shaking, that now, with the thought that soon he would be forced, *forced* to resume his work, they were totally steady, as steady as the blackness between stars.

Chapter Twenty-One

"Has the whole world gone to the devil?"

His mask of control shattered by the unexpected news, Erik Krogh bolted to his feet like a jackrabbit, barely stopping himself from throwing the full weight of his tall, Teutonic form at the seated Devin.

Devin leaned back coolly in his chair and stared at Krogh with the sort of silent disapproval only an Englishman could muster.

"You'd do well to remember," Devin said. "That you have no authority here other than what I afford you as a *courtesy*. In exchange, I expect you to keep from making inappropriate outbursts, especially with the press so eager to make clowns of us all."

Krogh was sufficiently chastened, though his body still vibrated with anger. He forced himself back into his stiff wooden chair.

Devin went on. "We've got to stop being our own worst enemy. We've made it easy enough with poor Mary Blyss bleeding to death under our very noses. With a new 'Ripper' killing, the press is now convinced Frankenstein and his monster are *not* the killers, leaving us responsible for the fact that the real criminal is free and on the street."

Krogh shook his head. "You can't let this happen. If they move the creature to an asylum, it will escape. It will kill again."

Devin shrugged. "The way I see it, that much at least is good news. Unlike our makeshift holding cell, Seward's Sanitarium has the proper facilities for containing a madman, even one who's impossibly strong. What disturbs me more is the fact that it'll be months before the medical experts are ready to give us a report. Maybe a year or more before there is a trial. *If* there is a trial."

Krogh was aghast. "No trial? How can you even say such a thing?"

Devin eyed him. "Well, whatever else he is, he's not sane, is he? I don't know how the insanity plea works in Germany, but here, since 1851 and the M'Naughten ruling, the issue pivots on whether or not the defendant knows right from wrong. Yes, this brute says 'good' and 'bad,' but I have a parrot that quotes Burnt Norton from T. S. Eliot and I doubt a case could be made against it for plagiarism."

"But it's killed. It's killed so many . . . " Krogh said weakly. "Torn them to pieces . . . "

Devin sighed. "Yes. Yes. I'd expected public outrage would make such a defense impossible, but with the death of Mary Blyss and the attack on Professor Lampini, their attention is back on the so-called new Ripper. With the public elsewhere occupied, the courts may decide to wipe their hands of it and accede fully to the wishes of Frankenstein's attorneys. They want him sent back to Germany, someplace called the Neustadt Prison for the Criminally Insane. Seward's was a hard-won compromise."

Krogh's shoulders slumped. "I have come so far, worked so hard, sacrificed so much, for this?"

"Now, Krogh, try to have some perspective. Much as it pains me, an insanity plea isn't unreasonable. Suppose some other brute had done this to your son, a wolf? Would you blame the creature for its actions?"

"Yes. And I would shoot it."

Devin smiled a little. "Bad example, then. What if it were a fallen tree? Who could you shoot then, God?"

Krogh leveled his gaze at Devin. "This creature has nothing to do with God."

Devin blinked and went on. "Well, be that as it may, I'm afraid the bad news doesn't stop there. My case from the start has been the new Whitechapel killings. According to the surviving Professor Lampini, he and Mary Blyss were stabbed by the same killer. At the same time, Baron Frankenstein was seen walking here to the Police Station. I no longer consider him a major suspect."

Krogh's face went white. "What?"

"That's the truth of it, I'm afraid," Devin said. "So while our purposes once seemed to dovetail, they do so no longer. If you can refrain from further emotional outbursts, you'll continue to enjoy my courtesy here until the immediate issues involving the prisoner transfer are resolved. My resources must now be concentrated elsewhere. I'm sorry."

"Dovetail?" Krogh said numbly.

"Intertwined," Devin said. "Connected to form a stronger bond. Would you care for me to spell it?"

Krogh nodded and pulled out his book. As Devin spelled the word, a young officer knocked at the door and said, "Stimpson is ready for you, sir."

"All right. Again, I'm terribly sorry it's all gone down like this, Krogh, old man, but there it is," Devin said as he rose.

Krogh stood as well, blocking Devin's exit.

"Before you go, would you tell me something else, please?"

"If I'm able."

"Do you in your heart believe it's even possible that Frankenstein built this creature from the dead?"

Devin looked at Krogh, eyes full of pity. "No sir, I do not. There is no evidence of that, and the argument itself, prima facie, is foolish. Perhaps the question you'd best be asking is, should *you* believe it? Did you see Frankenstein sew him to-gether? No. Did you witness this stunning creation, with lightning striking kites and preternatural electric forces funneled into obscure machines? No. You did not. The man downstairs is a freak, to be sure, but I have no reason to suspect he is not a freak of nature."

Devin firmly shook Krogh's hand. "I do wish you the very best."

With that, he stepped around Krogh, out of his office, and strode down the hallway.

As Krogh watched, he remembered the expression, *Mad dogs and Englishmen* . . . and wondered if the two words were synonymous.

What would he tell his son upon his return? He imagined Rikard's eyes lighting up as Krogh opened the gate to the little garden in front of his small, thatch-roofed cottage. The lad would come running, thrilled to see his father after so long. Krogh would lift him into his arms, along with the crude pros-thetic he now had for an arm, and hug him for the longest while. But then that blissful moment of reunion would pass and the boy's first questions would be, "Did you get him, Father? Did you kill the monster?"

And Krogh, having promised his son justice, having spent all his family's money, all this time from home, would have to say, "No. They caught him, but then they let him go."

No. That would not happen. He had to find a way to do what was right, even if it had to be done himself, even if he had to die in the process. It would be difficult, but not impossible.

After all, he still enjoyed Devin's courtesy.

Whenever the monster closed his eyes and slept, he dreamt he was trapped, unable to move while dark-azure demons stood by, straining their smooth little arms and legs as they tightened his bonds. His body hurt so much from the strain he thought it might burst, until, finally, he awoke.

And the scene was exactly the same.

He was trapped. He was held. Not even the view of the bars and the window in the hall beyond them had changed.

Awake and asleep, though, he would grunt and pull and grunt and pull until the light and shadows in that window changed from the moving sun. Then he would grunt and pull some more, until, at long last he could move one hand just a fraction of an inch. He was never sure which hand it would be, sometimes one, sometimes the other.

But no sooner did the chain rattle than the blue devils slammed their heavy hammers into the spikes. As they worked, the cell would fill with a sharp, explosive clanking that pierced his skull and hurt his teeth.

And the chains twisted and tightened.

In waking as in sleep.

With one difference.

Each time he pulled a hand free, it happened just a little sooner. For the longest time, no one noticed the difference, not the monster, not the blue devils.

But now, days later, they all knew. They all knew he could pull free in half the time, and that he was getting faster. He could feel it in the way his arms strained against the chains. He could see it as fear in the blue devils' eyes as they desperately slammed the spikes into the crumbling floor and walls.

He was getting stronger.

And his prison was getting weaker.

Chapter Twenty-Two

In the days that followed, the London streets near the Savoy Hotel enjoyed far less traffic, while the mob in front of the hotel itself dwindled to near nothing. This was partly due to the fresh Ripper attacks, which had drawn attention back to Whitechapel, but also partly because on this particular day the weather service had predicted a minor electrical storm in the evening.

As Frankenstein walked along, looking up, he was pleased to believe the prediction was correct. The dark, sooty sky was unusually cloudy and already a few thick drops had fallen. He'd also had no further contact from the police and guessed that Krogh had not passed on his message.

All for the best, he thought, since it had made keeping Elizabeth's disappearance a secret, and his own journey this evening back to the alleyway where he'd met the Ripper far easier. It was as if the fates, for a change, were buoying his efforts, as if now they wanted him back at work.

Minnie's cooperation concerned him, but she'd met his instruction not to answer the door, for anyone, with relief. "I'd be happy never to answer another door so long as I live, Baron," she'd said. Victor Moritz, of course, would do anything to ensure Elizabeth's safety. In any case, there was no choice but to trust them both, just as he had no choice but to be here again in the filth, seeking conversations with the shadows.

"Are you here?" Frankenstein said to the dark.

"I assume we have a deal, then?" the dark answered.

As last time, the alley seemed completely empty. A little surprised by the quickness of the response, he held his ground.

"It's not that simple. I have questions and some demands of my own."

"You're hardly in a position to make demands, Mr. Baron. But if it will get the process proceeding, what are they?" the Ripper said.

"First, I want to see you. An examination will be necessary before the procedure, but for now, just step out from the shadows," Frankenstein said.

"Very well," the Ripper said. "But be warned, no one has looked upon me for many years and lived to tell about it."

There was a rustling Frankenstein couldn't place, like a giant bat unfolding its wings. Then, from the corner of shadow opposite the one he expected, a figure of medium height emerged. He was wrapped in a black cloak and wearing a deerstalker hat. His skin was mottled, hair dark as Frankenstein's, but curly and glistening. His eyes were what stood out best: they were dead, goblin things. The only other time in his life Frankenstein had seen such eyes were on the monster. Seeing them on this man now, he found himself believing that this truly was Jack the Ripper.

What has *kept him alive all these years?*

The Ripper swept his right hand down the length of his form. "As I said, sir, not much of a body. It's changed some over the years, not for the better. I've grown thicker and have difficulty finding proper clothes. Though it's served me, I shan't be afraid to lose it," he said. "Now, what else is there of your demands?"

"I must know about Elizabeth. I must have proof that she's alive," Frankenstein said.

The Ripper shrugged. "I keep her warm and fed. She's inclined to scream, but I don't think it my doing. As for proofs, what sort can I give that won't reveal her hiding spot? I could give you a piece of her, show it to be nice and fresh, if you like."

Frankenstein shivered. "No! No! Touch a hair on her head and I'd sooner die than help you."

"That'll be as you wish, Mr. Baron. Rest assured, I'll return her as soon as I'm in a new body," the Ripper said. "And know that should I die under your blade, I'm sure she'll not be found."

"Very well. But what if I succeed? If I put your brain in a new body, what then? Will you still go around slaughtering people?"

The Ripper bobbed his head. "Well now, I haven't given that much thought. I won't have a need to, but I've grown very fond of it. You should try it sometime. I'm sure a man such as yourself—"

"No! There must be no more killings," Frankenstein said. "I'll have no more blood on my hands. The killings must stop at once."

The Ripper blinked his dark eyes. "At once? My wounds from your monster still leave me weakened. I'd hoped to revive myself with fresh food and would be doing myself a great disservice to agree to that."

Frankenstein shook his head. "You've no proof to give me Elizabeth is alive, so I must trust you on that. You must trust me on this. And I must work alone, I won't have you lurking about. It would make me nervous and then there might be a mistake, and mistakes in this sort of work can cost months, do you understand? Months."

"That I do. Anything else, your majesty?"

"I'll need a way to contact you when everything is prepared," Frankenstein said.

"That much I've thought of," the Ripper said. "Leave a personal advert in the papers addressed to Mr. Lusk that names the date. Leave a second to Mr. Abberline naming the place. I'll see them. Is that it?"

"Yes," Frankenstein said.

The Ripper smiled and put out his hand. "Shall we two gentlemen shake on it, then?"

Frankenstein shook his head in disgust. "No. Make no mistake about what I think of you. You're a vile thing, the most base imaginable. The only time I'll touch you is when you're under my knife."

The Ripper pulled back his hand and sneered. "A harsh judgment. You, a man who studies life, and me, such an interesting example of it. I am, after all, good sir, the very thing you're looking for. Need. Hunger. Isn't that life at its purest? Isn't that what you're after, no matter what boundaries you cross? Do you *really* think us so different?"

For a moment, Frankenstein felt as if he were looking at himself through a funhouse mirror that distorted the worst of him and minimized the good, but he shook the image from his head and declared, "You and I are as different as night and day."

The Ripper shrugged, stepping backwards into the shadows. "We all have our dreams and our callings. But do hurry. Your wife waits, and she seems, sir, to be the delicate type."

With that the Ripper vanished, leaving Frankenstein alone to wonder what he had become. If he truly did this thing, if he knowingly put that hideous brain in a powerful body, a brain, worse even than that of Tom Nodding, how could he trust a mere promise that it wouldn't kill again? What horrors might it unleash were it physically capable?

Frankenstein gritted his teeth and swore that though he had never killed anyone, he would kill this man.

Later in the evening, cold rain slapped Minnie's disgruntled face as she stuck her head out the hotel window. A string ran from inside out into the night and up to the makeshift kite that danced in the wind above the roof of the Savoy. As her bony fingers tugged the snarled line off the iron latticework that snagged it, she muttered to herself, comfortable that the rain would keep her master from hearing.

"Clear the line, he says. Clear the line! And I says again, what about taking Mr. Moritz to a proper hospital?" She scrunched her face to imitate the baron's grim expression. "Those fools can't do what *I* can, he says, so if you want him to keep his foot, do as *I* say! Keep it? I says, but it ain't even attached! Let *me* worry about that, he says. Hmph! I says. And what's all this got to do with my poor baroness?"

A boom from the dark clouds startled her. She wanted to screech, but held it in. The last time she screeched at the thunder she made the baron drop a vial of chemicals and he had such a look, she thought he might strike her.

Her work done, she turned back toward what their London hotel suite had become. Victor Moritz, held in place by belts and stripped sheets, lay atop two tables. The baron hovered over him, sniffing at his knives and needles to make sure she'd dipped them all in alcohol, as ordered. Then he looked at a gray metal box with dials on it, one he'd unpacked from those "special" steamer chests he wouldn't let her touch, and snapped his head toward her.

"The kite *must* go higher! This hotel hasn't the proper elevation and the storm is too small! Hurry! Hurry!" he shouted.

She waved her hands at him and turned back to the window. "All right! All right! I'm moving as fast as I can!"

She lifted the roll of string and started unspooling it.

"Faster! Faster!" he cried.

She went faster. "You don't want it caught up again, do you?" But he wasn't even listening anymore, leaving her to mutter to herself again. "Hmph! Thinks I'm his trained monkey, he does . . . "

"Henry, Henry . . . " a low voice said.

It was Mr. Moritz, trying to talk, poor thing. Minnie, still unthreading the string, watched from the corner of her eyes and strained to listen. The tall man had been in and out of consciousness since he'd been strapped down. Now he seemed awake as you please.

"Henry, I've changed my mind. You mustn't, it's unholy," Mr. Moritz said, his voice all pleading. "I beg you as your friend."

The baron leaned over him, bringing his face too close for comfort.

"Friend, is it?" the baron said. "Then explain why you were trying to abscond with my wife."

Minnie, wanting an explanation, too, nodded her head sharply in agreement.

Mr. Moritz's face flushed with shame. "Henry, she was losing her mind! What was happening to you was killing her. I couldn't let that happen. I had to try to take her away."

The baron regarded the prone man. His anger faded, letting a heavy sadness shine through. "You may be right, and to tell you the truth, I'm sorry you didn't get away with it. But all that's changed and I'm the only one who can save her now, even if it means engaging in my experiments again. And I must make these tests. So, look at it that way, Victor, is my work so unholy, as you call it, you'd sacrifice Elizabeth to stop it?"

Victor Moritz turned away, his answer unspoken.

Baron Frankenstein went back to threading his needle.

"There, you see? There are no choices. This small effort will help me determine how to better control the amount of the life-giving ray to use. If I succeed, I can build a body for the Ripper that will live for just a day, long enough for Elizabeth to be freed, short enough so his harm will be contained forever. Instead of building an immortal creature by accident, I'll build a mortal one on purpose. So stay still, old friend, and have your foot back, unholy or not. Because you acted only out of concern for Elizabeth, I'll try to make it as painless as possible."

Victor Moritz, bound to the table in any case, closed his eyes.

Minnie winced as she saw the baron's needle pierce the flesh of his exposed ankle. Catching her from the corner of his eye, the baron glared and covered his work with a sheet.

It was just as well. She didn't want to watch anymore anyway.

Chapter Twenty-Three

Sitting on the filthy mattress of his little hovel in Whitechapel, Erik Krogh thought, *Even if it can heal itself over time, a bullet to the brain would surely do it. If not one, then two, or three.*

He folded the note he had written to his wife and son and pinned it inside his shirt pocket. His boots were polished, his clothes ironed. Everything was almost ready. He looked over his Luger one last time. He rubbed the angled grip, assembled and disassembled the leaf-spring, and checked all the bullets in the cartridge.

And if the body still moves about once the mind is dead, I'll be ready for that, too. I'll fire into the brain, then cut the head off.

He took the hacksaw he'd purchased with the last of his money and slipped it into the small brown carrying case that had once carried his luggage. His other paltry clothes he'd tied in a bundle and left in the trash, so as not to impose on the landlord.

He'd gone through all the motions, thoughtless, like an automaton.

Like a body without a brain.

As he walked the short distance to the station, he wondered if he were a good enough liar to pull the thing off, if they wouldn't hear his plans in some hesitation of his voice. But by the time he greeted the two officers standing outside the main doors, and they smiled and touched their caps, he realized no one, except perhaps Devin, had ever paid enough attention to him to notice any differences in his behavior.

Krogh chose to arrive around noon, when most of the staff would be enjoying a final lunch before the creature's transfer. Within an hour, the station would bustle with activity, possibly even the press would be there, if someone had leaked the date that Devin had tried so hard to keep secret.

So this would be Krogh's one and only chance.

There was just one man on guard at the door which separated the holding cells from the first floor office area, then two more directly in front of the creature's cell. They watched the creature round the clock, sledgehammers, chains, and new spikes forever at the ready. Since the monster's capture, all the remaining cells had stayed empty, prisoners taken to other precincts.

A bullet to the brain would have to kill him. Two. Maybe three at most.

The desk sergeant barely nodded at him. The man at the door to the holding cells, having seen him so often in the company of Devin, quickly accepted his explanation that he was to check on the prisoner one last time before the transfer.

It was the two remaining guards at the end of the hall, who stood in the noon light from the little window, who would be the real problem. Krogh was deeply sorry he could think of no way past them without killing them. He was glad he only recognized one, Bailey. It would make it easier to concentrate on saving bullets.

Three bullets at most. The most it could take to kill the monster would be three bullets to the head.

So it would be two men dead. What of it? The monster had killed over forty, mutilated how many more? Just a final act of madness in a mad world.

Mad dogs and Englishmen.

The Luger waited in his pocket. His hands were free as he motioned toward the iron bars.

"Open it up for me, will you? I'm to have a final look," Krogh said.

Bailey, the plump boyish officer he knew stepped up with the keys. "Be extra careful Inspector, he's been rustling a lot today. More than usual. Maybe he smells the transfer coming."

The other one spoke up nervously. "Well, if Dr. Seward's sedatives don't work, there'll be a hundred men here to herd him into the wagon, right, Inspector Krogh?"

"By then, there will be nothing to worry about," Krogh said, trying to keep his mouth from twitching into a grin.

As Bailey pulled it, the door squeaked loudly. Hearing the sound, the monster's eyes opened. Upon seeing Krogh, its face twisted.

"He remembers you," Bailey said.

"Where . . . is . . . Frankenstein?" the monster said.

Bailey and the other guard looked at each other. Bailey grinned. "See? Told you he could talk."

The other fellow shook his head. "I don't believe it. Quiet as a church mouse for days, then he opens up with a few words like that."

Ignoring them, Krogh maneuvered into the cell.

"Inspector Krogh, do you think he understands us? Like an idiot savant?" Bailey asked.

"Idiot savant, listen to you talking like a Cambridge don," the other guard chuckled.

Bailey smiled. "Hey, is that good enough to write in your little book of phrases, Inspector? Idiot savant? I think I can spell it for you."

Krogh turned to both of them and nodded politely. A bead of sweat trickled down the side of his face. "Yes. Thank you. Let me open my book."

Slowly, he slithered his hand into the darkness of his pocket and wrapped it around the Luger.

"I . . . d . . . i . . . "

"Could you both come a little closer, please?"

"Sure thing, Inspector."

As Bailey and his friend came forward, Krogh drew the gun with a heavy heart. Before Bailey even realized what it was, Krogh fired directly into his forehead. Krogh was surprised at how small the entry wound was. Barely visible. But the other guard, just behind him, had been splattered with blood.

"Oh—" Bailey said.

Krogh was unsure if he were registering surprise, or continuing his spelling. In any case, he was pleased to believe that he had not suffered much.

As Bailey crumpled to the ground, Krogh turned the pistol on the other guard. This one was shaking, as if just about to understand what had happened. Before he could move, Krogh fired. Regrettably, the bullet hit him square in the nose, making a little black hole of its point. This forced Krogh to fire again. The second man dropped.

Three bullets. Not bad.

The monster was howling, his chains rattling loudly. If the gunshots didn't bring the others running, this racket surely would. Krogh had only seconds.

He stepped up to the creature. It twisted its head this way and that, gnashing its teeth and snarling. He had to be sure his aim was true. Another second was all it would take. He pressed the barrel against the monster's forehead. It writhed wildly, as if it had been touched with hot metal.

Krogh reasoned it knew what it was, and feared the pain.

Krogh smiled and squeezed the trigger. The gun fired as the monster twitched its head sideways. The bullet careened across the skull, opening a thick wide wound, but it did not pierce the bone. Worse, the creature now shrieked like a pig being slaughtered.

"Damn you, stay still!" Krogh shouted.

But the creature's writhing, newly desperate, had only served to loosen his chains a bit, giving him more room.

There were footsteps down the hall. They were coming. They would see.

In a mad flash, Krogh leapt atop the creature, straddling it with his legs. He held the monster's bony, bloody head with one hand as he tried to force the gun into its mouth.

The monster huffed and bucked like a wild horse, but Krogh managed to move his left hand down to the creature's lips, which he tore at in an effort to get it to open its mouth.

It snapped and bit, severing the first knuckle of Krogh's pinky. Pained and furious, Krogh gave up on the mouth and shoved the gun's barrel into the creature's nostril. He was about to pull the trigger again when he heard a loud scraping, like metal against stone.

Something heavy slapped against his back and side.

A chain! One of the chains has come loose!

Before he could do more than realize that, the monster's arm followed. It wrapped around Krogh's back, grabbed his face with his hand and pulled. Krogh fired, but he couldn't see where the bullet went because the monster's fingers were ripping the skin near his eyes.

He felt himself fly across the cell, twisting as he went. Then he slammed against a stone wall. Things cracked all along his back. Air burst from his mouth as it might from a popped balloon. He hit the ground, landing on top of Bailey's dead body, thinking he would never be able to rise again.

Breathless, he watched as the stuff of nightmares rose, shedding its remaining chains as if they were ill-fitting clothes. It stood and snarled as three more officers arrived on the scene and piled into the room. It slammed both of its arms into the first one. Krogh could actually see the man's shoulders collapse.

Swinging again, it knocked the other two out of the way and headed for the door.

In the doorway it paused, just for an instant, and turned to look back at Krogh.

There were more footsteps and shouting. The monster stumbled out into the hall.

Krogh was surprised he could still move. Even more surprised he could pull himself free from the corpse and stand. As he hovered above the men he'd killed, and the monster's three newest victims, the oddest thought occurred to him:

It's not over yet.

Now, perhaps they would be forced to destroy the monster. The dead men could be explained by his efforts to shoot the creature. He could still perhaps return home, and, given enough time, forget what he had done.

A howl quickened his limping steps. At the end of the hallway, he saw the monster beating at the closed doorway as a crowd of officers outside struggled to pull it shut.

The creature's back was to him. How many bullets did he have left? He walked up and stopped, two yards away. Then he aimed and fired. Coming in at an angle, the bullet again glanced off the skull. The monster howled. Its hand shot up toward the spot where the bullet hit. It turned and glared.

"Krogh," the creature said. Ignoring the door, he came forward.

Moving backwards, Krogh fired again. A complete miss.

He fired again. The bullet tore into the creature's neck. Blood spurted and began gushing down its chest. For a moment, as the creature staggered, Krogh imagined he had won.

But then it came forward again.

"Nyragghhhh!"

Krogh feared he was out of bullets, but it didn't matter, because he never had a chance to fire again. The creature lifted him, by his neck and crotch, marched him down the hall, and slammed him into the little window opposite its cell.

Krogh watched the creature's face as it strained and pushed. It was using him as a battering ram. He felt himself limply slam into the glass, the metal, and the stone, felt his bones crunch as the creature hammered him into the opening, again and again. Hopelessly disoriented by pain and shock, Krogh couldn't tell if the window were crumbling, the hole getting bigger, or his body, worn away by the assault, was getting smaller. He only knew that he was getting pushed further and further into the wall, until finally, he fell outside and saw unfiltered daylight in the sky above him.

The monster hovered over him. Their eyes met. For a moment, as Krogh looked into those goblin eyes, at the deadness that did not belong at all to this world, he realized how foolish it had been to think he could kill such a thing.

This was the monster, after all, Krogh realized. Not some mere experiment by an obsessive nobleman. This was the one that skulked behind every human fear, that had been chasing humans in their nightmares since the first man first dreamed. The one that takes our children, the one that eats our souls, the one that kills us all.

The tortured creature lifted Krogh one last time, tearing his shirt at the pocket. Krogh's little note tumbled out. Sounds came from all around, screams and tramping feet, screeching brakes. The monster turned to them, and, doubtless sensing Krogh was as good as dead, let the body fall.

Krogh landed on his side, whatever was left of his rib cage collapsing under its own weight. He could no longer move, but at least he had the note in his field of vision. There was a tear in it, from where the pin had held it, but the words were still legible:

I love you both. Do not take my failures as your own.

———◆———

At roughly the same moment, before the news could spread, the long, bony fingers of Mr. Burke drew the blinds of his storefront closed as quickly as he could, as if fearful the sunlight might want to eavesdrop. Ghostlike, he moved his tall, thin form toward the shop door and flipped the sign to indicate that his medical supply store was closed.

This accomplished, a pleasant smile blossomed on his face and he resumed his position behind the counter. He looked again at the piece of paper on which his esteemed guest had scribbled a considerable sum as proposed payment for some special services.

Born to wealth and title, Frankenstein had little understanding of the intricacies and niceties of bargaining, and even less patience for a process he deemed a nuisance. Every moment wasted here was another he could spend on a dozen needed preparations. But, since it would no longer do for him to be seen in the graveyards of London, this particular arrangement was the most crucial of all, so he'd have to bear with it.

When Burke kept staring at the figure and didn't respond quickly enough, he blurted out, "Isn't the amount satisfactory? I require the best specimens possible in a short amount of time. I can pay more if need be."

Burke's pleasant smile spread wider. "Baron, let me assure you, for the type of money you've indicated here, I could get you any bodies in London, living or dead."

Frankenstein furrowed his brow. The man's reach was far. Recalling Stimpson, the morgue attendant at the police station, a darkling thought leapt to the forefront of his busy mind.

After considering it a moment, Frankenstein asked, "Do you mean that? *Any* body?"

Burke stiffened slightly, as if his pride had been insulted. "Yes, sir. Any body."

Frankenstein's eyes danced from the dusty plastic models, to the shelves, and back to Burke. Did he dare?

The Ripper was a callous killer. He'd hurt Elizabeth if he could. But what if his experiment failed? What if he failed to control the ray and made the Ripper eternal?

That was always a possibility, however slight, but now, the baron had a better idea, a more *appropriate* idea, one whose success might even mitigate the enormity of his failures.

Chapter Twenty-Four

The hills of Hampstead Heath were the highest points in London, and these stairs, carved from the bedrock beneath its grassy hills, led to one of the deepest; an unused, uncompleted tube station that would have been called North End. The station, begun in 1907, was abandoned because the proposed above-ground access was on conserved land, and not enough people lived in the area to make fighting over it worthwhile.

The stairwell went a long way down. One hundred and ninety-seven steps, according to the metal sign hanging in the gloom. Inspector Devin looked down into the abyss, shook his head, and ordered one of the six patrolmen with him to find something to prop open the door.

"Don't want to get stuck in here."

"No, sir."

As he stared, the blackness in the center of the staircase welled, as if ready to push between the cold steel handrails, spill over onto the concrete steps, then rise up toward them, as if it were an ocean of shadow and the tide was coming in.

"Come on, then. Let's get on with it."

The men shifted on their feet, fell in behind him.

Sink or swim, Devin told himself, pointing his little electric torch at the first of the many steps. *For the sleep of reason brings monsters.*

As they descended, the sound of the thunderstorm outside muffled, then vanished. Soon, all they heard was the echo of their own footfalls.

Over the last two weeks since the prisoner's escape, there had been many casualties. By Devin's own estimation, the least among them was his career. The murder of Mary Blyss under their noses had strained his position. The fact that the foreigner he'd aided, the late Inspector Krogh, was suspected of freeing the prisoner and shooting two men had crippled him politically. Almost mercifully, last week's stunning robbery from the police morgue had done him in.

Devin, mundane imagination and all, had learned just yesterday that he was to be taken off all his cases and possibly put on suspension pending a review.

He'd been methodically clearing out his desk at Scotland Yard, sorting personal items from those belonging to the office, when bright-faced Bartleby from the Research Division bounded in.

The man was so excited he gibbered more than spoke, and his usually ruddy cheeks had been rendered pink by excitement. It took a few moments for Devin to realize the man was gesticulating at a page in the evening paper. Two personal ads had been circled in red grease pencil. Though grateful for the distraction, Devin was too distracted to see any connection between the two.

Bartleby, with baited breath, was happy to explain.

"Lusk, Abberline," Bartleby said, pointing to the names in the ads.

Devin shrugged. Bartleby pointed and said again, "Lusk, Abberline."

"Yes," Devin said. "George Lusk was head of a neighborhood watch-group that hunted the original Jack the Ripper. The famous letter 'From Hell' is addressed to Mr. Lusk from the Ripper. And Abberline was the Whitechapel inspector who headed the investigation. Yes. What of it?"

"Chief Inspector, look, one names a date, tomorrow, the other a place, the North End Station," Bartleby sputtered.

Devin leaned over and looked closer as Bartleby concluded, "It's a message about the Ripper, or *to*, or *from* him."

Devin frowned. "But there is no North End Station."

Bartleby positively brightened. "Oh, but sir, there is."

Of course the following night was the wettest of the year. Of course they had to slosh through a hundred yards of mud to get to the entrance, which was little more than a door and a cinderblock building sitting in the middle of a field. Of course it was a ridiculous longshot that these ads had anything to do with anything.

But Devin knew it would take a ridiculous longshot to nab the killer now. He'd been inactive since the Mary Blyss slaying, and expert opinion was that he'd gone into retirement, or back into retirement, if you believed in ghosts. So Devin had to check it out. For better or worse, his higher-ups were happy to let him make a fool of himself one last time.

And here they were, walking down into hell, the air growing heavier and dustier with each step.

From Hell, to Hell. With love.

"Do you really think the Ripper might be down here, sir?" one of the men said.

"First of all, he is not Jack the Ripper. Second of all, no, I do not," Devin said. "Otherwise I'd have brought a lot more men. Furthermore—"

A low moan came up from the deep: short, indistinct, but plaintive. It stopped them all in their tracks.

"That sounded like . . . " one of the patrolmen said.

"Don't be ridiculous," Devin said, though the sound chilled him. "Probably just a cat. A metal girder stressing from a change in temperature. That door hasn't been opened in years."

They resumed their walk, but one of the patrolmen kept talking.

"I was at Commercial Street when it escaped. Just like being in the trenches again; body parts flying, blood and broken bits of building everywhere, and above it all, the monster screaming, just like that."

Devin reared and hissed, "If there *is* anyone down there, I'd just as soon not announce our presence."

Monster. Useless word. Monster. After all, what *wasn't* a monster? A lion was a monster, if it chased you. A spouse was a monster, if they bore down on you with a rolling pin. The storm brewing overhead was a monster, according to the weather service. Devin's raw, bitter shame, that was a monster, too.

But there was nothing preternatural about any of that, was there?

The sound didn't come again, but even Devin had to admit to himself that he was wondering if it could be the escaped prisoner. Wounded, hurt, hit by bullets again and again, he'd vanished after his escape. The theory was he'd reached the sewer system. Without a sighting since, everyone was starting to believe he'd died down there. But if he hadn't, maybe he moved through the tube tunnels, trying to head out of London, or toward fewer people.

Hampstead Heath was a natural location for both.

Pointed down, the weak light of Devin's torch made out a wide-open area. In a few more moments, they arrived at the bottom.

The North End Station wasn't even a station, really, just a section of the curved tube tunnel that had been widened, but not even tiled, leaving the unfinished concrete exposed. No platform had ever been built, and the last step opened onto a small flat area that barely held the seven men. To further examine the area, they had to climb down a series of iron rungs, which brought them down to the level of the train tracks.

All around them was darkness.

I doubt anyone's around here, then. They'd need light, wouldn't they?

He shone his light on his watch fob. "Next train in seven minutes. Let's be sure not to be on the tracks when it arrives, shall we?"

The men chuckled as Devin scanned their surroundings. His torch dimly pierced an area fifty feet from them, where the curved tunnel narrowed again, but none of the blackness beyond. He had better success lighting the few open tunnels that lay across from them, perpendicular to the tracks.

"Passageways to the other tracks, or access halls to elevator shafts that were never dug," Devin said. "Let's split up, have a look. Ashby, Foss, and Barton take the main shaft; Griffith and Hayman the right; Collins come with me up the middle. Let's get on with it."

Shortly, seven yellow circles shone on bare walls, dirt, and concrete. "We meet back here after the train's passed, about eight minutes. Use your whistles if you see anything other than a rat or a cat," Devin said, and then he moved on.

Mud and gravel scrunched beneath his soggy shoes. He led the young patrolman with him across the tracks and into the first tunnel, where their twin beams lit a square of ceiling and floor.

"Not a cross tunnel," Devin said, noting the shape. "May be elevator access, or storage."

After several yards, the tunnel opened into a large rectangular space, tiled with the typical white squares of the London transport system. They hovered at its entrance, the space too large for their lights to cover. Devin made out old crates, awkwardly stacked, their raw wooden surfaces covered in a thin layer of grit and dust.

"Storage, then," Devin said.

Something rustled.

"Did you hear that, sir?"

Devin didn't answer, but his torch light danced across the crates, the walls, and floor, trying, but failing, to find the source.

"Probably a rat, but let's have a look," Devin said, stepping in.

The sound of their footsteps was sharper here than on the stairwell or in the main tunnel. The scraping of their soles against the floor hit the tiled walls and crashed back at them with a tinny echo that made it impossible to tell even where their own footsteps came from.

"Collins, shut off the light and stand still a minute," Devin said. "If it's an animal, the more we're hidden, the sooner it will show itself."

The young bobby hesitated, then complied.

As Devin flicked off his torch, the web of black that threatened them on the stairs swallowed them whole. Strange flashes, like light, skittered before his eyes.

"Give yourself a moment to adjust. And listen, listen," Devin whispered.

Devin started listening himself. Air whistled through the train tunnel they'd left behind. Somewhere, drops of water fell through dusty air and plinked on the ground. Eyes growing accustomed to the gloom, Devin pivoted his head toward the entrance and noticed a dull brown glow. He frowned.

Is there light down here? Did we miss it because of the torches?

The whistling grew in intensity, interspersed by a strange crackling.

What the devil is that? The train? It's early.

Devin's reverie was broken by a loud thud, the sound of a body dropping.

"Collins?" Devin shouted. He reached for his pistol with one hand and flipped on the torch with the other. With both hands occupied, he couldn't whistle for the others, and instead tried to reorient himself in the room.

Collins was gone, at least nowhere to be seen. At first it seemed as though nothing had changed, but then Devin noticed some dark spots on the ground.

Blood?

He bent down for a better look. Yes, they looked like blood, but something was off. He leaned down closer, put his pinky finger in the fluid, and brought it under the torchlight.

His old eyes must have been playing tricks on him, because he could swear the liquid was pulsating, like it was alive. It was impossible. Blood was not supposed to behave that way.

And the sleep of reason brings monsters.

A terrible howl turned his head. A lumbering form rose from behind the old crates holding a limp Collins aloft by his coat. Though Devin had seen it in the light, in chains, here the sallow white face and misshapen skull had a different sort of power. He, for all his mundane imagination, suddenly found he had no qualms about calling this thing "it."

Being a man of reason, Devin did not expect to survive this encounter, but being British, he had to try. He shone the flashlight in its face, to distract it.

"Nyargghhh!" it wailed as it put its arms to its face, dropping the unconscious Collins the short distance to the ground.

He could clearly see how its flat, giant head was full of scars from the attacks of men who had tried to kill it. With Collins reasonably out of range, Devin fired, hitting it in the shoulder.

It wailed and rushed forward, pushing Devin out of the way and stomping off into the depths of the room. Devin raced toward Collins, happy to be alive himself, but then realizing something was wrong. It should have killed him instead of running, unless it'd been hurt more than they thought during its escape. Perhaps it'd wandered here to lick its wounds.

But what a coincidence that would be—looking for the

new Ripper and finding the creature. Too much a coincidence. Devin felt dizzied by the possibility he'd never really entertained, the monster, Frankenstein, and the Ripper all in league.

Devin knelt by Collins, put two fingers to his throat, and felt a steady pulse.

Good, just knocked out. Now to warn the others.

Grabbing his whistle, Devin started blowing. When there was no immediate response, he rose and stumbled down the corridor, back to the main tunnel, and blew again. This time, he heard the distant rumble and whine of the coming train.

Frantic, he blew again and again, but each time, the train grew louder, overwhelming the shrill sound more and more.

The train flashed by him, a kaleidoscope of snaking gray metal and yellow light shining through blackened windows. It roared off down the tunnel, making even the far darkness glow. Devin waited as it receded, then blew his whistle again.

But there was nothing, nothing. Where were they?

He turned off his torch, hoping darkness would make it easier to see their light. Instead all he saw was a brown glow down the tracks, which, for the longest time, he believed was the train in the distance.

When it didn't change or diminish, when instead it seemed to flicker brighter, Devin realized it wasn't the train at all. There was something more than the monster down here.

Suddenly fearful of drawing further attention to himself, Devin lowered the whistle from his lips and crept forward. As the brown haze grew brighter, it seemed to flash, like a series of photographer's flashbulbs. The closer he got, the more he also heard. There was a crackle, a hum, and a low rumble, not at all like a train, but clearly from some sort of machine.

As he neared a bend in the tracks, he realized the lights and sounds were not from the main tunnel at all, but from a fourth, side corridor. He brought himself to its edge and peered inside. Because of all the light within, the view was easy, and complete.

And Chief Inspector Devin stumbled at last over the edge of his beloved mundane reasoning, into a world whose rules he could not understand.

There were crates, like the other room, but these were unpacked. Wires and all sorts of electrical gear filled the walls. Voltage meters rose and fell. Electricity arced between spheres, danced in the reflection of parabolic mirrors, crackled along tall poles and spat across black boards as if trying to escape and run wild.

In the center, where most of the wires led, was a long table with a body on it. It was wrapped completely in gauze held in place by safety pins, looking like an Egyptian mummy, though anything but ancient. A series of evenly spaced half rings, grouped three together, went all the way up its form, save the top, where flat silver circles of metal touched the sides of the unseen head.

Hanging directly above the body was the oddest device of all: two spheres of metal rings at either end of a long pole. In its center were more rings, vertical, rising up to the height of the ceiling.

And there, in the midst of what looked to Devin like the unfathomable insides of a wireless radio, stood Baron Frankenstein, dressed in a drab green lab coat, his hands covered in rubber gloves, his back arched, his head leaning forward as he screamed at the only other moving figure in the room.

"I said no more killing!"

The target of his rage was a man, thick, misshapen, attempting to hide his bestial form in the folds of a gentleman's cape. But he could not hide the animal nature of his voice as he snarled back. "I must protect myself . . . and you, Mr. Baron! Would you have us both arrested? And your wife dead?"

Blood still dripped from the man's long knife.

It was then Devin noticed the bodies of four of his patrol-men on the floor. Two were clearly dead from long cuts in the torso. The third, though bloody, still moved, while the fourth was too obscured to evaluate.

Frankenstein hovered over a fifth body, which had been placed haphazardly atop some of the empty crates. He was poking about a bloody wound in the man's abdomen with his long, fingers, moving them like the probing legs of a spider. "You stupid, blind, stubborn fool. The time I spend mending these men will take me away from the experiment! The storm is nearly at its peak and our window of opportunity will only be open so long!"

"Then leave them to bleed to death!" the man said.

"No!"

The man raised his blade. "Leave them Mr. Baron, or old Jack will cut you open worse!"

Frankenstein stopped and eyed him, his face a placid sheet except for the sneer. "Go ahead. Kill me if you like. Then you can try to remove your own brain and put it in the body!"

The man clenched his fists and shook. "Ahhh! You're a senti-mental clown! You'll be the death of your wife, Frankenstein! Not I!"

"Shut up! You're only making this take longer. Make yourself useful, check the lines for the kites. I had to run them all the way up the ventilation shafts. We must be certain the wires are all taut and untangled."

The man blasted some air through his nose. "Where are the shafts?"

Frankenstein's tone softened slightly. "The tunnel on the right, toward the back. Follow the main wires."

The man ambled off.

As Frankenstein pierced the officer with his needle, he winced and wriggled.

"Try not to move," Frankenstein cautioned. "You'll ruin my stitching. That's one advantage to working with the dead, they don't squirm about while you're trying to reconnect them."

Devin's mind swam in the flood of information, leaping from one impossible conclusion to another: *Could* everything *Krogh have said be true? Could that man be Jack the Ripper?*

It didn't matter. It could all be sorted out later. Right now he had two dead, three wounded, and the killer still loose. Frankenstein, he figured, would not put up much of a struggle, so the so-called Ripper was the one to contend with first.

Crouching low behind the crackling equipment, Devin made his way toward the tunnel the Ripper had disappeared down. He felt his meager hair stand from the static electricity in the air. As he passed close to the crates Hayman had been laid upon, Devin briefly caught his eyes and gave him a nod. The man said nothing, but his face relaxed, leading Frankenstein to comment, "There, you see? It's not so bad."

With the baron thus occupied, Devin slipped into the corridor, pistol out and ready to fire. The sound from his movements was masked by the hum and crackle of the equipment behind him, so he moved quickly and soon spotted the Ripper, talking to himself as he fidgeted with a series of tight wires that led through an open square in the ceiling.

"Thinks I'm his whore," the Ripper said, gnashing his teeth. "What am I supposed to do with this? What? The only use I know for a wire is as a garrote!"

Devin ducked as the Ripper turned from his work and shouted down the hall. "How in bloody hell am I supposed to make sure the wire is loose, your majesty?"

Frankenstein's voice came back, "Just tug on it then let go. If it gives, then rises, the line is free and the kite is fine!"

"All right, all right," the Ripper said, again turning his back on Devin. He wrapped his thick fingers around the first black line, pulled, then released it. He was about to move to the second line when Devin closed the distance between them, rose, and pressed the barrel of his gun to the back of the Ripper's head.

"Don't make a move or a sound, or I'll happily blow your filthy head off," Devin whispered.

The Ripper froze, but strained his eyes to look around. "If you wanted to do that, you could have already, sir," he whispered back.

Devin shook his head. "Much as I'd like, it's my job to arrest you and bring you to trial."

"So you like to play fairly? How about you put the gun down and we settle this fairly, with knives?"

"You misunderstand. You are under arrest. Now slowly, put your hands behind your back," Devin said.

The Ripper complied. As Devin clicked the handcuffs on him, the Ripper said, "Might I at least have the pleasure of a name, sir?"

"Chief Inspector Devin," Devin answered. At once, the Ripper began to cackle.

Devin tightened the cuffs, making them dig into his thick hairy wrists. "What's so funny, you devil?"

"I read about your dismissal in the papers. So, you finally did your job, but a bit too late, eh?" the Ripper said. "Too late for Mary Blyss in any case."

His next cackle was cut short when Devin rammed the Ripper's forehead into the concrete wall.

"I'm going to try very hard not to make any more mistakes. Now, move!" Devin said, shoving him forward.

They appeared at the head of the tunnel just as Frankenstein tied the knot on his final stitch.

"Baron Frankenstein," Devin announced. "You are under arrest. Put your hands where I can see them."

Frankenstein's already pale face went a deathly shade of white, almost reminding Devin of the monster's bloodless skin. Rather than comply, he seemed to go into some sort of tantrum, turning this way and that, twisting his hands and shaking his head.

"No! No, no, no! Not now! Not now! He's kidnapped my wife! He has Elizabeth! That's the only reason I'm doing any of this! If I don't help him, she'll die! You must let him go at once! You must!"

"Stand still, Baron," Devin said. "We'll get the information out of him."

"I think not," the Ripper said calmly, directing his comments at the frantic baron. "At least not for thirty days, and by then she'll dead of hunger."

Frankenstein's eyes went wide. "No, no! You must let him go, you must!"

Devin raised the gun, fearful the baron might try something foolish. "I'm telling you again to stand still, Baron. I'll shoot you if I must."

Frankenstein kept pacing, rubbing his hair, slapping his thighs, pulling at his fingers.

"I said, STAND STILL!" Devin shouted. To better make his point, he fired the gun toward the ceiling. Bits of concrete dust tumbled from the spot where the bullet lodged.

Frankenstein froze, chest heaving. "Very well, Inspector. My wife's fate will be in your hands."

Devin waved him closer. His body remained motionless, but Frankenstein twisted his head slightly to the side, briefly giving him the appearance of a pale reptile.

"Wait a moment. Do you see that long device hanging above the body? It's called a cosmic diffuser. Right now, it's building up a charge from lightning hitting kites flying in the storm above us. Unless I release that charge, all this equipment will explode with enough force to collapse this tunnel and bury us all," Frankenstein said. "You must let me discharge it."

Devin eyed the strange equipment, trying to decide whether to believe him or not. The crackling increased in intensity. The whole room seemed to hum with power. "All right, Baron, shut it down, but do it quickly."

Frankenstein moved slowly and deliberately toward one of the many control panels and indicated a large lever in the center. "This will disconnect the wires from the kites and allow the energy to dissipate safely. Just let me pull it and you can do with me what you will."

Devin nodded.

His black eyes on Devin, Frankenstein pulled down on the lever.

Electric arcs cascaded through the equipment, crackling louder and faster en route to the thing the baron had called a diffuser. Before Devin realized what was happening, he felt the gun in his hand pulled toward the diffuser by a tremendous force. As he struggled to hold the gun, a hot white arc flew from one of the diffuser's spheres directly into his gun. At once his whole body felt stiff, paralyzed.

Then everything went black.

Voices sparred in blackness.

"Damn you, sir! Will you take these handcuffs off me now?"

"No, you'll keep them on until the experiment is complete! I've seen what your hands do when they're free."

"This is not acceptable. This is not a part of our arrangement."

"Then I suggest you do what all life does when faced with a new situation: Adapt."

There was an odd smell in the air, the clean, sharp aroma of air churned by the sea. Ozone. But, surely he wasn't at the beach?

As Devin regained consciousness, though his hands and legs were tied, he could move his body again. Wriggling, he opened his eyes and let in a slit of light, a slit occupied by the face of Henry Frankenstein.

The baron was leaning forward over the bound inspector, his head floating like a snake's, brow furrowed, sharp eyes focused, a sparkle in them as he spoke.

"Good to see you coming around, Inspector. I'm sorry to say you've experienced a very powerful electrical shock. You've got a bit of a burn on your right hand that will make operating your firearm a little difficult until it heals. You'll also probably have a terrible headache for while, but other than that, you should be fine," he said.

"What did you do to me?" Devin asked.

Frankenstein smiled slightly. "Part of what I told you was true. The Cosmic Diffuser has been building up an electric charge. I released it, however, into the room. The odds were in my favor due to your location, but I have to say I was a bit lucky that the charge found your gun. Do believe me when I say I'm very glad you're awake and well. I very much want a man of reason to witness what's about to happen here," Frankenstein said.

As he stood and backed up more of the room came into focus. He could see now that the Ripper was seated, his hands still chained behind him by the handcuffs.

Frankenstein lowered his gaze and motioned toward the Ripper. "The first thing you have to understand is that I am not a murderer. This man is. He says he is the original Jack the Ripper, kept alive by consuming a brew that utilizes a fresh human uterus. I disbelieved this claim at first, but having examined him, I've discovered certain anomalies in his physical form that lead me to believe his strange story may well be true."

"Preposterous," Devin said.

Frankenstein shrugged. "Perhaps, but a man such as myself has gotten used to trafficking in the preposterous. Nevertheless, he is responsible for the recent murders."

"If you're innocent, release me, and help me bring him to justice," Devin said.

Frankenstein laughed bitterly, bringing out his natural sneer. "As if a jury of my peers *could* be found. No, Inspector Devin, much as I'd like to, I can't. You see, as I said earlier, he has my wife and won't tell me where she is until I've put his brain in a new, immortal body."

He pointed toward the thing on the table, now covered in a sheet. "That one."

The Ripper shouted, rising. "Don't tell him, you idiot! Now I'll have to kill him!"

Frankenstein wheeled at the Ripper and spoke as if to an unruly dog. "And I said no more killing! I want something more than a beast to understand what I'm accomplishing here! As for your precious identity, I promise you, it won't be a concern."

The Ripper huffed and glared. "It had better not be."

Calming himself, he turned back to Devin. "Some people believe life came from some powerful spirit taming a primordial chaos, call it God if you like, who invested it with shape and purpose. Others, scientists, believe life formed randomly under natural conditions, most likely in the sea. As it turns out, that's true, but it's only part of the solution. You see, I discovered that life came from the sky, not from some old man dictating terms, but from the lightning. Electricity, which we've only begun to tame, is just the smallest, most visible face of the force that resides in those fantastic currents. There also exists in lightning frequencies we can't yet imagine, among them the pure ray, beyond the ultraviolet, that first called forth life from the primordial soup."

As the baron spoke, he seemed carried off by his own words, as if his body could barely contain the concepts he was trying to communicate.

Devin used the opportunity to try to wriggle free. When a searing pain flared in his right hand, he realized the baron had spoken the truth about a burn. There was also some sort of bandage on it that made moving his pained fingers doubly difficult.

"What hit you was the undifferentiated force," Frankenstein said. "In that state, all it can do is damage." He swept his arms across the collected equipment. "But here, these carefully calibrated machines can filter out all the other aspects and leave only the pure ray, which will bathe this body that I made from the pieces of the dead, and, as you will see, give it life."

"And this is how you made the demented creature? The one who killed all those people?" Devin asked.

Frankenstein frowned, then nodded. "A mistake. A bad brain was used. I begged Krogh to let me correct it, but he refused, and look what became of him. I pray the nightmare of its existence is finally over, that it found some quiet corner and finally perished."

Devin frowned. "Then you don't know? It's still alive, and here in the tunnels."

Frankenstein lunged forward. "What? *Still* alive?"

Devin nodded. "Yes, and not far. It's wounded, but not so much so it couldn't knock out one of my men and threaten me."

Frankenstein shook his head slightly and stared ahead, focusing for a moment on nothing visible. "Even all those wounds, even all those gunshots, and the ray would not let it die. Stunning," he said softly. "Stunning."

The Ripper's reaction was more direct. "Let me go!" he screamed. "That thing nearly killed me twice! I'll not have it come at me with my hands behind my back!"

Frankenstein sneered at his captive, obviously relishing his fear and pain. "No. The storm is at its peak. We must act now. You and I will be done, and then I'll deal with my first creation."

The Ripper calmed. "Now?"

Frankenstein checked a dial and nodded. "Yes."

Something inside Devin snapped, and he finally shook with fear and believed. "You can't!" he cried. "You must realize it would be madness to give a killer a powerful body like that! He would be unstoppable! It would be nothing short of evil to accede to his wishes!"

The Ripper smiled. "Oh, he's not evil, or he'd have let me kill you and your men. This one's different than me. He just thinks he loves his wife."

"Baron Frankenstein, you mustn't!"

The baron turned from his equipment to face Devin one last time, his features softening. He came close and spoke quietly so the Ripper would not hear. "I know you've no reason to, but you must trust me. There is a point. One which I suspect, if you do not agree with, at least you'll appreciate."

Devin was not comforted and went back to working on his bonds.

Frankenstein turned to the Ripper and helped him to his feet. "I'll require one last thing from you."

The Ripper glared and gritted his teeth. "At this rate, sir, I have little left. I've half a mind to take a finger from your woman for every indignity you've made me suffer here."

"I'll have your book," Frankenstein said. "Your precious formula for immortality."

The Ripper laughed. "Fine. Take it from my jacket pocket. I'm sure you'll enjoy the pictures, sir. I've committed every blessed line to memory. It's a part of me now."

"Yes, I'm sure it is," Frankenstein said. He reached into the Ripper's pocket and withdrew a small musty bundle. He placed it on a table, then turned his eyes toward the ceiling.

"Do you hear it?"

Before either could answer, he dived for one of the larger consoles and began adjusting the dials with his long, steady fingers, his hands twitching in tune with the pulsing meters.

"Normally, I'd raise the body to the highest level possible, so it could experience the full effects of the ray, but I've found a heavier gauge wire here in your country, Inspector, that I believe negates that necessity," Frankenstein said, staring at the dials. "Yes. It's working. There'll be some sparks, you might want to close your eyes a moment."

He flipped a lever and at once electric arcs undulated through the metal and across the air. As the white flashes moved, he turned more dials, flipped more levers, as if coaxing and adjusting each spark as it went along its way. As Devin watched, he realized Frankenstein's movements were like the electricity itself, seemingly erratic, explosive, but full of power and purpose. It was a dance between the two, between the man and the primal force he trained before their eyes.

The sparks leapt into the air, as if trying to free themselves, but he brought them back down. When they seemed so dim they would die, he breathed new fire into them. When they splayed, he honed them, when they split, he drew them into one.

He rode the current and, in time, it bowed to his will. It was as if he'd grabbed starlight and dragged it down into the room.

The spheres at either end of the cosmic diffuser began to glow brighter and brighter, throbbing to white heat, fading to black, then throbbing again, full of every color imaginable, and even achieving a few that Devin swore he'd never seen before.

After a time, though, the strange, and some would say unholy, partnering simply stopped. With a series of flicks Frankenstein turned the equipment off. The hum lowered, the crackling ceased, and all that was left of the magnificent display was a few wisps of smoke and the smell of smoldering wires.

Sweating, panting, Frankenstein pulled off his rubber gloves and rushed up to the wrapped body. He pushed the diffuser aside as if it were an unwanted toy, ripped off the circular bands, and tossed them carelessly about the room. Gently, reverently, he knelt by the fingers of its hand, held his breath, and stared.

Within seconds of having his attention, they trembled, flexed, and clenched.

Still breathing heavy, Frankenstein rose and faced his captive guests.

"It's alive," he whispered hoarsely, and though he remained motionless, Devin could see a powerful shudder run the length of the baron's body.

"Wait," the Ripper said, his own voice trembling with concern. "If it's alive already, how are you going to get my brain into it?"

Frankenstein turned to him, his black eyes glowing with a madness that put the Ripper's to shame. "You fool. The only thing I'd put your brain in is the grave."

Before another word could be spoken, Frankenstein started to pull off the bandages. As soon as its white, bony legs were free, he helped it to sitting and started to remove the rest, revealing, bit by bit, a short but powerful form that was only vaguely female.

The white gauze came off the hands, revealing long curved fingernails that were more like claws. Pulling the bandages from its chest and torso revealed a horrid white body, full of scars which Devin recognized as being as haphazard and hurried as the attacks of the Ripper himself.

"Recognize it?" Frankenstein bellowed. "Any of the pieces perhaps? The hands? The mangled abdomen? No?"

He pulled back the bandages on the head revealing a face wrinkled from the decay of death, but still possessed of the sweet monkey features of Mary Blyss. What once had been a gay mane of brown hair now stood jagged and white, circling her partially rotted face like a child's drawing of sunbeams.

The eyes rolled wildly in their sockets, as if they were the only things alive in her and now found themselves buried in an otherwise dead body.

"How about the face?" Frankenstein asked. "Don't you recognize your last victim? I think she'll recognize you."

Devin watched in horror as the frantic eyes of Mary Blyss settled on the Ripper and filled with hatred. They seemed to be struggling to pull the rest of the body along toward him. All at once, the creature lurched to standing. As Frankenstein steadied it, it mewled at him in a horrible voice, like hot air forced through a filthy chimney.

"Curssachhhhhh!"

The Ripper wobbled and struggled to his feet, fear dancing in his wretched expression. "Sir, this, this is a most foul betrayal! I'd imagined we'd had a deal, and my part of the bargain would have been kept."

Frankenstein shook his head. "There was never any deal between us, only your blackmail, so here's a bit of mine in return. I used to think the brain a mere piece of tissue, but I've learned the hard way it contains at the very least the echoes of the life it experienced, and, at most, perhaps what the superstitious would call a soul. You would kill in any body you were given. But here now at least, you face your own victims."

The Ripper stumbled backwards, knocking over the crate on which he'd been seated.

"Kill me, sir and you kill your wife!" he screamed.

The thing took two steps forward. The head craned and snapped its teeth, as if the rest of the body were chains that held it back.

"Curssachhhhh!"

Frankenstein glared at the frightened slayer of whores. "I can't kill you. I'm no murderer. But my children seem to have a knack for it."

Devin, still struggling with his own bonds, called out, "Baron, don't be insane! You can't just let it kill him!"

Frankenstein threw a glance at Devin. "Don't you see the beauty of it, Inspector? It's up to him." Then he turned back to the Ripper, who'd walked himself backwards into a concrete wall and now eyed all the possible exits from the room.

"Tell me," Frankenstein said, as the handcuffed Ripper tried to balance the need for speed with a greater need to remain standing. "Tell me where my wife is and I'll tell you how you can still live."

"No! Never! Let the bitch die!"

"Then I'll let it have you."

"Hoorsahchhhhhh!" it hissed, coming forward, gnashing its teeth.

The Ripper looked around like a trapped beast. The new creature was picking up speed and only a few yards away. He kicked a small crate at it. It caught it in one hand, crushed the wood in its fingers. It didn't even turn its gaze from him as the shards and splinters tumbled to the floor.

"Damn you! Damn you to the foulest pit, sir! I will have my revenge."

"Unless you speak quickly, I'll have mine now!"

Devin noticed that Frankenstein's face had changed, his tone was a bit more hurried. He seemed worried the Ripper wouldn't be able to keep out of the new creature's clutches long enough to give him the information he sought.

The Ripper's eyes lurched back and forth between Frankenstein and the coming creature. It seemed to Devin the two were engaged in a deadly game of chicken, each wanting the other to flinch first.

Wincing, the inspector returned his attention to his hastily tied bonds and tried to work at them again. His gun, he could see, was atop a crate a few yards away. With all the excitement going on, it was just possible he could retrieve it.

Finally the Ripper let loose a hoarse, bestial cry. "All right! I'll tell you! She's in a flat on the second floor of 43 Thrawl Street, bound and gagged, but no worse for wear! Now call your creature off!"

"Forty-three Thrawl Street! I must go to her at once!" Frankenstein said, peeling off his lab coat.

The new creature took another step forward and raised its claw-like hands. The Ripper ducked in terror, moving his shoulder out of the way.

"Frankenstein! Help me!" he cried

Devin gritted his teeth and pulled his hands again. Pain soared through his arm like the electricity that had burned it in the first place.

Frankenstein narrowed his eyes. "I wonder if you gave any of your victims a chance to cry out. This is what you've wrought after all, your own crimes come to face you. But I'll keep my side of this bargain. I muted the ray. This creature has no more than two hours to live. If you can avoid it for just that long, you'll be free for Inspector Devin to arrest you and have you hanged."

"You bastard!" the Ripper cried, trying to leap out of the thing's way. This time he stumbled and fell on his back. As the creature hissed and came for him, he pushed himself backwards with his legs along the filthy floor, like a bloated, crippled spider, helpless before the fly.

Frankenstein headed for the corridor.

"Baron," the inspector called. "Stop where you are, please."

Devin was standing and had even retrieved his pistol, which he held shakily in his bandaged hand. Frankenstein eyed the weapon.

"I don't doubt you'd be able to squeeze the trigger, Inspector, but I do doubt you'd hit what you aimed for. And there is equipment in here, still charged, that could easily blow us all to atoms. But what do you want from me? All I want now is to save my wife. You must let me go to her. She could be starving, or worse, as we speak. Do you want the Ripper? He's yours if my creature doesn't get him first. But what do you want with me? By now you must believe I didn't kill those women."

Devin fought to hold the gun steady. He was sure the recoil from even one shot would cause him terrific agony. "I'm not certain what to believe anymore, Baron. But murder wasn't the only crime committed," Devin said.

Frankenstein smiled slightly. "What else? The theft of prostitutes' bodies that no one was ever going to claim for burial anyway? Blame the man who sold them to me, if you like, but I dare say the Ripper's victims might thank me for their chance at justice."

Devin eyed the frantic Ripper as he scrambled about the floor, inches ahead of the horrid thing that pursued him.

"Is that justice?" he asked.

"It may not be the letter of the law, but what about the spirit? Let me go, please. I must see to my wife."

The gun wavered in his hand. "What about your original creature?"

Frankenstein sighed. "It's a tormented beast with an overflow of life. It only wants to die. It believes I can help it do that, and will do as I say. Why not just leave it to me? I can promise it will trouble you no more. What's your choice, after all? Should you try to recapture it, more will die and then my attorneys will have it transferred to an asylum in my home country, in effect returning it to me, anyway."

"You'd kill it then. That's murder."

"Inspector, you have a first-rate mind trapped by second-rate beliefs. I gave it form, I gave it life. I'd only be correcting what I did in the first place."

"Does a mother have a right to kill her child, then?"

Frankenstein shook his head. "I don't know. But we both know the monster is no child."

"No, it's not," Devin said, and he finally lowered the gun.

Frankenstein nodded in brief thanks and sped off down the corridor.

"Help!" the Ripper cried. He rolled onto his back and started squirming across the floor on his belly.

"Get behind me," Devin said.

The Ripper struggled to get closer, but the new creature kept coming. It was smaller but stockier than the monster, but Devin knew if it was half as strong, it could rend both of them into pieces. The only reason the Ripper had survived this long was probably because the new thing had yet to discover its own strength.

When the Ripper was near enough, Devin raised his gun in the air and fired. The kickback jammed the gun into his wrist and he gave off a little moan.

Mary Blyss's head snapped up at the sound, startled. Bit by bit, the rest of the body followed along. She searched for the sound, looking up at the new tiny hole in the ceiling. Devin used the few moments to kneel down and, with his good left hand, grab the chain between the cuffs on the Ripper's hand and pull him to standing.

"Now stay behind me!" Devin said.

The Ripper, barely balanced on his feet, nodded.

By now the creature was no longer interested in the bullet hole. Mary Blyss's eyes once again began to search for the Ripper. They quickly spotted him, hunched behind Devin as the two tried to back toward the room's only exit.

Again, the eyes pulled the body along.

"Hsaachhhh . . . chsssss!" She snarled at Devin, warning him out of the way.

The body was getting more adept at obeying the eyes. Rather than a slow, shambling gait, it stumbled toward them in a half-run.

Devin and the Ripper were out of the room, almost at the corridor that led back to the tracks, but the Ripper wasn't moving quickly enough, letting the thing get nearer.

"It's almost on us!" Devin shouted. "Can't you go any faster?"

"No," the Ripper said. "But maybe you can slow her up for me!"

With that, the Ripper butted Devin in the back, sending him straight into the clutches of the female thing.

Devin felt small but powerful hands wrap around his elbows, then felt his body suddenly move as she pulled. He wasn't clear if she'd grabbed him, or the two had just become entangled, but for a moment, his own eyes met those two horrified, trapped orbs.

Then it twisted at the waist. He flew through the air like a sack of leaves, but hit the console like a middle-aged, overweight man, his head shattering the glass of several dials. As he crashed to the ground, for the second time in less than an hour, Chief Inspector Devin went unconscious.

Chapter Twenty-Five

Jack the Ripper had lived long enough to know not to look back when he was being chased by something that might kill him. Other than a curiosity about exactly what the creature could do to human flesh, he didn't particularly care what became of Devin. Fleeing with the same animal intensity he brought to his killing, he barreled into the main tunnel, nearly tripping on the steel tracks, then headed for the exit as fast as he could.

It was only when he reached the iron rungs that led to the small concrete landing, with the staircase to freedom beyond, that he realized he couldn't possibly climb them with his hands cuffed behind his back.

With the tunnels here all dead ends, and the nearest stations miles away, he was, in effect, trapped.

"Aghhh!" His shout echoed down the tunnel.

"Hsachhh . . . krgggllshhhhh!" the cry came back.

A quick rustling followed, then the sound of small feet on dirt and gravel, moving fast enough to indicate that having learned to walk, the thing was now trying a full run. He peered into the dim light that filled the main tunnel, but saw nothing. Still, the steps were getting louder, faster.

Having eluded the world for decades, he was damned if he'd be done in by a whore. Not even a whore, a collection of bits of whores, whores he'd already cut up. If he only had his hands free, if he only had his knife, he could just cut it up all over again. He'd do it again, somehow. Then he'd find Frankenstein and take care of his bitch of a wife.

Done with what little thinking he could manage, he shook with rage, then moved backwards, slamming his hands into the concrete wall, as if he could batter an exit for himself. When this hurt too much, he tried his forehead, ramming it so hard into the stone he thought it might crack.

Instead, wetness dripped from his brow, along his cheeks. A few salty drops slipped into the sides of his mouth. He lapped at them, relishing the taste as if he were savoring one of the wombs that gave him life.

He moaned with the pleasure of it, almost forgetting where he was.

It was only when the scraping footsteps and rasping hiss were right behind him that he came to his senses and again ran off into the dark, slamming into the opposite wall, then feeling his way into a side tunnel.

Here, the light from Frankenstein's makeshift lab was gone, and there were only shades of black, darkness. The darkness had been his salvation so many times. The darkness in which he could slit a throat before its owner could cry out, the darkness in which he could disappear from all London. It was all one dark, really, and he'd always been safe in it.

He pressed his lips against the dank concrete walls, rolling his bloody forehead against it in a vain effort to stop the bleeding. The smell of blood mixed with damp stone pleased him. It reminded him of the dank cave of Sawney Bean, the sweet place that had been a grave for hundreds of unwary travelers, but for him a stone womb.

Stepping lightly, he moved forward until he found a corner of the rectangular space. Then he turned, putting his cuffed hands to the corner. He stared out into the nothing, and waited. If Frankenstein hadn't lied, all he had to do was wait the creature out a few hours, then it would die, all on its own.

If Frankenstein hadn't lied. All he had to do was wait. He'd done it before.

He let the hate drain out of him, the heat, even the breathing. He flexed his stubby fingers against the corner, then let them fall to stillness as well. It was his greatest trick, to become motionless, invisible. He'd done it for hours once, while the police shifted around a few feet in front of him, never guessing he was there.

"Crshhankkkk!"

It had entered the room. He could almost see it now, the wild-star mane of its head outlined against the lesser black behind it. It'd slowed upon entering and its movements were uncertain, giving him hope.

It *couldn't* see then. All he had to do was stay still.

As he calmed himself further, he let his eyes focus, let his brain learn to distinguish the dark grays from the blacks. Then, he saw more of it, and more of the room.

"Schachhhh . . . hssssss . . . "

It was stumbling, hitting crates, flailing with too-long arms. Its balance seemed worse than it had in the main tunnel, as if it might tip over at any moment.

Could it be dying already?

But then it steadied, stood up straight. The Ripper thought he could hear the bones in its spine crack as it stood. Its arms went down by its sides, like thick listless ropes, as if it were trying to conserve what little strength it had left. A terrible smell came from it, like the rotting stench of the grave.

It was all he could do to keep from laughing.

But then, within the blackness below the outline of its hair, he saw something glisten, something catch a spark of light, from somewhere, and send it shooting back. The sparkle twitched and moved, left, then right.

It was the eyes, the whore's dead eyes. They were somehow

shining with their own light, even in the utter black. They moved, not even in tandem, but they looked as if they were separately scanning the room.

When they stopped, when they steadied, they seemed to be looking at him.

"Shchruchhhhshhh!"

It came forward, a step at a time, headed straight toward him. For a few seconds he couldn't believe it, but then reality dawned.

It sees me.

The eyes burned into him, black things almost like his own, except for the glistening. He hesitated for a fraction of a second, then tried to lunge past. One moment its twin arms hung dead and lifeless, the next, they leapt up and lashed out and snagged him by the shoulders, wrapping around him, its bones like steel.

He gave a powerful kick to its legs, swore he'd hit them, but only wound up crashing to the floor. He lay there, helpless, thinking he could try to bite it as it came for him.

"Rachhhhhh!"

It straddled him, raised its long bony hands above its head. One blow would probably crush his skull.

But the blow never came.

Instead, the arms locked, the hands shivered. The eyes danced about in the head, suddenly looking frightened and alone.

Lying on his back, hands still trapped behind him, the Ripper laughed long and loud, his gravelly voice echoing through the tunnels.

"Mary Blyss! It's Mary Blyss! And you still can't raise your hand to me, can you?" he howled, triumphantly. "Killed and dead and raised from the grave as a monster yourself and you still can't raise your hand to your betters! What a joke you are, you stupid whore! One way or another now, I'll cut you up again!"

The eyes of Mary Blyss moved about in the skull, faster and faster, as if they wished to burst free of their bone prison.

The Ripper kicked at its legs and it fell.

"Maybe I can stomp you to death!" he shouted, shifting himself to a seated position. "Just hold still!"

As she twitched and writhed on the ground, he thought he might really do it, but then something else in the room moved. From behind the stacked crates, the flat head appeared first, the steel clamps that held the top of the skull in place glistening. Then came the face and the body so huge, he'd called it Behemoth.

"Nrgggghhhh."

The sight of the monster silenced the Ripper's laugh, but quickened his efforts to rise to his feet. Sluggish, the monster stepped over. A weak slap of its hand on the Ripper's shoulder sent the killer back down to the floor. From the ground, the Ripper turned and saw the two things shift and stumble toward one another in what seemed a mixture of confusion and curiosity.

The monster seemed to recognize the twinkle in the dark disjointed eyes. He shook his head and waved his hands in the air plaintively.

"Uhn . . . uhn . . . "

The eyes of Mary Blyss twisted. Its head bobbed.

"Schhuihchhhh . . . " Then it lowered its head.

Were they speaking? Could they speak?

The Ripper shifted, hoping to get away while they were occupied with each other, but the monster growled and raised a hand to him.

He didn't strike himself, though. Instead, he pulled the female creature closer, raised her arm, and brought it down hard on the Ripper's face.

Two teeth were knocked loose. The Ripper spat up blood.

"Aghh, you devils!" he said.

"Uhn . . . uhn . . . " the monster said.

"Schhhahchhh!" the female creature replied. She seemed pleased.

The monster raised the female's arm again, and again brought it down. This time, the Ripper just whimpered. After a few more swings, while he was still conscious, the Ripper saw that the new creature had started to bring her fists down upon him without any help.

Once she finally got the hang of it, she turned out to be quite proficient.

When Inspector Devin and his men finally appeared, they found they needed several bags to collect the remains of the Ripper.

Outside, an hour later, the storm had cleared. The fields of Hampstead Heath smelled fresh and clean beneath a crystal sky with many stars. Under the branches of a tall old oak that had stood at least a hundred years, two grotesque figures sat next to one another. One, ever so slowly was recovering from its many wounds. The other was rapidly dying.

Having carried it here to this quiet spot, out of the ground, for the longest time the monster just watched the new creature. He stared at its parts and pieces, he stared at it all together, fascinated, as its breathing grew more and more shallow.

The monster knew from the stitching, from the different sizes of all its pieces that this was truly another being created like him. He also knew the dead from which it had been made. It held one hand and remembered it as Cyra's. It stared into the sad black eyes and knew they belonged to Mary Blyss. Some of the other pieces, it didn't recognize at all, but that didn't bother him.

It was different than the last creature. This one didn't seem to hate or fear him. Mostly, it seemed confused about everything, confused about even why it lived at all.

The monster sensed his new companion's life was fading, but didn't understand why it wasn't violent, like all the other deaths he'd seen, with bloody wounds and torn limbs. This was so quiet, so peaceful, like water pouring out of a bowl, like music from a violin fading as the player walked away.

He held its fingers, felt them tremble and marveled as the last of life's energy slipped out of them. They collapsed like sticks and he petted them, first with his palm, then with the back of his hand.

When its black eyes stopped moving completely, the monster was sorry and happy, all at the same time.

"Good," he said. And he petted the still hand once more.

A figure in an overcoat approached. The monster turned to it.

"Frankenstein."

"Yes."

The monster waved his hand toward the body in his lap and spoke in halting words. "You make her?"

Frankenstein nodded. "Yes. Yes I did."

The monster turned to him, furrowed his thick brow, and said, "Thank you."

Epilogue

The night was clear and the seas so calm they reflected the starry sky like a flat mirror. Despite the magnificent display, Captain Rodriguez, a dark-haired Spaniard with a few well-earned strands of white, found himself staring instead at the famous passenger he'd been asked to pretend he did not know.

"He tells the strangest stories, your Mr. Moritz," the captain said. "About monsters and killers, and the dead returned to life."

Henry Frankenstein shrugged as he smoked a cigarette and stared at the sea. "My friend is undergoing a difficult recovery," he answered. "You'd do well not to pay him any heed."

Rodriguez laughed. "I am paid well not to. Is your wife feeling better?"

The polite smile on the baron's lips faded. "Her recovery is difficult as well. I'll be glad to have her home again."

The captain nodded and stepped back. "You should try to get her some air on this lovely night. It looks as though someone pulled the stars from the sky and sprinkled them on the water."

"Yes," Frankenstein said. "I'll try."

He took a final drag on the cigarette, then tossed the burning stub out over the dark water. For a moment it looked like a comet, hurtling between the stars, but then, in a flash, the tiny glow was extinguished.

He bade the captain goodnight and stepped toward the cabins. He peered through a porthole at Moritz and saw him toss and turn.

He'll get over it, soon enough, Frankenstein thought.

Once certain Rodriguez wasn't watching, he slipped past the cabin area and climbed down into the storage hold. There, among the many bags and crates faithful Minnie had assembled for their journey home, he found the tall one he'd packed himself, the one full of air holes, the one the men who loaded it said reeked of some sort of animal. But they'd been paid to be quiet, too.

Frankenstein walked up to the crate and put his ear to it.

"Do you hear me?" Frankenstein hissed. "Do you understand? You must remain absolutely quiet unless you hear my voice calling for you."

The reply was quick and clear. "Yes. I understand."

Satisfied with the response. Frankenstein returned to the dock, then steeled himself for another encounter with his wife.

He walked into her cabin. His own was right next door, for it had become impossible now for him to stay with her long. Though her brain groaned for the release of dreams, she did not sleep any longer, and his presence only seemed to upset her more.

She started when he opened the door, then twisted her head left and right.

She lay on her pillows, hair washed by Minnie, a wild look to her lovely eyes. Some of the weight she'd lost in captivity had been regained, but not enough yet to make her face look flush and full.

"Come outside, Elizabeth. Come look at the sea, at the stars. Breathe in some fresh air. You'll see, my darling, the nightmares are finally over," he said.

"Oh, no, no Henry, they've only just begun. I can't go out there again. He'll take me. He'll drag me down to the bottom of the sea and never let me breathe again," she said.

Thinking she spoke of the Ripper, he tried to be reassuring,

"The man who tormented you is dead. He can never trouble you again. I've saved you, my love."

She turned to him with a bemused expression. "Oh, no, Henry. He can never die. He's inside me now. In me, in my head, spinning, in my skin, crawling, he's dug down so deep he'll never come out! Never! You must give me one of your knives to cut him out! You must!"

Henry answered in a half-moan, "Elizabeth, please! Please calm down!"

She started to writhe, to moan back at him. "Cut me! Cut me! Cut me!"

Henry Frankenstein rubbed his hair back and covered his ears with his hands. Shaking his head, he reached into a small drawer and withdrew the vial of opiate he had packed from the hotel. He plunged the needle into the rubber stopper, filled the hypodermic, and stepped toward his wife.

"Here! Here! This will calm you, my darling," he said. He pulled her thin arm out from the blanket and rolled back the sheer sleeve of her nightgown. "This will help you rest."

As he pushed the needle into her arm, she regarded him with a curious, alien look.

He pretended not to see it. He pretended everything was just fine. Then he stepped back and watched grimly as her whole form twisted, writhed, shuddered, then finally settled. Her eyes, though still lost, no longer quivered. A few moments later, they closed and her breathing steadied.

An addict, Henry said, stepping back from yet another of his creations. Part of him, a gross, small, insect part of him thought, *At least . . . maybe now . . . she'll know better what it is that I am . . .*

He wished he could take the drug himself, to still his beating mind, but he couldn't. He had to stay clearheaded for the daunting tasks ahead.

He stepped from the cabin, felt the sway of the ocean, and confused it for dizziness. He grabbed for his handkerchief, to wipe some sweat from his forehead and felt something hard and stiff in his pocket. Slowly, he withdrew the Ripper's ancient book, flipped through the rotting pages, and marveled at the technical accuracy of the drawings, though noting where they could stand some improvement.

The Ripper thought the monster had eternal life. Perhaps he'd been right. Perhaps, by accident, Henry Frankenstein had not just challenged death, but defeated it. Utterly.

That had always been the second part of his plan, first to discover the secret of life, then the secret of immortality, a secret which this book, if he could sift through its arcane superstition and uncover the scientific meat, might help him unlock. He had the mind for it. He knew he could do it, combine it with his own discoveries, learn to distill the great ray's properties with even more precision.

Then, perhaps he could even fix the monster's defective brain, grow back what had been damaged in Tom Nodding's life. What a feat that would be! Then, no one would call him mad. It'd just been failure, after all, a mistake that had created these nightmares. Now, perhaps he could finally fix things.

That's all he'd ever wanted to do, fix things.

Fix life.

Fix death.

Fix everything.

Once and for all. And then he wouldn't care if they all did think he was mad.

Fools.

The End

Acknowledgments

First, my thanks to agent Amy Stout, editor Rob Simpson, and associate editor Victoria Blake for giving me this terrific opportunity to pen an ersatz sequel to two of my favorite films, James Whale's *Frankenstein* and *Bride of Frankenstein*. I've always wanted to see what might have happened had the amazing but tortured Colin Clive survived to play the seminal mad scientist a third time. Those two original films, holding up strong seventy-five years later, have inspired, thrilled, and tickled me for ages. If I've captured just a little of their flavor here, I am deeply satisfied.

Double thanks to Lesley Logan both for being an early reader and for all the cool Whitechapel maps and 1930s London guides. Likewise, many thanks to fellow Frankenstein fan Steve Holtz for his quick and insightful first read, and his continuing friendship over three decades. Double plus thanks to my dear friends at the Who Wants Cake Crit Group (Dan Braum, Nick Kaufmann, Sarah Langan, K. Z. Perry, and Lee Thomas) for their comments on early chapters.

An extra double plus debt of gratitude to Nick Kaufmann, the man who came up with the title. I wanted it to be something "of Frankenstein," and what better to fall between the bride and the son but a Shadow?

Last but not leastly, many more thanks than I can muster to my dear wife Sarah for putting up with my caffeine-fueled efforts to complete this on schedule. It is indeed, alive.

This was a real treat for me to work on—I hope it's an equal treat to read.

About the Author

Stefan Petrucha published his first comic in 1987 and his first novel in 1997. His Timetripper series from Razorbill is currently earning raves from critics and readers alike, while his recent work on the Nancy Drew graphic novels won the 2006 Benjamin Franklin Award. He is perhaps best known for writing Topps's *X-Files* comic, which has been collected into six trade paperbacks on sale here and abroad. In 2007, his new horror anthology series from HarperCollins, Wicked Dead, will debut with co-author Thomas Pendleton.

Petrucha lives (assuming the closing has taken place by the time of publication) in Amherst, Massachusetts, with his wife and fellow writer Sarah and their two daughters, Maia and Margo. He hopes one day to be wealthy enough to purchase a watchtower laboratory where he can conduct his experiments away from the prying eyes of the villagers, but first he has to get the kids through college.